THE LIBERTY BRIDE

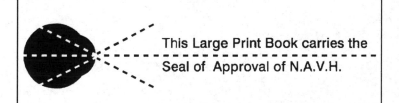

This Large Print Book carries the
Seal of Approval of N.A.V.H.

THE DAUGHTERS OF THE MAYFLOWER

THE LIBERTY BRIDE

MARYLU TYNDALL

THORNDIKE PRESS
A part of Gale, a Cengage Company

Farmington Hills, Mich • San Francisco • New York • Waterville, Maine
Meriden, Conn • Mason, Ohio • Chicago

Copyright © 2018 by MaryLu Tyndall.
All scripture quotations are taken from the King James Version of the Bible.
Thorndike Press, a part of Gale, a Cengage Company.

Thorndike Press® Large Print Christian Romance.
The text of this Large Print edition is unabridged.
Other aspects of the book may vary from the original edition.
Set in 16 pt. Plantin.

LIBRARY OF CONGRESS CIP DATA ON FILE.
CATALOGUING IN PUBLICATION FOR THIS BOOK
IS AVAILABLE FROM THE LIBRARY OF CONGRESS

ISBN-13: 978-1-4328-6165-0 (hardcover)

Published in 2019 by arrangement with Barbour Publishing, Inc.

Printed in Mexico
1 2 3 4 5 6 7 23 22 21 20 19

Daughters of the Mayflower

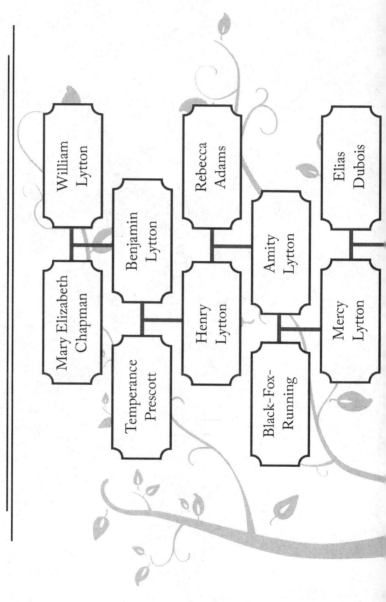

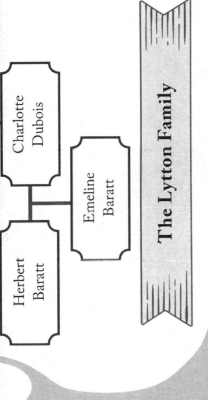

Herbert Baratt — Charlotte Dubois

Emeline Baratt

The Lytton Family

William Lytton married Mary Elizabeth Chapman (Plymouth, 1621)

Parents of 13 children, including Benjamin

Benjamin Lytton married Temperance Prescott (Massachusetts, 1668)

Born to Benjamin and Temperance

Henry Lytton married Rebecca Adams (New York, 1712)

Children were Goodwill and Amity

Amity Lytton married Black-Fox-Running, a Mohawk warrior (New York, 1737)

Only child was Mercy Lytton (aka Kahente)

Mercy Lytton married Elias Dubois (Massachusetts, 1759)

Children included Charlotte

Charlotte Dubois married Herbert Baratt (Maryland, 1788)

Children included Emeline

CHAPTER 1

The Atlantic Ocean off the Coast of Virginia,
August 6, 1814

What would it feel like to drown . . . to float
listlessly down . . . down . . . beneath the
chilled waters of the Atlantic? To feel salty
fingers wrap around you, their deadly talons
tugging you farther into the murky darkness, your lungs burning until they
screamed for air that would never come . . .
until finally, cloaked in a silent, peaceful
tomb, you floated into eternity. . . .

Emeline Baratt pondered these things as
she gazed upon the dark waves from the
larboard railing of her father's merchant
brig — or rather, privateer — *Charlotte.* The
pondering sliced an icy knife down her
back. Was it the thought of dying or the
chilled mist of the morning that caused her
to suddenly draw the warmth of her cloak
tighter about her neck? Perhaps both.

Unable to sleep as usual, she'd come up

on deck just before dawn. It was the only time of day she was left unhindered by the many sailors on board who felt it their duty to protect and entertain their employer's daughter. On her long journey across the pond from Calais, France, she'd endured more than enough male attention to last a lifetime. Whether their desire for her was motivated by her dowry, their need for a wife to take care of them, or her "exquisite" beauty — as many of them claimed she possessed — she did not know. Nor did she care. As far back as she could remember, she had never wanted to marry.

A sliver of a moon frowned its disappointment down upon her. A scowl with which she was quite familiar, having seen it enough on her father's face whenever she'd dared to tell him of her dreams. Mockery always preceded his frustration, a complete dismissal of all that was important to her. Yet she knew he meant well. He wanted to see her settled and cared for. He wanted grandchildren. And while he didn't voice it, she knew he wanted to be free of the burden of her support.

"At two and twenty, you should be married with a bevy of wee ones frolicking about your skirts," he had told her after he'd discovered her painting away the afternoon.

"It is the godly and proper station for women — raising children and caring for a husband. Not wasting your time with frivolous art that will never sell."

That frivolous art was the most beautiful seascape she'd ever painted and a secret commission from the mayor's wife, who'd admired Emeline's work from afar.

She never finished it. The next day her father whisked her overseas to Brighton to spend a year with her great-aunt, a wealthy daughter of a baron.

"What you need is a woman's influence, someone to teach you how to be a proper lady." He waved his hand through the air and huffed. "Perhaps you'll even find a husband. God knows you've rejected every eligible gentleman in Baltimore."

Indeed she had. A smile lifted her lips at the memory of those suitors vying for her affections like puppies for their mother's milk. But she would not be any man's pet. Why tie yourself down to a life of endless scrubbing and mending and cooking and tending? She'd done enough of that in the past fourteen years caring for her father and two brothers after her mother died and then most recently her aunt. If that was to be her life, what was the point?

She gazed at the churning water again.

She *could* jump.

The brig pitched over a wave, sending the deck tilting and wood creaking, jarring her from her morbid thoughts. Gripping the railing tighter, she sighed and gazed at the blanket of golden light swaddling the horizon, fluttering threads of gold and azure over the inky swells. Soon the deck would be abuzz with sailors, joining the two night watchmen and helmsman standing at the wheel. Soon she would have to go below to spend her final day at sea cooped up in a cabin the size of a privy closet. At least she had her charcoal and paper to keep her busy.

She may even finish her sketch of the captain if one of the sailors didn't come down with some phantom illness she had to address. Possessing medical skills she'd learned while accompanying her uncle on his rounds in Baltimore was yet another thing that kept her forever tending to everyone else's needs.

Everyone's but her own.

La, but she sounded bitter. *Forgive me, Lord.*

The pound of footsteps and groans of men unhappy to be awakened from their sleep rumbled behind her. A brisk wind flapped loose sails and stirred the curls dangling about her neck, and she drew a deep breath of the sea air. She'd grown so accustomed to the scent of brine, wood, and tar these past six weeks she'd all but forgotten what land smelled like.

She'd nearly forgotten her father's face as well — at least the look of chagrin it usually held. Would he be happy to see her? Perhaps her absence for nearly two years had softened his resolve to force her to marry if she returned without any prospects. Or would he be angry that she returned no better off than when she'd left? Without a husband and with but a pittance of an inheritance from her eccentric aunt.

She supposed his anger would win out, especially since he'd been forced to risk one of his merchantmen-turned-privateers to bring her home during wartime. Not just any privateer, but his best one, along with his best captain, Henry Lansing, notorious not only for capturing three British prizes but also for his skill at breaking through the British blockade of American ports.

Now that they neared the American coastline, they'd need his skill more than ever.

"Good morning to you, miss." One of the sailors smiled at her on his way to the foredeck as more men emerged from below and hurried to their posts.

Facing the sea once again, she drew back

her shoulders. She had made up her mind. She would give up her art, marry within the year, and settle down to the life that was expected of her, a life that would please her father, society — and most of all, God.

No more wasted time, no more painting, no more frivolous dreams . . .

She dropped her gaze once again to the misty sea. She *could* still jump. Death would come within minutes, and then she would be taken to heaven. To be with Mama.

"Oh Mama, I miss you so." She gripped the locket hanging around her neck as the sun peered over the horizon, soon becoming naught but a golden blur in Emeline's teary vision.

More sailors greeted her.

Wiping her eyes, she leaned over the railing and watched the line of bubbling foam rise and fall over the hull.

It would be so simple.

But of course she wouldn't jump. She straightened and glanced over the dissipating mist. From this moment forth, she intended to be a proper lady. And proper ladies certainly did not hurl themselves into the sea.

"Lay aloft! Loose top sails, Mr. Brook!" the boatswain shouted behind her.

Sailors leapt into the shrouds and skittered to the tops like spiders on a web. Within minutes, sheets were dropped, flapping idly before they caught the wind and ballooned in a thunderous roar.

Lowering her head, she prayed for forgiveness for her negative thoughts. She prayed that God would take away her dreams and help her be a godly woman. Then, perhaps then, He would choose to bless her and not punish her.

Warmth caressed her eyelids, and she opened them to the sunrise kissing the waves with saffron and whisking away the remaining fog. Perhaps an omen of God's favor at last. She started to turn and descend to her cabin, when a dark shape on the horizon caught her eye. Squinting, she watched as it grew larger . . . a leviathan emerging from the mist.

"A sail! A sail!" A shout came from the tops.

They hadn't seen a single ship in the entire crossing. Odd since America was at war with Great Britain. Odd also because the captain had warned her that they may encounter some trouble.

She scanned the deck and spotted him mounting the ladder to the quarterdeck where he took the telescope from his first mate.

Another shout came from the tops. "She's flying the Union Jack, Cap'n!"

"What in the blazes! Where did she come from?" Captain Lansing bellowed, scope still to his eye. "Why was she not spotted earlier?"

"There was a heavy fog this morning," the boatswain offered.

"We are at war, man! Fog is no excuse!" Captain Lansing gripped the quarterdeck railing, his face mottled with rage.

"She's heading our way, Cap'n, signaling for a show of colors."

"By God, then we'll show her our colors! Raise the flag! Beat to quarters! All hands make sail!"

The string of orders sent the sailors dashing here and there as the first mate shouted further commands to the crew.

More sails were loosed. Wind glutted them like white pregnant bellies. Emeline stood frozen, watching the harried crew race about, their eyes sparking in fear. The ship veered to larboard. She caught the rail and slammed against the bulwarks.

"She's running out her guns!" the first mate yelled.

Emeline dared a glance back out to sea. A Royal Navy frigate advanced toward them in a sea of raging white foam.

A spindle of terror wove down her back. She couldn't move. Could hardly breathe.

A foul curse spewed from Captain Lansing's lips, followed by something about bearing off and starboard guns. . . . Emeline could no longer make much sense of his words.

Boom! The roar shook both sky and brig. Her heart seized.

Someone shouted, "All hands down!"

Her last thought before dropping to all fours was that God so rarely answered her prayers.

CHAPTER 2

"Captain's orders. You and Mrs. Keate stay here until it's safe." In his haste to join the battle, the sailor's mate all but shoved Emeline and the quartermaster's wife, Hannah, into the tiny cabin and slammed the door.

Safe? Emeline shared a terrified glance with Hannah as shouts ricocheted above them and feet pounded over the deck. The eerie grate of iron set every nerve at attention to what she assumed were the guns being run out.

"Now, now, dear." The older woman took Emeline's arm and tugged her to sit in one of the chairs. "It will be all ri', you'll see."

"All right —" The deck suddenly tilted. Emeline toppled from the chair, lost her footing, and slammed into the bulkhead. Dazed, she clawed the wood, her shriek drowned out by the mad dash of water against the hull.

"Oh dear, you hurt yourself." Hannah's

kind face came into view as she dragged Emeline across the small space and forced her to sit. Within moments, a cloth pressed on her forehead.

"Just a wee scratch. Nothin' to worry about."

The wood creaked and groaned as the brig heaved to starboard. Emeline gripped the arms of the chair while Hannah merely bolstered her stance and remained in place. She withdrew the rag. A red line marred the gray fabric.

Boom! The distant explosion roared overhead. Emeline covered her face and crouched into the chair, too afraid to scream or even breathe for fear the shot would crash through the cabin, through her body, and rip her to shreds.

It didn't. But it *did* hit above deck as the snap and crunch of wood pierced the air, followed by a gut-wrenching scream.

"I should see if the injured need help." Gripping the chair arms, Emeline attempted to rise, but the ship careened yet again, sending her hairbrush and toiletries crashing to the floor from the table.

Shouts increased in volume and intensity, the captain's chief among them. Wind slapped the sails, the sea roared against the hull, and footsteps pummeled the deck like an angry giant.

"You can't go up top now, dear. It is too dangerous."

Emeline wanted to cry, but her eyes were as dry as her throat. "This can't be happening!"

"Try to calm yourself." Hannah dabbed the cloth on her head again.

"Calm? How can I be calm when we are in the middle of a battle at sea?" Emeline eased the woman's arm away. "And against the mightiest navy on earth!"

This time Emeline made it to her feet and instantly regretted it as the brig pitched. She gripped the bunk chain before she toppled to the deck. It nearly yanked her arm out of its socket, and she fell anyway. Pain seared a trail up her tailbone.

Sinking onto the bunk for support, Hannah reached a hand for her. "Never you fear about that. God be wit' us."

Forty years had not stolen an ounce of vigor or vim from Hannah. Though they *had* rounded out her figure and added a few silver streaks to her chestnut hair. She had been Emeline's companion on the long journey across the pond, but in truth, she'd been more of a mother figure — something Emeline had not had since she was eight.

Taking Hannah's hand, she allowed the

older lady to pull her up onto the cot. "How do you know God is not with the British?"

Hannah shrugged. "Don't matter wha' side 'e takes. 'E's still wit' you and me."

Stern voices — brisk and harried — echoed from above. The brig tilted to starboard again. An explosion shook the ship so violently it seemed every timber would turn to dust. The sound pulsed in Emeline's ears. Beside her, Hannah's lips were moving, but Emeline could make nothing of the words . . . something about a broadside.

"We must 'ave fired a broadside," Hannah repeated, staring at Emeline with concern. "Are you all ri'?"

"I want to go above. What if the brig sinks and we drown, trapped in this cabin?" The irony was not lost on her that she'd only that morning been brooding on a watery death.

Easing an arm around her, Hannah drew her close, but Emeline leapt up, stumbled over the shifting deck, flung open the door, and barreled into the companionway. She supposed proper ladies didn't barge on deck in the middle of battle either, but if she were going to die, propriety made no difference.

Hannah's shouts followed behind her but were quickly muffled by the mayhem above.

Emeline emerged into a scene of such chaos, blood, and destruction she nearly retreated back to her cabin. She *would* have retreated if a cloud of black smoke hadn't completely enveloped her, stealing her breath and stinging her eyes. Coughing, she batted it away, when a sailor rammed into her. She stumbled to the side. Hannah grabbed her arm before she fell and dragged her against the quarterdeck as the metallic scent of blood combined with gunpowder sent bile into her throat.

Men scurried back and forth, following the captain's orders. Gun crews swarmed the ten cannons — or *guns,* as they called them — on the port side, reloading them with shot and powder. A charred hole smoked from the starboard railing. A huge gouge had been blasted from the main mast between main and topsail. The enormous pole whined and teetered, remaining upright by a mere breath and a prayer. Splintered wood, stained with blood, showered the deck, slicing the bare feet of the sailors as they hurried past. Above, sails flapped impotently in search of wind. The brig slowed.

Curses showered on them from above where the captain stood.

"They've got the weather edge, Cap'n,

and coming fast on our port quarter!"

An agonized moan drew Emeline's attention to a sailor sprawled over the deck by the foredeck ladder. Before Hannah could stop her, she gathered her skirts and dashed toward him, dropping to her knees at his side. A spear of wood protruded from his neck while blood gushed from a wound on his head. She scanned the scene, looking for anyone to assist her in bringing him below, when another boom split the sky. The sailors crouched.

Was this the end? Would she die aboard this ship? Her heart pounded in her ears, drowning out all other sound and slowing time. *Thump . . . thump . . . thump.* Sailors moved across the deck as if wading through oil. The captain was shouting something, his lips opening and closing ever so slowly, but his words sounded hollow and muffled. Emeline glanced down at the injured man and blinked, trying to regain her senses. Grabbing his hand, she closed her eyes. "Oh God, help us."

A splash sounded and the clamor on board resumed.

Emeline peered over the railing to see the British ship coming alongside with the muzzles of at least fifteen guns mocking them from its side.

A confident voice bellowed over the water. "This is His Britannic Majesty's frigate *Marauder.* Lay down your arms and surrender at once or be blown to bits!"

First Lieutenant Owen Masters took a position beside his captain on the main deck of HMS *Marauder* in preparation to receive the prisoners on board. Though the American merchant brig had put up a good fight, in the end they were no match for one of His Majesty's frigates. At least that's what Owen kept telling himself . . . that there had been nothing he could do to save them — not without exposing himself. Yet now as he watched the last of the cutters rowing their way, he cursed under his breath. Thus far, the *Marauder* had not captured an American prize, and hang it all, this complicated things.

Just when he was finally in a position to be of use to his country, now he had prisoners to protect.

The boat thudded against the hull, and a group of marines moved to stand on either side of the entry port, arms at the ready. Second Lieutenant Benjamin Camp, whom Captain Blackwell had sent to inspect the American ship, leapt on board first, approached his captain, and handed him documents. Captain Blackwell quickly perused them. His subsequent "Humph" indicated they now had proof that the American ship was indeed a privateer.

The privateer's captain and his officers clambered up the ladder and onto the main deck. Hatred burned in the American captain's eyes as he jutted out his chin. More sailors leapt on board behind him.

Beside Owen, Captain Blackwell eyed the prisoners with disdain. "Welcome aboard His Majesty's frigate *Marauder.*" He held up the documents. "I see you are the privateer *Charlotte* out of Baltimore."

"We are but merchants, Captain" — their captain approached, his face moist with perspiration and red with anger — "returning from Calais with a cargo of —"

The remainder of his words were blown away in the wind as all eyes shifted in unison to the entry port where a woman was helped aboard by one of the prisoners. Not just any woman, but the most stunning creature Owen had ever seen. Apparently, by the gaping mouths and wide eyes of those around him, his opinion was shared by the crew. Sunlight glittered topaz in hair that dripped like sweet honey along her elegant neck. A modest gown of blue taffeta clung to a slight figure that exuded elegance and femininity. Men instantly drew close to help her aboard, but instead, she turned to assist an injured sailor behind her. A bloody bandage seemed to be all that held his neck to his head, and the tenderness with which she led him to the side made Owen swallow. She assisted three more injured men on board before she finally lifted eyes the color of emeralds to scan her surroundings. And the terror he saw within them made him want to dash to her side and offer his comfort.

An older woman climbed on board and joined her, followed by the last of the Americans and the ten British sailors who had accompanied Ben. Forty Americans in all. They'd left another forty on board the brig to be transported to a prison hulk in Plymouth — just enough men to be contained and not risk a mutiny.

The ship rolled over a wave as a blast of wind flapped a loose sail but offered little respite from the searing sun.

Captain Blackwell cleared his throat and addressed the American captain again. "You are no merchantmen, Captain. I have your letter of marque in hand."

"If you please," the American captain began with a smile that seemed to cost him dearly. "I'll agree to the letter, but we have made no use of it. As you can see, it is dated two years past, and since then, we have found no reason to attack British ships. In truth, we were conveying the ship owner's daughter back home." The gruff-looking man with a chest the size of a water barrel gestured toward the beautiful lady. "Then we were headed back to the West Indies."

"To pirate."

"To trade. As is our profession."

"Hmm. Eighty men. A large crew for a merchantman." Captain Blackwell chuckled and some of the sailors joined him.

The American captain's weather-lined face was devoid of amusement. "There are many dangers in these waters."

Captain Blackwell eyed the man from head to toe, then cast a cursory glance over the American crew. "Nevertheless, consider yourselves prisoners of the Crown. And your ship a prize of war."

The hot sun poured molten heat upon them, and the American captain wiped a sleeve over his forehead. "I assure you, we are no such thing!" He waved a hand toward the young lady. "Would a man allow his daughter to be escorted on a privateer?"

"A foolish man would, I'd say."

"I assure you, Captain. Mr. Baratt would never put his only daughter in danger."

"Then perhaps he should not have put her on a privateer during wartime."

Defeat lined the American captain's face as he shifted his stance. "What are you to do with us? With my brig?" The man glanced behind him at the *Charlotte,* where midshipmen prepared her to set sail.

"You will be put to work on board this ship until I can escort you to a prison hulk in Canada. Meanwhile my prize crew will sail your brig to Plymouth to repair and refit her for service. Royal Navy service," he added sharply.

Sailcloth flapped impotently above them as grumbles traveled among the prisoners. From the looks of defiance on their faces, Owen believed that if they were armed, they'd brave an attack, even outnumbered six to one.

That's the spirit! He'd not seen another American since his rendezvous with a supply boat off the coast of Wilmington, North Carolina, a month past, and their presence brought a surge of patriotism.

"Dimsmore," Captain Blackwell addressed the marine first lieutenant. "Lock the prisoners below. Lieutenant Masters" — he turned to Owen — "see that the injured are taken to sick bay."

"And what of the ladies?" Owen gestured

toward the two women backed against the railing as if they would rather jump overboard than face their fate. The younger one still attended the injured men by her side.

"Hmm." Blackwell rubbed his chin. "They do present a problem."

"A very eye-pleasing problem," Second Lieutenant Benjamin Camp whispered to Owen from his other side. The two shared a smile.

Dimsmore began rounding up the prisoners as Captain Blackwell made his way toward the women. He halted before them, and the younger one raised her brazen gaze to his. Though Owen detected a slight quiver in her lips, determination sparked in her eyes.

"Do you know medicine, miss?"

"A bit, Captain," she said without emotion.

"Good. We lost our ship's surgeon two weeks past. Lieutenant Masters, have one of the marines escort this woman and her companion" — he glanced at the older woman curiously — "to sick bay to attend the injured. Keep guard over them there. Then find them a cabin separate from the other prisoners."

"Aye, Captain."

Blackwell glanced up at the sun. "Raise all

sails, Mr. Masters, and proceed to our destination. I'll be in my quarters." With that he spun on his heels and marched away.

Owen turned to face his friend. "Take us out, full and by, Mr. Camp."

"Aye, aye, full and by." Ben turned and began ordering the crew as Lieutenant Dimsmore shoved the prisoners down a hatch. The marine's cold eyes passed over Owen as they so often did, but this time, a malicious smile curled one side of his mouth. Certainly, the vile man did not suspect anything. Owen had been more than careful.

Shrugging off the thought, he scanned the crew. "Mr. Yonks, Mr. Manson, Mr. Denrick," he shouted, drawing the attention of three sailors. "Escort the injured to sick bay at once."

"Americans too, sir?" Manson asked.

"*All* the injured."

Above him, topmen unfurled sheets while sailors on both larboard and starboard watches hauled on the ties and halyards. Soon the lowered sails grabbed the wind like ravenous dogs, and the ship jerked to larboard. A cloud swallowed up the sun, offering them a reprieve from the heat.

A feminine shriek drew his gaze to the women where Denrick yanked the injured

American from the younger lady's arms to drag him below.

"You're hurting him, you fiend!" Grabbing the injured sailor's shirt, she tugged him back, and for a moment the poor man pivoted back and forth like holystone over the deck.

Owen gripped her wrist and wrangled her from the man's shirt before nodding for Denrick to take him away. "You will attend to him soon enough, Miss . . . Miss . . ."

She jerked from his grasp and backed away. At least as far as the railing would allow. The older woman wove an arm through hers and faced Owen like an avenging angel.

"Miss Baratt," the younger woman finally said, her green eyes sparking at him with both fear and anger.

"Very well, Miss Baratt and Miss . . . ?" Owen lifted his brows at the other woman.

"Mrs. Keate, quartermaster's wife." Proud brown eyes flared at him from within a round, kind face.

"There is naught to fear. We are gentlemen here." Owen glanced over the marines standing nearby and selected one he trusted. "Mr. Blane, take these women to sick bay and stand guard over them."

"Naught to fear, you say?" Miss Baratt snipped. "There is much to fear. We are now

31

prisoners of war, are we not?"

"We do not harm women."

Mrs. Keate huffed. "Not wha' I hear."

The comely one said nothing, merely stared out at sea before those incriminating eyes met his again.

Blane nudged them from behind. "This way, ladies."

Owen cursed under his breath as they were led belowdecks. How could he protect these innocent women? More importantly, how could he protect them *and* himself?

All while doing his job as an American spy.

CHAPTER 3

Arm in arm with Hannah, Emeline glanced over the filthy space that passed for sick bay and did her best to force back her tears. The marine, Mr. Blane, gave them one last shove from behind before he took his post against the bulkhead. Other sailors carried the injured — most of whom were moaning from their injuries — and deposited them on sailcloth laid across the floor as if they were naught but sacks of wheat.

Emeline held a hand to her nose as the stench of stale vomit and gun smoke as well as other indescribable odors assailed her. To her left, a cabinet full of what appeared to be medicines stood against the bulkhead. Beside it, chisels, hammers, saws, and every imaginable blade hung along the wall.

A table made from barrels shoved together with a bloodstained slab of wood on top stood in the center of the room. It wasn't really a room, but just the end of a long deck — second level down — that opened to a row of cannons still run out for battle.

In all honesty, it looked like a medieval torture chamber rather than a place where men were healed.

Even the ever-stout Hannah trembled beside her.

Why, God, why? When I promised I would behave.

She hadn't time to ponder the answer as a sailor flung the worst of the injured onto the table. "Here you go, miss." He gave her a salacious perusal before he left.

Groans of agony reached for her from all around, pleading with her to do something . . . anything to ease their pain.

Emeline's breath came swift as she leaned toward her friend. "I don't know what I'm doing, Hannah."

"You did a fine job 'elping the men on board the *Charlotte.*" Hannah patted her hand.

Emeline gulped and stared at the saw hanging on a hook. "But I did not have to cut off any legs!"

"Let's see wha' needs to be done first." Hannah squeezed her hand and gave her a nod of confidence that did naught to ease Emeline's nerves. " 'Sides, I thought you loved adventures, Em. Think of this as jist another one."

"I love exciting adventures, not *deadly* ones."

"Posh!" Hannah snorted. "If there weren't no risk, you wouldn't need faith."

But Emeline didn't need faith. She already believed God rewarded those who obeyed.

And punished those who didn't.

Nevertheless, she must do what she could for these poor men. Pushing aside fear for her own predicament, she rolled up her sleeves and approached the sailor on the table. He was British with a splinter the size of a sword blade stuck in his leg. Perspiration dotted his forehead, and his chest rose and fell erratically beneath a blood-splattered shirt. Wild eyes met hers as she examined the wound.

"You will be all right, sir." She attempted a smile. "Nothing a few stitches won't fix."

This seemed to allay his fears as he breathed out a huge sigh and nodded.

His confidence in her — though based on naught but his own foolish hope — gave her strength, and she got to work. With Hannah's help, she found needles, twine, laudanum, bandages, and several herbal tinctures. There were six injured sailors: two British and four Americans. Thank God, none of them required actual surgery.

Regardless, the next several hours passed in a blur of removing splinters, cleaning out wounds, stitching gashes, and applying bandages.

All while trying to see in the fading light of a flickering lantern and maintain balance on a heaving deck.

An ache etching across her lower back and bloodstains splotching her gown, Emeline moved among the hammocks — where the marine had hoisted the injured after she tended them — offering them whiskey-tainted water.

As she did so, she also offered each a smile, even the two British sailors. One of them had barely a whisker on his chin, and she imagined he had a mother back home worried sick for the safety of her boy. The other — Thornhill he'd given as his name — was the first man she'd ministered to. Well into his fifties with a bulbous nose, arms as thick as masts, and a whitecap of hair atop his head, he had followed her every movement when she cleaned out the gaping wound on his leg. Yet nary a shriek, cry, or wince gave indication of his pain.

She set the ladle down on the table and rubbed the back of her neck. Now that the crises for these men were over, her own crisis rose to tighten around her heart. She was a British prisoner on board a British man-of-war during wartime. Could things get any worse?

A dozen possibilities rampaged across her mind — imprisonment in one of those dreadful prison ships, endless enslavement on board this ship, transport back to England to be tried as a traitor, abuse at the hands of her enemies, or perhaps — her heart nearly failed her at the thought — even ravishment.

Oh God, I'm so sorry for whatever I've done to deserve this.

If she had known what would happen, she *would* have jumped overboard that morning. Like Jonah tossed into the sea to save the ship from calamity, perhaps she could have spared the crew of the *Charlotte* from enduring a punishment meant only for her.

Standing on the quarterdeck, feet spread apart for balance, Owen squinted against the sun slipping behind the American coastline to his left. Per his captain's orders and the fleet's command, they had sailed on a north-northwestern course all afternoon toward the Chesapeake, where they were to team up with Admiral Cockburn's fleet blockading the bay. Captain Blackwell had come on the bridge once or twice to check on things, but otherwise he remained below as was his way. Unless of course, they came across another ship. That he trusted Owen with the command of the *Marauder* never failed to make him smile. If the captain only knew . . .

"Two points to larboard, Mr. Pardy," Owen commanded the helmsman then turned to the master. "Take in fore-topsail, if you please."

The master began braying a string of orders, sending sailors scrambling to task.

Owen gazed at the patch of land barely visible off the larboard beam. *America!* How he missed his homeland. It mattered not that he'd been absent for eight years, he couldn't wait to return. *Had* returned in fact two years ago just before the war broke out. He'd recently passed the lieutenant's exam and the *Marauder* had been assigned to transport British prisoners, who'd escaped from England to America, back to stand trial. He'd managed to slip away from the shore party and make his way home to his mother, who lived in Norfolk with her brother and his family.

Granted, they were overjoyed to see him again, grown and successful and "finally making something of himself." His mother wept continually, refusing to stop embracing him. But when he expressed a desire to become a privateer in what would surely soon be a war with Britain, his uncle, who had recently been appointed general counsel for the Department of the Navy, pleaded with him to return to the British fleet and spy for America.

Owen instantly regretted telling him that the *Marauder*'s next assignment was to cruise the American coast. Besides, how could he convey information from a ship he so rarely left?

"Just one bit of vital information. That's all we need," his uncle had said. "Egad, but you are in the perfect position on board a frigate. The Royal Navy use their frigates to pass messages between other ships in the fleet, do they not? You'll be privy to most of their plans."

"But certainly I can do more good for my country as a privateer!" Owen returned.

His uncle had leapt to his feet, eyes flashing. "We have many privateers, but if you agree, only one spy on a British ship. Think of what you could learn. A major attack at sea or land, and you would know of it!" His uncle took up a pace before the hearth. "When you come across information that will affect the outcome of the war, desert your ship and bring it to us. War will break out soon, boy. Madison has had enough of British aggression. Our army and navy are nothing compared to Britain's. Wars are won by good intelligence, Owen, and spies provide that. We need as many men on the inside as we can get."

Owen rubbed the back of his neck. "Even if I am privy to battle plans, how am I to get them to authorities on land?"

"Supplies — you'll need to come ashore for supplies. And surely your ship will take part in land raids. Jump overboard when you are close to shore, if you have to. You can find me at the Department of the Navy in Washington. Your country needs you, boy. Now more than ever."

Owen could not deny the pride he'd felt at his uncle's confidence in him. He'd never known his father. The man had abandoned him and his mother when Owen was ten. Hence, he'd never known a man's instruction or guidance or a father's pride in his accomplishments. Still, when he had hesitated, his uncle had sealed the deal with an offer too good to refuse. If Owen provided crucial information, his uncle would fund a privateer for him to captain for the remainder of the war.

A brisk wind swept over the ship, and Owen closed his eyes for a moment, breathing it in, listening to the creak of wood, dash of water, and clap of sheets. To have his own ship to command, to be free of British regulations and rules, to sail upon the seas wherever he wished . . . and all in the service of his country. It would be a dream come true!

Yet so far, he'd not been privy to any crucial information. Things were about to change, however. Joining the blockade fleet would grant him opportunities to go ashore on supply runs and raids, where it would be easy to desert the Royal Navy and gain his freedom.

He only needed one piece of information — battle plans, tactics, something huge that would greatly affect the outcome of the war, something he could pass on to the American generals that would change the course of events and give his countrymen a fighting chance.

In the meantime, as much as he hated it, he must remain on this ship. The British navy with all its rules and regulations was enough to leech the life out of a man, and he rued the day eight years ago when his mother had acquired a commission for him through a well-placed family relation in England.

"To make an honorable man out of you,"

she had said. "To make straight your way-ward ways so you won't end up like your father."

Instead, all the eight years of restrictions had done was to make Owen more deter-mined than ever to live out his days in reck-less abandon, beholden to nothing and no one.

The sun slipped behind a mountain of green to the west, spreading maroon and golden waves over the treetops. A breeze swept up from the sea, and Owen removed his cocked hat, allowing the air to cool the sweat on his forehead. Up ahead, a forest of bare masts rose to the evening sky — ships guarding the entrance to the Chesapeake — and beyond them to the west sat his home-town of Norfolk. This was the closest he had been in two years. But he could not go home yet.

"Stand by to take in fore-topsail!" he bel-lowed to Mr. Wells, the midshipman of the watch. "Reef the courses!"

He needed to slow their approach before he signaled the other British ships.

Lieutenant Benjamin Camp left the group of sailors he'd been instructing and took up a spot beside Owen. Wind tore through the light hair beneath his hat as blue eyes shifted his way. Ben had been one of the few bright spots in the past eight years of drudgery. A good friend, a good man — a far better man than Owen would ever be. And the only person who caused Owen to feel a slight twinge of guilt at his betrayal.

His thoughts drifted to the American prisoners and to one American in particular. He needed to see how she fared and then escort her and her companion to their cabin.

"All in all, a good day, wouldn't you say, Owen?" Ben clasped hands behind his back and squinted at the last rays of the sun.

"A great day for Britain, indeed. A worthy prize and prisoners to boot."

"Beautiful prisoners." Ben winked. "I saw the way you looked at her."

Owen snorted. "You mean the way *every* sailor looked at her?"

Ben smiled. "She was quite lovely, wasn't she? And I know your weakness for the gentler sex."

"She's our enemy," Owen spat out, hoping to end the conversation.

"Which makes her all the more vulnerable to your attentions." Ben gave him a stern look. "Behave the gentleman, Owen."

"Whatever do you mean?" Owen jerked back his shoulders, feigning indignance.

"She's a prisoner and not one to be taken advantage of."

43

"I own that I may be a rogue as you say, but I would never take advantage of a woman. Can I help it if they all flock unbidden to me?"

Ben shook his head and chuckled. "God may have given you a handsome face and an innate charm, but it is a gift to be used for good and not evil."

"I *have* been using it for good. *My* good." Owen winked.

"You are incorrigible." Ben shook his head. "If we succumb to every temptation sent our way, we are no better than animals."

"Have you considered that perhaps that is all we are?"

"Bah! I will convince you otherwise one of these days."

Owen smiled at his friend's constant attempts to entrap him in religious conversations. "I await that miraculous moment."

Ben smiled in return, then leaned on the railing and shouted to the master to take a sounding.

"Speaking of ladies," Owen said. "I must be off to get them settled. Send for the captain. He'll want to signal the ships."

Leaping down onto the main deck, Owen descended a ladder onto the gun deck and followed a flickering light to the far end where the surgery was located. The lovely American was busy tending to the men, so intent on her ministrations that he hesitated at the edge of the room to watch her.

Blood stained her gown, but she didn't seem to care as she flitted about from hammock to hammock, offering a smile and a drink. She had treated six men, two of whom were British. And he could not see that she'd shown any favoritism at all. In fact, as she halted now before one of the *Marauder*'s sailors, she offered him the same kindness as she had just given the American before him.

The older woman followed her, carrying a bucket.

Finally, she moved away from the last patient, placed her hand on her back, and stretched her shoulders. He'd never seen the likes of it. A lady — of some means and status from all appearances — unaffected by blood, getting her hands dirty, and truly caring for the injured, enemy or not.

The ship teetered, and he shifted his boot to catch his balance.

The angel turned. Her eyes latched upon his, fear replacing the exhaustion he first saw within them . . . along with something else he couldn't quite place.

Even with her stained gown and loose hair

tumbling from her pins, she was a true beauty. And no enemy at all. Hence, he must do his best to protect her and the other prisoners while not raising any suspicions as to his own loyalty. Not an easy feat, by any means.

Emeline didn't know what to make of the handsome lieutenant leaning against the bulkhead, arms crossed, staring at her as if he'd never seen a woman before. How long had he been there? How much had he seen? The marine he'd ordered to stand guard remained at attention, eyes focused forward, so unflinching during the past few hours that she'd been tempted more than once to tickle him just to get a reaction.

But of course proper ladies didn't tickle strange men.

The lieutenant continued to stare at her. No, more like admire or perhaps study as one would a new form of species. He stood there in his crisp blue uniform with nine gold buttons down the lapel and a grin on his lips as if he knew a grand secret. Dark brown hair was slicked back in a queue. His jaw was firm, his nose straight and regal, and a small scar cut across his left cheek. But it was his eyes that drew her in. She was not unfamiliar with the particular way he was looking at her, and she almost turned her back to him. But there was something else in their brown depths — a wildness, an intensity that made her throat feel suddenly parched.

Setting down the bucket, Hannah rang out a wet cloth and finally noticed the man.

He started toward them. "You make a good ship's surgeon, Miss Baratt."

He remembered her name. She tore her gaze from his. "I am a woman and thus cannot be a surgeon, sir. Not on a ship or anywhere else." Not that she wanted to be. "Come to lock us in irons?"

"If that is what you prefer." He grinned, a roguish look that set her off balance. Or was it the sudden tilting of the deck? "But I am to escort you to your cabin when you are finished here. The captain wishes you to join him for dinner."

"You may tell the captain I do not wish to eat with my enemy. Nor do I have a change of clothes with which to do so."

The lieutenant seemed amused. "A gown will be provided."

Hannah fisted her hands at her hips. "Where is my husband?"

His gaze shifted to her, but Emeline saw no indication of anger or even annoyance on his face. "Locked below with the other prisoners."

"I demand to see 'im at once."

"You'll make no demands on board this ship." His voice was deep, commanding, and confident, and Emeline could see why men obeyed him. Then as if a cloud moved from above him, his expression softened. "I'll see if I can arrange a visit."

"Shall we, ladies?" He swept an arm out, and with it, the scent of the sea and spice wafted over her.

Retreating, Emeline wiped the back of her hand over her cheek and glanced over her patients. "I should remain to tend to these men."

"Your concern is most admirable, Miss Baratt, but I will have Mr. Oakes tend to their needs. He's been stepping in ever since our surgeon was blo—" He slammed his mouth shut. "Now, if you please?" He gestured behind him.

"You may forgo the pleasantries, Lieutenant . . . Masters . . . was it? I know full well I have no choice in the matter."

This seemed to elicit yet another smile.

"You both would do well, miss" — his eyes shifted between Emeline and Hannah — "to behave and stay in the captain's graces. He would not be opposed to tossing you both in the hold with the other prisoners for the remainder of the war."

His tone carried no threat but oddly bore a hint of pleading, as if he actually cared what would happen to them.

Still, he was a British officer *and* her enemy, and by the look in his eyes when he glanced her way, he definitely had untoward intentions.

CHAPTER 4

Hannah hefted the gown over Emeline's head and assisted her arms into the sleeves. "Such a lovely dress. Strange they 'ad it lyin' around when no women are aboard."

"Strange, indeed. And I don't like wearing it at all." Emeline allowed the lilac gown to drop to her ankles then stuffed her locket inside the bodice. Grabbing the purple velvet sash, she tied it around her waist. Lace ruffles fringed the neckline, puffed sleeves, and hem, creating a very alluring look, but she wasn't in any humor to be alluring.

She'd done her best to freshen up with the basin of water and lye soap the cabin boy had delivered, but the metallic scent of blood and sweat still rose from her skin.

She glanced down. "Whoever owned this gown was much better endowed in the chest than I am. I hardly fill out half of it on top."

"Ah, dear, but it looks lovely on you

anyway. 'Ere, sit down."

Emeline lowered to the only chair in a cabin not much bigger than the one she'd had on her father's brig. "Why am I making myself presentable anyway? I don't want to eat dinner with these men, enemies all of them."

Hannah began working on Emeline's hair. "That handsome lieutenant don't seem too bad. He were kind to us. Better than expected, I'd say."

"That's because he wants something, Hannah. He doesn't even know us. Why else would he be kind?"

"Posh, now, don't be too quick to judge. These men may be Brits, but they're God's creation too. 'Sides, he were right about one thing. It would be good to stay in the captain's graces."

"I will not lower myself to play the coquette with the man."

"I'm not sayin' you should, dear. But why not convince 'im you're not 'is enemy?"

"Of course I'm his enemy. I was born and raised in Baltimore."

"But you spent the past two years in England." Hannah raised a brow, her eyes twinkling.

"I don't understand."

Grabbing pins from the table, Hannah

began piling up Emeline's hair. "They don't know why you were sent there or for 'ow long. Why not tell them your loyalties are wit' Britain?"

Outrageous! She'd never be able to accomplish such a deception. Besides, proper ladies didn't lie. "Don't be ridiculous. They know my father owns a privateer."

Hannah stood back to examine her work, hands on her hips, her cheeks rosy and eyes alive. "Well, it will 'ave to do. You look stunning as always. And many Americans 'ave family back in England loyal to the Crown."

Emeline was pondering these things when Lieutenant Masters appeared at her door to escort her to dinner. A marine stood beside him.

The handsome lieutenant dipped his head. "I've made arrangements for Mrs. Keate to visit her husband."

No sooner had he spoken the words than a shout of glee sounded from behind Emeline as Hannah rushed forward.

" 'Ow kind o' you, sir."

"Mr. Tamson will escort you below, allow you to stay for twenty minutes, and then bring you back here where I've ordered a steward to bring your supper."

"Thank you, Lieutenant." Hannah stepped into the narrow hallway and cast

Emeline a glance of reassurance.

"My pleasure." He proffered his elbow for Emeline to take, but instead, she shut the cabin door and gripped her hands in front of her.

Clearing his throat, he started walking. "This way then."

Why he'd offered his hand, she couldn't say, because the narrow hall would not accommodate two of them side by side. It was impossible not to notice how tall he was. His hatless head skimmed the deckhead even as his shoulders brushed against the walls on either side. The scent of lye and spice and the sea showered back over her — a pleasant enough scent.

"Thank you for allowing Hannah to see her husband, Lieutenant," she said as they passed a ladder leading down and then a closed door. "Though I can hardly credit the kindness to an enemy."

"*Enemy* is a relative term, Miss Baratt."

She found his reply odd as she peered around him to see a marine standing guard outside another closed door.

He nodded to the marine who opened the door for them. Then halting, the lieutenant gestured for her to enter first.

Clutching her skirts, she turned sideways, attempting to squeeze past without touching him.

No such luck. Her bodice brushed against his chest ever so slightly in passing.

"Even enemies can be kind now and then, Miss Baratt," he whispered in a sultry tone as she passed, his warm breath wafting upon her. Against her will, her face heated, and she was sure it had turned red in the process. The rake!

She hurried into the cabin, doing her best to hide her embarrassment. Five men seated around an oblong table rose to their feet, all eyes latching upon her. Candles set in silver holders flickered from the table, which was filled with steaming bowls, pitchers, platters of meat, and baskets of biscuits. Such a feast she had not expected on board a ship and certainly did not get on board the *Charlotte*. Her traitorous stomach growled, thankfully drowned out by the purl of water against the hull and the creak and groan of the ship's timbers.

Beyond the table, stern windows revealed a night sky sprinkled with stars while the rest of the cabin was well appointed with furniture and trinkets of the highest quality — a mahogany desk littered with various maps, navigational instruments, quill pens, and an hourglass; a sideboard on which sat a silver-lidded claret jug and several cut-glass decanters; a cot, massive trunk, and fitted racks that held books of every size and color.

Uncomfortable beneath their gazes, she allowed Lieutenant Masters to lead her to a seat between two men on the right side.

"I am pleased you could join us," the captain said as he gestured for her to sit, a polite smile on his face. He was an attractive, commanding man, around forty years of age, with a strong chin and jaw and dark eyes to match his hair. Streaks of gray spanning from his temple made him look more distinguished than old.

She slid into her chair. The lieutenant assisted her from behind before he took his own seat across from her next to the captain. Two men flanked her. A marine to her right and another officer to her left, barely out of boyhood from the smoothness of his face.

"Did I have a choice?" she replied curtly, causing a few of the men to laugh.

The captain gave a tight smile and took his seat, as did the rest of them. "Allow me to introduce my officers, Miss Baratt. You are acquainted with my first lieutenant, Owen Masters." He gestured to the lieutenant sitting at his right. "Beside him is Second Lieutenant Benjamin Camp."

The light-haired man with the pleasant

face nodded her way.

"Next to him is Master Jacob Tempe."

The gruff-looking seaman barely afforded her a glance.

"On your left," the captain continued, "is Midshipman James Sharpe, and on your right, Lieutenant of the Marines Luther Dimsmore."

The young midshipman's face reddened as he glanced her way, while the marine offered her a sneer.

Despite her hunger, all she wanted to do was run back to her cabin and slam the door. She hated being on display. She had no idea why these men wanted to dine with their enemy. Unless it was to taunt her, to belittle her. Or worse, to gape at her because they'd been on a ship too long without females.

Without so much as a prayer or word of thanks, the men began grabbing bowls and platters and heaping food upon their plates. Emeline took a small portion of rice and fish, though suddenly her stomach felt as though someone had tied an anchor to it and dropped it overboard. The marine to her right took the liberty of pouring some amber-colored liquid into her glass. The scent of alcohol stung her nose.

And as much as she wanted to take a sip

to calm her nerves . . .

Proper ladies did not partake of spirits.

"Do you have any water, Captain?" she asked.

For some reason her question seemed to please him as he set down his spoonful of rice and smiled her way. "A rare luxury on board a ship, Miss Baratt. I think, however, you'll find there is not enough rum in your water to dull your senses."

"Which is why I'm thankful we also have this Madeira," Lieutenant Masters said as he poured himself a drink from a separate bottle.

"And if ever there was a man who could hold his liquor, it would be you, Owen." The light-haired lieutenant beside him chuckled.

"Hold it, indeed, for who would release such a pleasurable repast?" Lieutenant Masters grinned and sipped his wine, causing laughter to abound.

Emeline frowned.

The marine lieutenant beside her — Dimsmore, if she remembered — added with a scowl, "It has gotten you into more than one brawl ashore, Masters."

Owen's eyes flashed. "Spirits? Or perhaps it is my charm with the fairer sex that invokes jealous rages in some."

Emeline could feel Dimsmore stiffen beside her. He shifted in his seat and pierced Owen with his sharp gaze. "Women are not playthings to be pulled off shelves, toyed with, and then discarded."

"I never toy and rarely discard," Lieutenant Masters retorted.

"You do both, sir!" Dimsmore seemed barely able to contain himself. "And with those who are not yours."

Disgust soured in Emeline's mouth, and she lowered her gaze. What sort of men were these?

The ship rolled over a wave, shifting bowls and platters on the table. No one seemed to notice.

"Enough!" The captain cleared his throat and cast a stern glance over both men. "There is a lady present."

Lieutenant Camp addressed her. "You must forgive these two, Miss Baratt. They oft behave like feuding schoolboys."

"A feud that will not interfere with the running of this ship!" Captain Blackwell interjected with authority. "Or my dinner."

With a growl, Dimsmore returned to his meal.

The captain faced Emeline. "Lieutenant Masters informs me that you were quite proficient at tending the injured."

Emeline stared at her food, unsure whether her stomach would accept it or would simply thrust it back out of her mouth and further embarrass her in front of these men. "I was happy to care for them."

"Wherever did you learn such skills?" Lieutenant Camp asked before plopping a piece of fish in his mouth.

"My uncle was a physician. As a child, I assisted him in his calls on the sick and injured."

"Unusual skill for a lady," Master Tempe muttered under his breath.

A bell clanged above, joined by the squawk of a bird in the distance. *Land.* They were so close. She had felt the ship come to a halt mid-afternoon, but she didn't know where they were until the cabin boy told her that they'd sailed into the Chesapeake and dropped anchor, awaiting orders.

The Chesapeake! Would they continue up the bay and sail close to Baltimore? But what did it matter? Even if she could jump ship, she couldn't swim.

Emeline continued to stare at her food, finally attempting a spoonful of rice. It tasted better than it should have in her current state, but then again, she hadn't eaten since last evening. Finally, she squared her shoulders and faced the captain. "What is to become of me? Why have you invited me to dine with you and your men?"

"Forthright. I like that, Miss Baratt." Grabbing his glass, he sat back in his chair. "We are gentlemen and officers, and although" — he glanced at Lieutenant Masters and Dimsmore — "we have obviously been far too long from society, there is no need to be anxious for your safety. Now eat. I insist."

Lieutenant Masters refilled his glass.

"As to what will become of you," Captain Blackwell continued, "that depends on you. If you behave and tend the sick as I require, it will go well for you."

"I am no ship's surgeon, Captain." Her pulse took up a violent race. "I can only patch minor wounds and distribute medicaments for simple illnesses. If you were ever to be in battle . . ." She swallowed and could speak no more.

Her gaze met Lieutenant Masters, and she thought she saw concern on his face.

The captain plucked a biscuit off a platter. "Until another surgeon is sent to us, you will suffice. It is better for you than the alternative — imprisonment, either here on the ship or somewhere far less pleasant."

She pursed her lips, attempting to suppress the tremble that ran through her. Hannah's words intruded on her thoughts. Perhaps she *should* declare her loyalties to England. Would these men even believe her?

"The cap'n don't take kindly to American privateers," Master Tempe added with a spiteful glance her way. "Traitors, all!"

This comment, though directed at her, set the men off into a discussion of the "blasted American privateers," especially those out of Baltimore.

"That nest of pirates!" Captain Blackwell cursed. "Who would have thought there were so many worthy seamen among the barbaric Americans."

She should object to the insult, but none of them seemed to notice her presence anymore. All save Lieutenant Masters, whose gaze kept drifting her way.

She sampled the fish, her stomach responding with great enthusiasm. She bit into a biscuit, tried the crab soup, then the fresh corn and cinnamon glazed apples. The ship must have been supplied recently to have such fresh food aboard — a luxury she hadn't had in over a month.

"Proper ladies don't stuff food in their mouths like pigs in a trough." Emeline could hear her father's words as clearly as if he were sitting beside her. She'd always had a

healthy appetite, and he'd always chastised her for it. She set down her spoon.

"Remember the time Owen was sailing that prize sloop to Plymouth?" Lieutenant Camp glanced over the men and laughed. "And he caught another privateer with it? With a crew of only ten men?"

"Brave of you when you could have easily avoided battle." Captain Blackwell looked at Lieutenant Masters as a father would a son.

Master Tempe shoved a sliced apple in his mouth. "I still owe ye my life, sir, for jumping overboard in that storm to get me when I fell in."

Lieutenant Masters shrugged. "I'm a good swimmer."

"Not many officers would have done that." Captain Blackwell took a sip of wine. "Or climbed to the tops to rescue that young midshipman."

"Aye, a brave move," Tempe added.

"Or a foolish one." Dimsmore scowled and poured himself more Madeira.

So the lieutenant was not only a womanizer but a reckless madcap. More reason for Emeline to steer clear of him. Especially since every time he looked at her, she felt as though he were peering into her soul. Why would he be interested in an enemy of his people?

"Speaking of bravery, Miss Baratt." Captain Blackwell leaned back in his chair. "Why would a lady sail on board a privateer?"

Emeline set down her spoon and surveyed the men, searching for the right words . . . the right way to lie to them. Or should she? They seemed reasonable men. Perhaps her stay here would not be so bad. Perhaps she should accept her punishment. Before she could answer, the door opened. A sailor approached the captain. "Message for you, Captain."

Unfolding the paper, Captain Blackwell perused the words, his kind face of only moments ago tightening with each line he read until his expression conveyed naught but fury.

She had never witnessed such a rapid transformation in a man's mood, and it made her realize that these men were no ordinary gentlemen as they claimed. They were warriors who would not think twice about taking the life of their enemy, and taking it brutally. Even hers.

Her heart crawled into her throat. Perhaps it was best if she convinced them of her loyalty to England. The lie may ensure her safety and aid her in keeping Hannah and the crew of the *Charlotte* safe as well.

"What is it, Captain?" Lieutenant Masters asked.

Crumpling the paper, Captain Blackwell glanced her way. "Nothing. News from Baltimore."

"Isn't that where you are from, Miss Baratt?" the young midshipman asked.

Her hands shook, and she gripped them together in her lap. "I was born there, yes." She hesitated. "But in truth, it is not where my loyalties lie."

Silence absconded with all sound in the cabin. Even the men's chomping ceased.

"What are you saying?" the captain demanded.

"I am saying I am loyal to England. I always have been."

"She's lying." Master Tempe slammed down his glass. Beside her, Dimsmore huffed and tossed the remainder of his drink to the back of his throat.

Lieutenant Masters narrowed his gaze.

Lieutenant Camp's expression scrunched in disbelief. "You expect us to believe such a thing after we discovered you aboard an American privateer?"

Emeline swallowed and lifted her chin. "I'll admit that my father owns a privateer.

But I have not lived in America since long before the war. My father sent me to stay with family in Brighton, to be educated by my aunt. I am an artist, you see, and among many other subjects, my aunt allowed me to pursue my drawing and painting. I have been there these past" — she pressed a hand on her agitated stomach — "ten years. In truth, I hardly remember Baltimore." For a minute she was sure everyone would burst out in laughter. To her own ears she sounded ridiculous — her bloated tone overcompensating for her lies.

Captain Blackwell eyed her. "Why didn't you tell us this when you boarded?"

"Because, Captain." She looked down, giving herself time to search for the right answer. "I didn't wish my father's crew to know."

"Then why not inform us when you first entered my cabin?"

"I wanted to know what sort of men you were. And I was frightened — still am, if you wish to know. I've never been on a ship of war before, nor with such boisterous company. I was unsure whether you would believe me."

"Hmm." The captain grunted. "Who is this aunt? I assume she can verify your story."

"Miss Martha Langson, daughter of Lord and Lady Newsome."

"Nobles." Lieutenant Masters snorted.

For the first time that night, Lieutenant Dimsmore turned to gaze at her, his perpetual scowl temporarily abandoned.

"Indeed, my aunt was the daughter of a baron, but she passed away three months ago, and my father called me home." She fingered a curl dangling at her neck. "Believe me, I did not wish to return. My father and I had a falling out before I left, and we have not spoken since." At least that much was true. And that her aunt had died.

For some reason, Lieutenant Masters sat back with a snarl and stared out the stern windows.

"Your father called you home during a war?" The captain's tone was incredulous.

Emeline stared at her lap. "There was an issue of arranging a proper guardian for me, and I had not received the monies my aunt left me."

Captain Blackwell studied her, rubbing his chin. "If this is true, then we have done a great injustice to you, miss. This certainly was not our intention."

"You may ask Captain Lansing why my father wished to bring me home. He was none too pleased at being called across the pond away from his trade in the West Indies."

"We will do just that, Miss Baratt. Mark my words."

Fear prickled over Emeline's skin. Had she made things worse with her lies? What if Captain Lansing knew more of her past than she assumed? If so, her deception would probably cause Captain Blackwell to follow through with his more unpleasant threats to her future.

CHAPTER 5

Sleep eluding her yet again, Emeline stood at the railing of HMS *Marauder* and gazed over the choppy gray waters of the Chesapeake. It was hard to believe that just yesterday morn she'd been doing the very same thing aboard her father's ship, and even morosely — though not seriously — contemplating leaping overboard rather than be saddled to a life of drudgery and societal expectations. La, how much had changed since then — and all for the worse. Either God had a rather peculiar sense of humor or He was still punishing her for her past rebellion.

Rays from a rising sun warmed her back and chased away the mist blanketing the water as four bells rang, announcing the midpoint of the morning watch. She'd taken a chance coming above without an escort, but after pacing her cabin all night while listening to Hannah's snores, she felt she'd go mad if she didn't get some air. The marines and sailors on watch gaped at her when she'd first come above, but then they'd quickly settled back to task. She assumed if any of them planned to take liberties, they wouldn't do it in plain sight of all.

Proper ladies did not gallivant without escort around ships full of men.

Nor did they lie.

"Lord, I'm sorry for the lie. It appears that no matter how hard I try to be good, to be a proper lady, I fail." Which was most likely why she was in her current predicament.

A cool breeze swirled around her, tossing her curls and flapping the edges of furled sails above. Emeline drew a deep breath and watched as beams of golden light glittered across the waves and reflected off a rising mound of deep browns and greens in the distance.

Land. *Her* land. Her country. The country she had denied last evening in front of officers of the Crown.

But what else could she do?

She frowned. That seemed to be her excuse more often than not for the things she did by impulse rather than by honor and decency.

Like the time when she was sixteen and she had sneaked out of her house before dawn and gone to the shore to paint the sunrise.

Or the time she'd put rat hair in Richard Boorden's soup when her father invited him and his family to dinner to arrange a potential courtship. She couldn't help but smile now at that particular memory. The poor man had dashed out the door and retched in the bushes before leaping upon his horse and galloping down the street as if he couldn't get away fast enough. He'd even forgotten his hat.

Or the time she'd been so engrossed in studying the paintings of a traveling art gallery, she'd forgotten to buy fresh fish from the market. They'd had nothing to eat for dinner except moldy bread.

She sighed. Her unruly antics had continued right to her last year at home. One of the worst rainstorms she'd ever seen had struck Baltimore, and she simply had to experience it firsthand. Hence, down to the shore she went to watch the foamy waves crash, to thrill at the way lightning painted the sky in vibrant silver, and to feel the rain soak her hair and skin — all impulses based on her sentiments without a care for her safety, her reputation, or her future. At least that's what her father so often told her.

"Proper ladies don't traipse around in the

rain. You're so much like your mother," he had shouted in exasperation, shaking his head and stomping away.

Which was the best and worst insult of all. The best because Emeline had loved her mother and had always wanted to be like her; the worst, for she knew how much he disapproved of her mother's actions when she'd been alive.

Tugging on the chain around her neck, Emeline opened the locket that held a miniature painting of her mother, done by the woman herself. Somehow, she had captured her zeal for life in her expression, her smile, and the look in her eyes. Emeline's own eyes moistened as she stared at the picture. If not for this portrait, Emeline might have forgotten all those wonderful things. Or even how beautiful her mother had been. "I love you, Mama."

Swiping away a tear, she closed the locket and dropped it beneath her bodice again.

"And now, Lord, here I am a prisoner of this horrid war. Just when I promised You I'd behave." She glanced up at the sky where gray clouds began to form. "I would have too. Please give me another chance." Before she ended up like her mother . . . sick, miserable, and dying.

The ship angled over a wave, and Emeline

gripped the railing as footsteps alerted her to a man approaching. Lieutenant Dimsmore appeared beside her. The morning sun made his uniform appear an even brighter shade of red as his blue eyes assessed her.

"Miss Baratt," he said with a smile.

"Lieutenant Dimsmore," she returned, knowing that his sudden kindness was due to his belief she was no longer his enemy.

"You really shouldn't wander about the ship alone."

She studied him. In the sunlight, he appeared much older than he had in the dim light of the captain's cabin. At least ten years older than her. Tiny lines furrowed his face, and there was a weariness to him she'd not seen before. The odor of alcohol and musk clung to him. But still, he was a handsome man, tall, broad-shouldered, firm features, with dark hair cut short to his collar.

"I don't know how you bear the stuffiness belowdecks," she said. "I took a risk and was rewarded with fresh air and a beautiful sunrise."

"Ah, such an appreciative attitude when you find yourself a prisoner."

"Am I still?"

His lips flattened as he stared into the bay. "I believe your story, Miss Baratt, though I was skeptical at first. You comport yourself as a British lady and not one of those cloddish, vulgar Americans."

Emeline hid a grimace. "Why thank you, Lieutenant. I can't say I've ever been quite so flattered."

Her sarcasm was lost on him as he lifted his chin to the wind.

Another bell rang from the front of the ship. Five rings this time, and Emeline could hear someone below shouting, "All hands ahoy! Up all hammocks, ahoy!"

Moans filtered through the deck, followed by the thudding of feet. Within minutes, the clank and grind of chains was added to the cacophony, and ten men from the crew of the *Charlotte* crawled through a hatch, large stones the size of a book in their hands. They removed their shoes and rolled up their stockings, as a hose, carried by two sailors, was hoisted above after them. Water and sand were strewn over the deck, and the men dropped to their knees and began scrubbing with the stones. The first mate, Aaron Mules, and the purser, Robert Nifton, were closest to her. Robert glanced her way, a momentary look of confusion on his face before he went back to task.

Her heart sank, and she faced the bay again, attempting to keep her anger at their treatment from her expression.

Dimsmore's eyes followed her curiously. "Does the sight of hard work disturb you, miss? They are treated better than they deserve."

"No, of course not. I quite agree. They are prisoners, after all."

Moments passed, the scratch and scrape of their scrubbing grating over Emeline's nerves. If only she could help them somehow. And why was Dimsmore still standing there? Surely he had duties to attend.

Finally, he cleared his throat. "Miss, I feel it is my duty to warn you." He glanced behind him then leaned toward her. "There are those aboard this ship who will not treat you with the respect your weaker gender deserves."

Weaker, fie! She forced a smile. "And here I was told you were all gentlemen."

"Well" — he stared over the deck as if looking for someone — "as you witnessed last night, Lieutenant Masters has quite a history with women. And not a good one. I'm afraid he will attempt to lure you in with his charms. He cares not if a woman is rich, poor, noble, common, comely, or ugly, he must feed his insatiable ego by gaining their affection." The man's jaw tightened.

"Again, you flatter me overmuch, Lieutenant."

His eyes widened. "Oh, I certainly didn't mean —"

"I know." She smiled. "And I thank you for the warning." Not that she had any intention of getting to know Lieutenant Masters, nor the man before her. Her goal was to survive and get off this ship and back home as soon as possible before she was forced to do anything else she shouldn't do and only increase God's anger.

More sailors leapt on deck from below, followed by several midshipmen and a few officers, Lieutenant Masters among them. He headed their way.

Emeline had noticed the change in him as soon as she'd announced her allegiance to Britain. It became all the more prominent when he'd escorted her back to her cabin. An ax couldn't have sliced the tension between them. Odd. Perhaps it was because he'd imbibed too much alcohol, evident in his uneven gait. Or perhaps his flirtations had just been an act of which he had grown weary.

He halted before them now, sunlight glinting off his shiny brass buttons. "Miss Baratt, the captain wishes to see you. He has spoken with Captain Lansing."

Already? Emeline's throat tightened. "Very well."

He and Lieutenant Dimsmore exchanged a look of disdain before Lieutenant Masters led the way to the captain's cabin. But Emeline took no care of the hostility between the two lieutenants. Of far greater import was that whatever Captain Lansing had told Blackwell, it would seal her fate.

Owen Masters led the lady onto the quarterdeck and down the companionway. *Traitor* was more like it. Any attraction he had toward her had instantly vanished at her declaration. And even more so when he'd spotted her with Lieutenant Dimsmore. Any female who spent time with that slobbering mongrel was not worthy of Owen's time. Unless of course, Owen was only using her to purposely frustrate the marine — as he had done on more than one occasion when he'd lured away Dimsmore's lady friends.

Not that this particular traitor hadn't presented a very alluring figure standing on deck with the wind waltzing through her curls set aglitter by the rising sun. That same sun cast a flawless golden hue over her skin that made Owen itch to touch it. He frowned. Perhaps his attraction to her hadn't completely vanished. But he had no intention of doing anything about it. Not even when, at the moment, her uniquely feminine body drifted past him — smelling of woman and sunshine — as she entered the captain's cabin.

Ducking beneath the beams, Owen followed and heard the marine shut the door behind him.

"Ah, Miss Baratt, do have a seat." Captain Blackwell rose from behind his desk and gestured toward one of the wooden chairs perched before it.

The rare smile on the man's face had the effect of lowering the lady's shoulders ever so slightly. Still, she remained standing, stiff as a salt-encrusted rope, as if she were on trial for her life.

"I'll stand, if you don't mind," the lady squeaked out.

"Very well. I'll get right to the point. I have spoken with Captain Lansing and he has verified your tale."

The woman smiled and released a huge breath.

"However" — the captain added, circling the desk — "only so much as to say he'd been ordered to collect you in France and escort you home and that you were none too happy about it."

The lady gulped. "Surely that is all you

need to believe that I am indeed loyal to England."

Captain Blackwell leaned back against his desk. "What did you intend to do once you arrived in Baltimore, Miss Baratt? Seeing that you would have been on enemy territory against your will."

The lady flung a hand to her chest and affected a rather defenseless tone. "I was petrified at the prospect, I assure you. Should anyone discover my loyalties, I could be hanged."

Owen prided himself on knowing the human character pretty well, and it seemed the lady was overdoing the theatrics a bit.

"Of course," she continued, twirling a finger through one of the golden curls at her neck, "I would have made plans right away to escape my father's clutches and return to Brighton as soon as possible."

"Why did you bother stepping aboard your father's ship in the first place?"

"I am a dutiful daughter, Captain, or try to be. I wanted to explain to him face-to-face that I wished to stay in England. He is my father, after all."

The captain seemed to accept her explanation, for he nodded. "Yet by what means would you survive since your aunt has passed on?"

Miss Baratt folded her hands before her, her fingers fumbling as if seeking anchor. "My aunt gave me an inheritance that will suffice as my support until I can marry."

Another smile appeared on the captain's face — so foreign, Owen had to blink to ensure he wasn't seeing things. "I find myself persuaded of your loyalties."

"Thank you, Captain." The lady's smile washed all harshness from Blackwell's face. "Am I free to go then? Can you put me ashore?"

"Bah!" The harshness returned. "I wouldn't do such a thing to a defenseless lady. It isn't safe for you in Baltimore at the moment. I insist you stay on board. As my guest of course. Aid the men with their medical complaints, and I promise I will ensure you are safely delivered home at war's end or back to England if you prefer."

"War's end, Captain?" Moving to the chair, she slowly lowered to sit. "But that could be years."

Captain Blackwell shared a glance with Owen that bespoke of knowledge he'd yet to impart. "I assure you, miss, that will not be the case. The war will soon be over, and Britain will be the victor, mark my words."

Miss Baratt held a hand to her stomach.

Owen wanted to do the same. But not for

the same reasons. A wave of excitement quivered through him. Finally he would acquire some valuable information vital to the war, and he could leave this godforsaken ship.

"In the meantime, Miss Baratt," the captain continued, "did I hear you say that you are an artist?"

The lady nodded, appearing as unsure where this was going as Owen.

"Good." Captain Blackwell rubbed his hands together. "I would like to commission you to do a portrait of me while you are here."

Miss Baratt shifted in her seat and lowered her gaze. "I couldn't possibly. Truly, I'm not that —"

"Pish." He batted away her objections. "I've always wanted one done, and since you are available . . . Give me a list of what you require, and I'll ensure you get it."

Miss Baratt opened her mouth to respond when a knock on the door preceded Midshipman Sharpe with a folded piece of foolscap. He handed it to the captain.

No one else would have detected the ever-so-slight twitch above the captain's right eye, but Owen knew him too well, had served under him these past eight years. He was a man of rules and regulations, honor and loyalty. A good man, in truth, despite the blood of England flowing through his veins and the Royal Navy saturating his every breath. The only thing that stirred emotion in Captain Blackwell — other than, apparently, Miss Baratt — was an impending battle in which he was assured victory.

"I must end our conversation, Miss Baratt." He folded the paper and extended his hand. The lady took it and stood.

"Of course, Captain. You have a ship to run."

"And a war to win." He bowed to place a kiss on her gloved hand. "In the meantime, should you have need of anything, Lieutenant Masters will see to it."

Owen suppressed a huff. Just what he needed. To be nanny to a traitor — a pampered British lady who would no doubt complain ad nauseam about the hardships of life aboard a ship. Never mind her. He had but one thought as he escorted the woman back to her cabin. To discover what news had the captain so excited and then get off this blasted ship and gain his freedom.

CHAPTER 6

Emerging from the companionway with Hannah on her heels, Emeline drew in a deep breath of fresh air, tainted with brine, moist wood, and a hint of earthy loam — the promise of home. She shifted her gaze to the left where she spotted land rising from the sea like a murky green cloud off the starboard railing. So close, she could almost reach out and grab it. Yet there might as well have been an entire ocean between them.

Halting, she lifted her closed eyes to the sun. It felt good to be on deck. She'd spent too much of the past two days in sick bay attending the injured or in the captain's cabin working on his portrait.

"I thank you, dear," Hannah said from beside her, drawing Emeline's gaze as they started their walk. "For takin' me on your walks. I 'ate bein' cooped up below like one of their pigs or chickens."

Emeline returned her smile. "The captain said I needed an escort, and who better than you?" Feeling uneasy, she looked up to see at least half the sailors staring their way.

"It gives me a chance to see Mr. Keate, I 'ope." Totally ignoring the gaping men, Hannah searched the crew for her husband as they rounded the capstan and headed for the foredeck ladder.

"I'm sorry, Hannah. I don't believe he's above deck right now." Emeline had already spotted the men from the *Charlotte,* cleaning out the guns and polishing brass. "They only allow ten men on deck at a time."

Hannah did not hide her disappointment. "I don't see why. Chained up as they are. They can 'ardly escape."

The clank of iron brought Emeline's gaze to Aaron Mules, the *Charlotte*'s first mate, scrubbing the foredeck ladder railing . . . or at least attempting to do so as the irons locking his feet together made mounting the ladder difficult.

"Mr. Keate is doing well though. You know he is." Emeline tried to comfort her friend.

"Yes. I saw 'im last night. So nice of Lieutenant Masters to allow me to sup wit' the crew."

Emeline glanced over her shoulder to the

quarterdeck where the lieutenant stood, shoulders squared and hands clasped behind his back. His cocked hat shadowed his expression, while rebellious strands of his dark hair had loosened from his queue and waved wildly in the breeze. Beside him Second Lieutenant Ben Camp said something and gestured her way.

She spun around. "Indeed. Though I cannot fathom why."

Sails glutted with wind as the frigate sped on its way. Their snap and thunder joined the gush of water against the hull. No sooner had Emeline left the captain's cabin yesterday morn than he'd ordered all sails raised, and they had rushed up the Chesapeake where they rendezvoused with a much larger ship of the line. A cockboat was lowered, and the captain and his lieutenants rowed over to the other ship, only to return at dusk. He must have received new information, for they tacked about and were now speeding back down the bay.

Halfway up the ladder, Aaron dropped his cloth. The wind tossed it across the deck, and Emeline rushed to catch it before it blew overboard.

She handed it to him, accompanied by her best smile, but he snagged it from her hand, eyes fuming, before he spit to the side.

Clenching her jaw, she clutched her skirts and passed him up the ladder, heart sinking. "I wish you'd tell them the truth," she said to Hannah after they both stepped onto the foredeck. "It pains me to see the hatred in their eyes."

"It's for the best, dear. The less people what know, the better." Hannah patted her hand. "The truth might slip, and then who knows what the captain would do with you?"

"Most likely lock me up below. Which is what I deserve."

"Don't be sayin' sich things, dear."

Emeline released a breath and leaned toward her friend. "Lying is a sin."

"Not during war," Hannah whispered back with a flash of her brows.

Despite the breeze, perspiration slid down Emeline's back. "Indeed? And just where is that written in the Bible?"

"God says not to murder, but then killin' in battle is acceptable. And remember King David actin' like 'e were insane so 'is enemy wouldn't kill'im?"

"I don't remember that. You certainly know a lot about the Bible."

"My papa taught me to read jist so's I could study the Word. 'E said it would bring me life. And 'e was right."

Emeline had to admit, other than sermons she'd heard in church, she didn't know the Bible very well at all.

Sails cracked above, and the deck slanted. Emeline stumbled to grip the railing. After nearly two months at sea, she should be used to the heaving and leaping by now. She should also be used to being stared at. She glanced over her shoulder once again to find Lieutenant Masters's eyes fastened upon her. Instantly, he shifted them away.

The ship bucked again, this time showering them with sea spray. Hannah chuckled. Emeline joined her, happy to have a reprieve from the hot August sun.

"Look lively, men!" Lieutenant Masters shouted. "Lay aloft and unfurl topsails. Halt taut!"

Other shouts followed, and men scrambled to task. Backing against the railing, Emeline braced her feet on the teetering deck and watched as sailors flew into the shrouds and climbed aloft. Others remained on deck, hauling ropes or "lines," as they called them, while other men busied themselves with repairs on lines and sailcloth, cleaning guns and weapons, and participating in drills. Every man had a duty, and every man was busy at all times. Such an efficiently run ship. So different from the

Charlotte.

The thought made her swallow a lump of dread. How was America supposed to win against such power and expertise?

"Where d' you suppose we are sailin' off to so fast?" Hannah gripped the railing and glanced above. A few of the newly unfurled sails flapped and growled like ravenous birds until they caught the wind in a jaunty *snap!*

"The captain must have important information to pass along to other ships," Emeline shouted over the wind.

Hannah's eyes sparkled with mischief as she leaned toward Emeline. "You should discover what it is."

"Whatever for? In case you haven't noticed, we are trapped on board this ship."

"Posh!" Hannah waved a hand through the air. "We could escape."

Emeline gaped at her friend. "Two ladies escaping from a Royal Navy ship of war? Hannah, you never fail to surprise me."

"If God wills it, it will happen. Remember Peter in prison?" The sun had turned Hannah's cheeks into rose blossoms, making Emeline smile.

Before a frown overtook her. "I'm no Peter." Not even close.

"God is no respecter of persons, my dear.

We are all 'is children."

Some of whom were in His disfavor at the moment, Emeline wanted to say, but kept the words to herself. Hannah would only chastise her for such a thought.

They continued onward, and Emeline felt that strange sensation again. But when she looked around, she found most of the sailors hard at work and only Lieutenant Masters looking her way. Odd man. Facing forward, she inched over the deck, clinging to Hannah for balance. At the front railing, she halted and closed her eyes, allowing the wind to rush through her hair and blast past her ears. And for a moment, she pretended she was on a ship of her own, sailing on a wild adventure to exotic ports where she would paint magnificent scenes of each locale. She smiled. What a wonderful dream.

But a dream only for fools.

Angry shouts coming from the main deck ruined their carefree moment, and Emeline took Hannah's arm and led her around the foremast then down the ladder.

Lieutenant Dimsmore stood amidships, his red uniform stark in the noonday sun, shouting at one of his men — something about the state of his uniform and his omission to salute the lieutenant properly. The fury tightening the lieutenant's face and his grating tone made Emeline feel sorry for the young marine he was scolding. She slowed her pace even as she heard Hannah give a disappointed huff.

"Somethin' 'bout that man. I don't care for 'im."

"He's just doing his job, I suppose."

"Maybe, but 'e's the one locked up my husband, an' what keeps 'im locked up. Wait." Hannah's press to Emeline's arm halted her. "That means 'e has the keys."

Emeline followed her gaze to a set of iron keys hanging on a loop attached to the lieutenant's belt. "Yes. But what can we do about it?"

A tiny smile curved her lips. "Why, get them of course!"

Emeline couldn't help chuckling at her friend. "To what purpose? Need I remind you, *yet again,* that we are on a ship?"

"Ah, but did you know that ole Robert Nifton can swim?" Hannah stuffed wayward hair beneath her bonnet.

"The purser?"

"Aye. And quite well if you're to believe 'im."

Emeline wiped the perspiration from her neck. "So what are you saying? We should steal the keys and free Robert so he can swim to shore?"

"That's exactly what I'm saying, dear."

"And what will he do when he gets there? Doesn't that leave the rest of us still here?"

Hair blew in Hannah's face, and she wiped it away. "Didn't you say you knew someone in the militia? We can send Robert to 'im."

Emeline stared toward shore, shaking her head. "I still don't see what good it will do."

"Maybe they can rescue us."

"Off a Royal Navy frigate?" Emeline gave her friend a berating look, to which Hannah only shrugged.

"Why would they bother?" Emeline added.

Finally, Dimsmore's tirade wore itself to completion, and the young man shuffled away. Emeline attempted to yank Hannah to the other side of the deck before Dimsmore saw them.

Too late. He started their way. And as if he had not just belched fury upon another human being, he smiled. "Miss Baratt, such a joy to see you grace our deck," he said, completely ignoring Hannah.

"Thank you, Lieutenant Dimsmore. My friend Mrs. Keate and I enjoy the fresh air."

He gave Hannah a cursory glance. "Then perhaps you'd enjoy a stroll after dark? The stars are stunning on a clear night."

She'd rather remain in her cabin and count the divots in the bulkhead. "The captain has forbidden me above deck at night."

"Without an escort, Miss Baratt." He leaned in to smile. "But I assure you, you will be safe with me."

Somehow she doubted that. Hannah gently elbowed her in the side. *La!* To what lengths did Hannah expect her to go to steal the man's keys?

Seconds passed interminably . . . proper ladies didn't steal, right? *Ohhh. Fie!* She faked a smile. "Then I accept your kind offer, sir."

He dipped his head. "Until then."

Hannah drew her away and smiled. "Seems you have an admirer."

Emeline huffed. "I should get below. The captain expects me to continue work on his portrait."

"How is that going?" Hannah asked as they approached the companionway. One glance up revealed Lieutenant Masters's eyes upon her yet again. Was he that deprived for the sight of a female? The man had done nothing but ignore her for the past two days.

"The portrait I have only just started," she answered Hannah as they descended the ladder. "The captain seems pleasant enough. Not at all as harsh as he first behaved."

Inside their cabin, Hannah shut the door and whispered, "Good. Perhaps you can pry some information out of 'im. That would give Robert somethin' to tell the Baltimore militia."

Emeline rubbed her temples. "You have such exaggerated faith in me, Hannah."

"Because I know you, dear. You 'ave a passion, a fervor for life, and a courage I've not seen in many women. If only you realized it."

Emeline sighed and stared out the porthole. "I don't want to realize it. For once in my life, I'm trying to be proper."

"Proper? Wha's bein' proper 'ave to do wit' it?" Hannah grabbed a handkerchief and dabbed the back of her neck.

"Hmm." Emeline frowned. "Regardless, my passion for life, as you put it, has brought me nothing but trouble." And she was through with trouble.

After doing her best to refresh her appearance, she left Hannah and made her way to the captain's quarters with one thought in mind.

Proper ladies don't spy.

■ ■ ■ ■

Sometimes Owen loathed himself. Well, perhaps *loathe* was too strong a word. *Disappointed* might be a better term. The Baratt woman was clearly an enemy. Nay, worse than an enemy — a woman who would turn against her own country! Yet he couldn't keep his eyes off her, purposely made sure he was on the quarterdeck when she came up for her daily strolls, looked forward to them, in fact. He could only attribute his uncanny attraction to the fact that he'd not had female company in months. Not since the last shore leave in Bermuda. Indeed, that was the reason.

She was comely, to be sure, but he'd seen beautiful women before — courted many of them. No, there was something else about her. Where most women would demand every luxury they could acquire aboard the ship, she hadn't asked him for any comfort besides the basic necessities she was given. And she didn't flirt. What attractive woman didn't flirt? It was one of the few weapons God had afforded the weaker sex. Miss Baratt had been given an extra measure of beauty with which to wield that particular sword. Still, she kept her blade sheathed.

In addition, she was kind — even to her enemies. He'd watched her with great interest pick up the rag the American sailor had dropped. Why? Even if he wasn't her enemy, she hailed from nobility — albeit quite removed — but someone of status who had lived in a noble home these past ten years would never lower themselves to assist a servant. Why, she even treated her lady's maid as if she were an equal, a friend.

Then there were the injured men, both British and American, whom she tended without prejudice. And tended well — sacrificing her own sleep last night to remain with one of the Americans who had developed a fever.

Hang it all!

And now she was speaking to Dimsmore. The peckish fatwit! How could she not tell what a snake he was? She may be a kind enemy, perhaps even humble, but she was definitely a fluffhead.

"You're quite smitten, eh?" Ben said from beside him.

"I beg your pardon?"

"With the Baratt lady." He gestured toward her with a nod of his head.

"Gad! Contrary to your opinion of me, I don't chase every skirt I see."

"Only the pretty ones."

"She's pretty, I'll give you that. But that's where her attraction ends."

"I've never known you to avoid a comely lady. Have you taken ill with one of those tropical maladies?" Ben raised a hand to touch Owen's cheek, but he batted him away.

"Perhaps I'm finally looking to settle down, and I seek a decent lady." The words sounded ridiculous on his lips.

Apparently Ben was of the same mind, as his laughter brought the gaze of a few sailors. "If so, then why not this lady? She has noble blood *and* an inheritance. In addition, I continually find her conversation at dinner entertaining."

Something Owen had also enjoyed. The lady was polite. She offered compliments and interesting anecdotes, and she didn't blather on and on about nonsensical things as some women were prone to do. "Then *you* pursue her," Owen snapped.

"I just may do that, thank you."

Owen's stomach coiled into a knot at the words. Yes, he definitely loathed himself.

Fortunately, land appeared off their starboard bow, changing the topic of conversation.

"I'm anxious to stretch my legs on land again," Ben said, planting his feet wider apart as the ship canted. "Hard to see it so close."

Harder than Ben realized. One slip over the side and Owen could swim to shore within minutes. "Perhaps we'll soon be sent on a raid."

"Perhaps, yet I don't relish the violence." Ben's mood suddenly soured.

"We are at war. Violence is to be expected," Owen returned a bit too harshly, though he was not surprised at his friend's comment. Ben was pure goodness, honesty, integrity, and kindness. If anyone could convince Owen that God was good, it would be Ben.

If anyone could convince him otherwise, it was men like Dimsmore. He watched as the ladies left his side and disappeared below, the muckrake staring after Miss Baratt like she was his last meal.

Yes, the sooner Owen got off this ship, the better.

The urgent message the captain had received two days ago contained information about a large land campaign, but the captain had given him no further details. So Owen would wait. And watch. If there was an invasion planned, he must discover the date, location, and number of troops and armament.

Still, such a plan could only mean one thing — the British believed they had the advantage and could soon win the war.

Owen smiled. Not if he could help it.

CHAPTER 7

The minute Lieutenant Dimsmore offered Emeline his arm as they emerged from the companionway after dinner, she regretted accepting his invitation. It wasn't that he wasn't handsome, gallant, and charming. He was all those things. But something about the man soured the food in her stomach she'd just consumed.

But once they reached the railing and she gazed up at the myriad stars flung across the sky like diamonds on black velvet, she realized his company might be worth it.

The bell at the forecastle rang three times, and she calculated it must be 9:30 p.m. in the first watch — something the captain had taught her. Drawing a deep breath, she gripped the railing and glanced up.

"It's gorgeous. God's creation. Makes one feel rather small in the scheme of things."

Dimsmore eased beside her. Far too close. "I knew you'd enjoy it."

She inched away slightly. "Thank you for the invitation."

"It gives me a chance to get to know you better."

"We eat dinner together every night, Lieutenant."

"Ah, but I mean alone."

She glanced behind her at the men on watch. "We are hardly that." *Thank God.*

Dimsmore slipped closer, and the pungent scent of alcohol stung her nose. She'd seen him imbibe quite a few drinks at dinner. Lieutenant Masters as well, making her wonder if they were in some sort of deviant competition to see who best could handle their liquor before falling over.

He placed his hand atop hers on the railing, giving her a start. She withdrew hers and faced him, longing to excuse herself and retreat to her cabin, but she had promised Hannah she'd attempt to get his keys. As unlikely as that was.

"Tell me of your childhood, Lieutenant."

The topic seemed to wipe the desire from his eyes as he faced the bay. "Not much to tell. I was an orphan. My parents were both killed in a fire when I was six."

Emeline followed his gaze to the dark water, laced in silver moonlight. "I'm so sorry."

He leaned on the railing. "I barely remember them."

"How did you survive . . . if I may ask?"

"I lived on the streets of Liverpool for a time, stealing food and clothing just to stay alive." Despondency settled on his features, almost making Emeline feel sorry for him.

"Then I was rounded up and sent to an orphanage, where I was educated." He shrugged as if the incident had not altered the course of his life.

"Thank God for that," Emeline said, and she meant it.

"God had naught to do with it, Miss Baratt. He abandoned me as a child and has not made an appearance since."

As much as she wished to defend God, the sudden fury and gravity of his voice bade her change the topic. "How did you come to be a marine?"

His shoulders rose. "I joined of my own volition. Worked my way up from private to lieutenant in only ten years. Unlike" — he glanced behind him — "many of the naval officers who receive commissions because of their connections and wealth." His tight expression matched his tone, and she wondered if he referred to someone in particular.

"I imagine they work quite hard as well."

"Humph. They have a life of ease on board this ship compared to the marines. We are the ones who keep order, who protect against mutiny. We are the ones who go on land to fight their battles."

Emeline swallowed. Anger and bitterness seeped from this man's being, and she longed to relieve herself of his company, but her eyes landed on the keys clipped to his belt. "You have done well for yourself, Lieutenant. You should take that to heart and be satisfied."

"Hard to do when lesser men around me get rewarded." He tightened his grip on the railing, then released it and drew a breath, no doubt trying to cool his temper.

She should allow him to do so . . . wanted him to regain his cheerful demeanor lest he lash out at her in his anger. But she needed to gather information, and his fury may allow something of value to slip. "I assume you refer to Lieutenant Masters. I have noticed the animosity between you."

The smile that had begun to erase the hostility from his face grew flat again. "Hard not to, I'm sure, miss. He is a raffish miscreant of the worst kind. You'd do best to avoid him."

"You fault him simply because of the privilege of his birth?"

"No. I fault him for the many acts of cruelty he has perpetrated on me, Miss Baratt."

"Such as . . . ?"

He studied her for a moment, but a cloud covered the moon, and she couldn't make out his expression. Finally he said, "Nothing that would recommend either of us, I assure you." He proffered his elbow, and she allowed him to lead her around the deck.

The keys jangled at his side, taunting her. She must get her hands on them. But how?

He led her up the foredeck ladder to stand at the prow where a cool breeze swirled around them, fluttering the curls at her neck. She grabbed one and fingered it like a lifeline, seeking a solution to her problem. Lieutenant Dimsmore stumbled and put a hand on the mast for balance, reminding her that he was rather besotted. He stared out to sea, and Emeline took the chance to study the keys in the light of a nearby lantern. A simple clip seemed to be the only thing holding them to his belt.

Shoving down her repulsion, she sidled up to him. "Your success in life is commendable, Lieutenant. It is rare to find such a handsome, honorable man. I can't help but wonder why you have not taken a wife."

This brought a rather wide smile to his lips. "You are too kind, Miss Baratt." He faced her and leaned back on the mast, taking her hands in his. "I suppose I haven't found the right lady."

She stiffened but did not pull away.

There was a coldness to this man. Instead of looking at her with an ounce of care, his gaze was one of predator to prey — or perhaps a pirate to treasure.

Over his shoulder, Emeline saw the marine who was standing guard turn and leave. A trickle of dread slithered down her spine.

She glanced up at Dimsmore and found his gaze wavering over her lips. La, was she going to have to kiss this man in order to get his keys? Nausea brewed in her stomach as she debated whether it would be worth it.

The deck tilted.

Emeline fell against him. His arms encircled her. His head lowered.

She reached for the keys.

Her hand gripped the metal ring. She dared to gaze up at him and found his slobbering lips inches from hers. His breath was hot and stank of rum. Disgust made her cringe.

She groped for the clip. There! She attempted to open it. It didn't budge. She tugged on the keys. They wouldn't move.

Fie!

She pushed from the lieutenant and backed away.

His eyes opened, shock and anger appearing on his face.

"Thank you for the stroll, Lieutenant, but I should be retiring. I have a long day tomorrow in sick bay."

"So soon?"

"I'm afraid so." When he didn't offer his arm, she turned to leave, but he grabbed it anyway and spun her back around.

"I had hoped . . . well . . . it seemed . . ." He pulled her against him and held her there with one hand, while with the other he raised her chin.

She pushed against his chest, fear ringing in her ears. "Let me go! What are you doing?"

Hands reached out of the darkness and shoved the lieutenant away. He stumbled over the deck and landed against the railing. "Leave her be, Dimsmore." The voice, deep and commanding, brooked no argument.

Gripping the railing, Lieutenant Dimsmore stood to his full height and glared at the intruder. "What business is it of yours, Masters?" He straightened his coat. "The

lady and I were merely getting acquainted."
He gripped the hilt of his service sword.

"Miss" — Lieutenant Masters's gaze swept to her with a look of concern — "do you wish to be left alone with this man?"

"Most certainly not." She stared at Dimsmore. "You forget yourself, sir."

He frowned, and his eyes flashed fury before a smile appeared on his lips. He dipped his head. "Forgive me, miss. I misunderstood your encouragement."

"I gave you no such encouragement."

"Then I am in your debt." Squaring his shoulders, he stormed past Lieutenant Masters, bumping him in the arm.

The lieutenant stared after him, his fists hard knots, and for a moment Emeline thought he would charge him and pummel him to the deck. But then he turned and faced her. Wind wisped the dark strands of his hair, and she wished she could see his expression, but his hat kept his face in shadows.

"Are you all right?"

"Yes, thank you." Her pulse was racing a bit too fast, and she was angry at herself for not getting the keys, but she was otherwise unharmed. It wasn't like a man had never attempted liberties before.

"I warned you about Dimsmore. He's not

a man you should keep company with."

"He says the same about you."

"Then I recommend you stay away from us both." His tone was clipped, angry.

Yet contrary to his words, he made no move to leave or escort her below. He merely stood there, gazing at her.

Oddly, she felt none of the uneasiness she'd felt with Dimsmore.

The deck lifted slightly, and the lieutenant steadied her with a touch then quickly released her. He scanned the ship as if he were looking for some excuse to leave.

"Why have you not asked anything of me?" he finally said, removing his hat and raking a hand through his hair.

"I have everything I need, Lieutenant."

He snorted and ran a thumb down the scar on his cheek. "I have never met a woman who was satisfied with what she had."

"Then perhaps you should spend less time in the company of port trollops."

Surprisingly, he chuckled. "Now, what gave you that impression?"

"Merely the talk at dinner. Or are you so drunk each night, you don't remember?"

He cocked his head. "Do my dalliances and spirits offend you?"

"Me? I take no care. But they offend God."

He grinned and looked away. "Ah, God is it? I doubt He knows what I'm up to."

The declaration both surprised and saddened her. In that way, he and Dimsmore were very much alike. But she wouldn't tell him that. "He sees everything."

Lieutenant Masters cocked a brow. "Yet He never attempts to stop me."

"He has given us free will."

"Then I choose to live my life the way I please."

As if to prove his words, the ship pitched yet again, and the lieutenant caught her by the waist — this time refusing to release her.

She glared up at him. "Am I freed from one scoundrel only to be assaulted by another?"

CHAPTER 8

Owen found he would like nothing more than to sample Miss Baratt's sweet lips. Hang it all! He released her, regretting the action immediately for the wind stole away her feminine scent.

"I make a habit of never kissing traitors," he said.

She eyed him curiously. "But I am on your side."

"Regardless, you turned your back on your country. Not an admirable trait."

"So that is why you despise me so." She stared over the shadowy bay.

"*Despise* is a strong word for someone I do not know."

"Yet I see it in your eyes when you look at me. And you *do* look at me quite often." She smirked.

So she'd noticed. He would have to stop that immediately. "You are the only eligible woman aboard this ship, Miss Baratt. All the sailors look at you."

Lifting her hand, she began twirling the curls at her neck — an adorable habit of hers he'd noticed. Along with her moist, soft lips that suddenly drew his gaze again.

He *did* want to kiss her. Desperately.

"Hmm. Since you loathe my presence, Lieutenant, why are you still here? Surely you have duties to attend."

"I cannot leave you unescorted."

"I can take care of myself. Besides, a traitor deserves whatever fate brings her, no?"

Owen crossed his arms over his chest. "Perhaps, but I have my orders."

This seemed to sadden her. "Very well, Lieutenant. You may escort me to my cabin."

He may, may he? Her supercilious tone grated, but he supposed that was her intention.

At the door of said cabin, before he could bid her good eve, she slammed it in his face.

Maddening woman! This was his reward for rescuing her from Dimsmore? Next time he would leave her in the man's slimy grip. He stood there for several minutes, too angry to move, oscillating between knocking and demanding an apology — or at the very least, a thank-you — and going to the wardroom for another drink.

Finally he decided to head down to sick bay to see his injured midshipman before retiring.

He leapt down the ladder and crossed the gun room that substituted for the crew's berth at night. Snores rumbled from dozens of swinging hammocks hanging from the deckhead, looking more like a school of grumpy whales than sleeping sailors. The stink of far too many unwashed bodies curled Owen's nose.

Only three men remained in sick bay, one American and two British — Seaman Thornhill, who slammed his eyes shut when Owen appeared, making Owen wonder if the man was pretending his illness, and Midshipman Langston, whom he found reading a book by a candle.

"Studying for the lieutenant's exam, I see." Owen drew up a stool and sat beside the man's hammock.

Langston lowered his book and smiled. "No time to waste, sir. I hope to take it soon as this war is over."

"Good man. How are you faring?"

"I am well. Miss Baratt said I can return to my duties tomorrow. Though in truth, I could use a few more days of studying. Besides, she's pleasing to look at and so kind."

"Kind?" The thought bristled Owen.

"Aye, doing so much more than old Clemens did. Checks on us often. Makes sure we get enough food and water. Talks with us, offers comfort. Sometimes she even sings."

"Sings?" *Of all the . . .* Owen clenched his jaw.

"She's even kind to Thornhill there" — Jack thumbed toward the seaman two hammocks over — "who constantly makes lurid comments. And the Americans too. That one over there, he says all manner of vile things to her since she claimed loyalty to Britain. But still she tends his wounds just the same. Probably saved his life."

Owen didn't want to hear any more. "Seems you're quite smitten."

"Naw, sir. She's far too old for me. But it's nice to have a caring female on board."

Owen chuckled at the comment, for the lady had to be close to his own age of five and twenty. "Well then, I shall see you at your post."

"Are we going to see action, sir?" The boy's eyes lit.

"Seems that way." Owen nodded and rose. "The captain is preparing for a big campaign."

Angry at herself for not getting Dimsmore's

keys, Emeline tried her best to concentrate on the task at hand — painting the captain's portrait while hiding her true loyalties beneath the man's incessant questions. Either he suspected her or he was truly interested in getting to know her. Both prospects sent a shiver down her spine.

Every day over the past week, she'd spent two hours in his cabin during the hottest part of the day. In that time she found him to be a strict and stern man, but fair, kind, and a good conversationalist.

Also during that time, HMS *Marauder* had been quite busy sailing up and down the Chesapeake, meeting with other ships of the line. No sooner did they drop anchor beside a ship than Captain Blackwell and his lieutenants would row over to confer with its officers, only to return in a few hours and set sail in the other direction. Even in the short time Emeline had known the captain, she could sense a new excitement about him. His eyes had a twinkle that wasn't there before, his step was a bit lighter, and every time he called his officers into his cabin, he seemed about to explode with new information.

Of course she was always excused before she could overhear anything of import.

But she *did* know one thing. Something

big was afoot, and keys or no keys, she simply had to discover what it was.

Dabbing her brush into a blob of brown paint, she stroked it over the canvas and decided to turn the questions onto him. Most men loved to talk about themselves, and she sensed this one was no different.

"Pray tell, Captain Blackwell, how did you come to be in His Majesty's service?"

He shifted excitedly in his seat by the stern windows.

"Be still, Captain," she scolded playfully.

"Ah yes, of course." He smiled and began to talk, regaling her with the entire story of his naval career. A fascinating one, to be sure, and one that more than entertained her. His love of the sea was obvious, as was his love of rules, regulations, and God. Indeed, she could learn much from this man.

"I see you are a man of honor, Captain. One who allows decency, morality, and the strictures of society to guide your behavior."

He must have noticed the approval in her tone, for the gold epaulets on his dress coat shook as his shoulders rose. "Indeed, Miss Baratt. I have lived my life accordingly, and the good Lord has marked His approval with many a success."

Exactly what she believed. Or what she

must believe from here on out. God rewarded good behavior and punished bad. No more frivolous pursuits for her, no more wild adventures, no more dreams of becoming a famous artist and traveling the world.

From now on, Lord, I promise to comport myself as a lady of good breeding and high society.

Sunlight trickled through the stern windows and dappled over Captain Blackwell's blue coat, sending Emeline dipping her brush in the yellow paint, hoping to capture it.

"And where do you go from here, Captain? I mean, after we defeat the Americans." She hoped he didn't notice her grimace.

"Why, I hope to make admiral one day, but of course that depends on so much. Regardless, I wish to serve my country at sea, for it is my true love."

Emeline bristled at the comment. "But what of your wife? How often do you see her?"

"Very rarely, I'm afraid. But that's the life of a sailor's wife."

"Surely she has children to keep her company in your absence."

Silence pervaded the cabin, save for the creak of timbers and gurgle of water.

"We could never have children, I'm afraid."

Suddenly Emeline felt sorry for the poor woman, left all alone months on end without even children to comfort her. "I'm very sorry, Captain."

"So are we, but God's will be done." Though his voice was edged in sorrow, she sensed his strong faith.

She ducked her head behind the canvas, feeling like an intruder into the man's emotion.

"I have grown fond of our time together, Miss Baratt," he said.

Hannah's suggestion to get close to the captain reasserted itself in her thoughts. "Thank you, Captain. I too have enjoyed our conversations." Though it was true, guilt pricked her conscience at her ulterior motives. *And* at her lies. Yet perhaps the captain had some of his own reasons for befriending her. Many a lonely man at sea had found temporary solace in the arms of another.

Bile rose in her throat at the thought that she may have to encourage such attention. She continued painting.

"If you'll permit me to say, Miss Baratt. If Eleanor and I were to have had a daughter, I can very well imagine her to be just like you. Talented, wise, educated, and kind."

Relief swept through her. A daughter — not a prospective lover. She smiled. An honorable man, indeed. His sentiment touched her deeply, something that rarely occurred with her own father. She laid down her brush and peeked around the canvas. "If you'll permit a moment of honesty, Captain. If God had deemed me worthy to be your daughter, I should feel quite honored."

Captain Blackwell smiled, rose from his seat, and started her way.

She meant it of course, but as he approached, guilt at her deception assailed her, making her feel nothing like a proper lady at all — and everything like a bedeviled cur.

He halted before her and was about to say something when a rap on the door interrupted them. At his "Enter," in marched Lieutenant Masters, hat in hand, ducking beneath the beams. Strands of his windswept hair hung about his stiff jaw.

A burst of salt-laden air swept in behind him and rustled the papers on the captain's desk.

His intense gaze swept over her before it landed on the captain. One curious brow lifted at the sight of them so close. His presence filled the room, and against her will,

Emeline's heart leapt in her chest.

Owen stood at attention. "Captain, we approach HMS *Shannon*."

"Very good." Captain Blackwell backed away from the lady, adjusted his coat, and grabbed his hat. "Miss Baratt, it has been a pleasure as always. The lieutenant will escort you to your cabin."

She nodded and smiled before focusing back on her painting.

Blackwell marched from the room, leaving Owen alone with the woman. He should escort her right away. He would be expected on deck. But his eyes were drawn to the portrait she so intently worked on.

Though only shadows and shapes took form on the canvas, he could see the figure of the captain emerging, the colors and textures quite alluring. "Exquisite." His thoughts emerged unbidden in a whisper.

Startled, she swerved to face him. "I didn't realize you were still here."

Did she take so little note of him that she wasn't even aware of his presence? He supposed he deserved that. They hadn't spoken since he'd rescued her from Dimsmore, and he wondered if he'd been too harsh. But seeing her sitting here in her blue gown, fringed in Chantilly lace, all innocence and golden curls, he felt himself softening toward her.

And he couldn't have that. "I should escort you to your cabin."

"Do you admire art, Lieutenant Masters?"

"I admire beauty."

She stared at him, and he could see in her eyes that she understood he referred to more than the painting.

He shifted his stance. "Your work is truly beautiful thus far. I own it will be a good likeness of the man. You've captured his severe essence, his authority."

She eyed him with a grin. "And yet I sense your disapproval of those qualities."

"He is a good man, and I have learned much from him these past years. Your time could be spent in worse company."

"You shock me, sir. I understood you to be a man who shuns rules and regulations." Her tone was playful, her green eyes twinkling.

So she *did* pay attention to matters concerning him. "That doesn't mean they don't fit well on others." He frowned. "A little advice, miss. Have a care for your reputation."

"My reputation is none of your concern, Lieutenant," she retorted, her playfulness gone. "I am merely painting his portrait.

That is all." She dipped her brushes in a cleaning solution.

"There is talk among the crew."

"You would do well not to listen to idle gossip, Lieutenant. Or" — she smiled coyly — "perhaps you are jealous?" The curls around her neck dangled like jewels.

Of all the . . . ! He couldn't help but chuckle. What a fascinating woman. Too bad she was a traitor, or he'd be delighted to banter with her, even woo her with his charm. "You flatter yourself, miss. But I give you fair warning. Do not toy with the captain's sentiments. I will not see him hurt." If the woman could turn on her own country, she could certainly turn on a man.

Oddly, her brow furrowed, and a brief flicker of unease traversed her expression before she began drying her brushes with a cloth. Her glance swept toward the captain's desk as if looking for something. "No need to escort me, Lieutenant. I should clean my brushes more thoroughly before I return to my cabin."

"I cannot allow you to remain here alone."

"I only wish to —"

Owen held out his hand. "Now, Miss Baratt. I am needed above."

With a huff, she laid down her brushes, stood, and followed him out the door. At her cabin, he bowed and spun on his heels before she could slam the door on him again. He heard it slam, nonetheless, as he made his way up the companionway ladder. For some reason, that made him smile.

On the main deck, he joined Captain Blackwell, Ben, and Dimsmore in a cockboat that had just been lowered and was ready to row to HMS *Shannon*. The meeting with the captain of the *Shannon* was short and to the point. Maps were spread out and battle plans marked. Coded messages were handed to Blackwell with further instructions.

But one thing — one very alarming thing — became clear. One piece of information that sent Owen's mind and emotions reeling.

The British planned to attack Washington, DC!

He could hardly believe it. The capital of his nation! His anger and outrage at the news had risen so quickly and so intensely, it had taken every ounce of his strength not to unleash hell on the officers surrounding the captain's table of the *Shannon*. But he must have allowed a flash of emotion to appear on his face, for Dimsmore stared at him most curiously after that.

Unfortunately, the crew of the *Marauder*

would not take part in that battle, but their marines and sailors would be required for another possible offensive planned against Baltimore.

Specifics of both battles were being kept secret at the moment, but soon all would be disclosed.

Owen hated to wait. He longed to jump overboard, swim to shore, and warn his uncle. But he didn't have dates or troop numbers yet. Just a few more days, a week at most, and he would know more. In fact, he would probably be sent ashore with the marines. After that, it would be easy to sneak away and report to his uncle in Washington. Then finally after all these years, he would gain his freedom, but even more importantly, he would be able to help America win this war and defeat the British once and for all.

CHAPTER 9

"Quit your pacin', dear. It only makes it hotter in 'ere."

The bulkhead grew larger in Emeline's vision until she could make out every stain, knot, and divot. Twisting one of the curls at her neck, she spun, her skirts swishing over the cot on one side and the table on the other. "I can't. I hate being confined in this cabin. I feel as though I'm in prison."

Before the words escaped her mouth, she realized what she had said and knelt before Hannah, sitting on the chair. "I'm a peevish goose. I'm so sorry, Hannah. I know your husband is locked below in a far worse place than this." She rose with a sigh and moved to the tiny porthole. "I should not complain." Standing on her tiptoes, she peeked out at the same scene she'd seen for the past two weeks — ripples of gray-blue water extending toward the distant blur of land.

"That's a'right, dear. I know 'ow you hate

losin' your freedom."

Emeline drew a breath of the stale, muggy air and rubbed the moisture from the back of her neck. "I hate this deception. Especially lying to the captain. Why, every day he seems more and more attached to me."

"That's a good thing, if you ask me." Hannah unbuttoned the top of her neck-high bodice and began fanning herself with an old cloth.

"Have you gone mad? He looks at me as a long-lost daughter. I am the worst sort of person to trifle so with the sentiments of a lonely man. God must be so displeased." Which would explain why their situation only seemed to grow worse.

"This is war, my dear. The closer the captain gets to you, the more 'e will trust you, and we need some good information soon." Rising, Hannah moved to the cot, lifted the straw mattress, and pulled out a cloth. She carefully unwrapped it and lifted it toward Emeline. A sharp chisel lying among the folds reflected a twinkle of mischief in Hannah's brown eyes.

"What?" Emeline could only stare at it. "Where did you get that?"

"One of the sailors repairin' the mast on deck put it down while 'e went to ladle some water for a drink."

"You stole it?"

"More like borrowed." Hannah winked, but then she stumbled slightly and rubbed her eyes.

Emeline poured a glass of water from the pitcher and handed it to her. "I know what you're up to. You intend to give it to Robert to cut through his chains."

"Tonight. It might take 'im a day or two. By then, it would be good to 'ave some information what he can report to the American forces." Taking a sip of water, she lifted brows toward Emeline.

"And you expect *me* to provide that?"

"You're the only one what can."

"Isn't it bad enough I'm lying and deceiving and spying on people who are kind to me? And now you want me to steal information?" Emeline fluffed out her skirts and plopped into the chair. "My father would die of shame."

Hannah wrapped up the chisel and stuffed it under the mattress again. "Your father would be proud."

"No, he wouldn't. He would say" — she lowered her voice and added a bit of pretense for effect — " 'Ladies don't engage in such devious and dangerous behavior.' " She sighed. "Besides, doesn't the Bible say we are supposed to be submissive?"

"To God, absolutely. To our 'usbands, within reason. But *not* to our enemies." The deck tilted and Hannah grabbed the table for support. "Posh! Why is it so bloomin' hot in 'ere?"

Emeline frowned. "Even if I should acquire some valuable information, how will he ever be able to sneak overboard?"

Hannah sank to the bed and closed her eyes for a moment.

"Are you all right?" Emeline knelt before her. "Your face is flushed."

"Jist 'ot and tired, I'm sure." She caught her breath and stared at Emeline. "It'll 'ave to be before dawn when they send the prisoners up on deck to do the 'olystoning. The marines are usually so sleepy they won't notice 'is chains missing in the middle of the rest. It would be an easy thing for 'im to slip quietly over the side."

Emeline wasn't sure about that. From what she'd seen, the marines were quite attentive.

"So's all we need is for you to glean some important information from the captain."

"Oh, is that all?" Emeline laughed. Yet, if she admitted it, being a spy sounded rather exciting. It was the deceiving part she hated. "I'm definitely going to hell."

Hannah chuckled. "I doubt that very

much, dear."

"Then why am I always forced to do the wrong thing?"

"I can't say, 'cept perhaps your idea of the right thing an' God's might be a bit different. 'Sides, why shouldn't women lead excitin' lives? God ain't no respecter of persons, race, or gender, an' 'e's created us for a life of adventure, not boredom. Look at me!"

True. Hannah had led a fascinating life. As a young girl, she'd helped her family defend their home in Boston from the British during the Revolutionary War. After she'd married Abner Keate when she was seventeen, she'd traveled with him, first on a merchant ship then on a privateer. She'd been to five different countries and seen things Emeline could only dream of. "You are an exception, my dear friend. Much more is expected of someone of my station."

"Bah on all stations! Ain't no need for 'em in America."

Emeline wished that were true. "Perhaps I am too rebellious at heart, and I always will be."

"We are all rebellious at heart, dear. That's why Jesus 'ad to die to pay the price for us. But followin' a bunch of rules don't make you righteous in God's eyes. Knowin' 'is Son does. An' havin' 'is Spirit inside you."

She pointed at Emeline's chest. "Don't it say in God's Holy Word, 'Where the Spirit of the Lord is, there is liberty'?"

Emeline had never heard that before. "But that doesn't mean we should do bad things like lie and steal and cheat."

"Of course not!" Hannah coughed. "God sets us free to follow 'im. Before we knew 'im, we was slaves to evil and wickedness. Now we can partake in all the adventures 'e has planned for us."

Emeline rubbed her tired eyes. "I don't understand how we can be free yet have to follow rules at the same time. It doesn't make sense."

"It will, dear, someday." Leaning over, Hannah coughed again, this time more violently.

Emeline poured more water from the pitcher into her mug and handed it to her. "Are you ill, my friend?"

"Jist a bit of a cough. I'll be fine. But I fear I'll miss our afternoon walk. I need to lie down for a while."

"Of course." Emeline helped her lie back on the cot and felt her forehead. No fever. Good. "I'll go without you and return to check on you later."

No sooner had Emeline closed the door than her heart began thrashing in her chest at the thought of what she must soon do. Sneaking out at night from her father's house, painting instead of doing her chores, attending the Independence Day parade alone against her father's wishes — those were simple things. But spying for her country on an enemy ship? As fun as it sounded, it could get her hanged. Along with Hannah and the rest of the crew of the *Charlotte.* How could she even entertain the thought for one minute?

But she *was* entertaining it; God help her, she was. She could almost see her father's face, red and lined with anger . . . the fear streaking across his eyes at the danger she was putting herself in, the fury at her foolishness.

She would pray and seek guidance. Yes, that was what proper ladies did, didn't they? And if God had set her free, as Hannah had said, He would surely answer her, despite her many failings.

Making her way down the wobbling companionway, she silently appealed to God for wisdom. She continued praying as she mounted the ladder onto the deck. But once she emerged, a blast of hot wind swept her petitions away before she could feel any peace that God had heard her requests.

As if sensing her discomfort — and longing to increase it — the sun moved from behind a cloud and speared her with rays as hot as branding irons. She quickly ducked into the shadows of the quarterdeck and waited for her eyes to become accustomed to the light.

A line of sailors to her right, under the command of Master Tempe, hauled on a rope that led to a yard above. One man sat on a barrel sewing up a hole in a sailcloth. A carpenter repaired the bulwark to her left. Above her from the quarterdeck, commands from the officers fired down upon the crew, keeping them attending their duties. Marines in their bright red uniforms with muskets in hand stood as stiff as masts along the railing. She felt sorry for them in this hot sun and wondered if the captain ever allowed the men to jump in the bay to cool off. Most likely not.

Shouts from the sails lured her gaze to the tops, and shielding her eyes from the sun, she spotted a sailor, stripped to his waist, balancing on the top yard as if he were born a monkey. Beneath him, two other sailors were holding something.

She felt eyes upon her and lowered her gaze to see Lieutenant Dimsmore addressing a group of marines. He'd apologized for his behavior the day after the incident, but since then, he'd kept his distance. For which she was glad. Though now, he smiled her way and started toward her.

Thankfully, Lieutenant Camp appeared at her side.

"I see you are without escort today, Miss Baratt."

Dimsmore spun around but not before she saw a scowl on his face.

Wind blasted over them as Emeline balanced on the teetering deck. "Hannah is not feeling well."

"I'm sorry to hear it. But no doubt with your healing expertise, she'll be on her feet in no time." Ben's blue eyes flashed with approval as he gave her a genuine smile.

"You're kind to say so, but in truth I fear I don't know much about doctoring at all."

"I beg to disagree with you, miss. And so would our injured sailors. You are a godsend to this crew. We are most fortunate that you are loyal to Britain."

Laughter from above drew her gaze again — *familiar* laughter — and she glanced behind her on the quarterdeck. Lieutenant Masters was not there. Shielding her eyes, she stared once again at the man who was balancing on the top yard as the ship rocked and heaved through the blue waters of the bay. There was no rope about him and nothing much for him to cling to, save a few lines and the mast. Yet he stood there, wavering in and out of her sight, as nonchalant as if he were standing on firm ground.

"Is that — ?" she asked.

"It is." Ben followed her gaze and smiled.

"La! What in the blazes is he doing?"

"Small repairs to the fly block."

Gripping the mast, Owen stood tall and gazed over the Chesapeake as if he were merely glancing out a window. Yet every time the ship leapt over a wave, every time the wind stuffed into a sail and jerked the mast, he dipped behind sails and lines out of her view. "Surely there are other, lesser-ranked sailors who could attend such a dangerous task."

"Indeed. As I have told him repeatedly. In truth, miss, he quite enjoys it."

"Foolish man. He could fall and die."

"I believe that's exactly *why* he enjoys it." Lieutenant Camp smiled. "A bit of a wild card, Owen is, I mean Lieutenant Masters. The opposite of our captain, I'd say. But the men adore him. And despite the antics, the captain admires him as well. He can always count on Owen to volunteer for the most dangerous missions."

"So I have heard during your dinner conversations." Emeline was as daring as

131

the next person — much to her father's chagrin — but there was a difference between adventure and stupidity. Then why couldn't she pull her eyes off this particular *stupid* man — a mixture of fear, admiration, and disgust causing her to squirm? The ship lurched again, but this time, Owen slipped from the yard.

Gasping, she inadvertently grabbed Lieutenant Camp's arm.

She felt him tense beneath her touch, ready to give some order, but then Owen swung himself seemingly without effort onto a yard.

"He's a fool," she spat out.

"Some would say so."

"Not you?" She dropped her gaze to Lieutenant Camp. The man had such a pleasant demeanor, she could well imagine him sitting in an English parlor having tea. Blond hair streaked lighter by the sun crowned a handsome, kind face. "You are his friend."

"He's a good man, Miss Baratt. He merely needs someone to temper his talents toward a more productive path."

"I doubt there is such a man."

"No, but there is God."

Emeline merely nodded, for she knew firsthand that God was good at tempering.

If He wasn't, she'd be painting landscapes in the French countryside, not imprisoned on a British warship. However, it was good to know that there was at least one British officer besides Captain Blackwell who was a godly man.

Several sailors on deck began clapping, and she glanced aloft to see Owen making his way down the shrouds. Finally he gripped the backstay and slid down to the deck with more pomp than was necessary, bowing before their cheers.

Grabbing his shirt, coat, and hat from a post where he'd left them, he sauntered toward Emeline and Ben, that ever-present annoying grin on his lips.

Yet it wasn't his smile she was looking at, but rather the flex of every muscle rounding his chest and arms as he moved, like a cougar on the hunt. *Oh my.* And his stomach — ripples of iron and steel, tanned bronze by the sun. A flush swamped her, and she dropped her gaze to the deck.

She really *was* going to hell.

He halted before them, showering her with the scent of sweat, the sea, and man. She didn't look up. She couldn't look up. How embarrassing! Yet staring at his bare feet, her embarrassment only rose. Fie, two of her feet could fit in one of his.

Ben chuckled.

A finger beneath her chin forced her gaze up to Lieutenant Masters. "Something interesting on the deck, miss?"

His hazel eyes shifted from Ben to her, and she thought she saw a spark of jealousy. But that couldn't be.

"Always have to make an entrance, don't you?" Ben clapped him on the back. "Better get dressed before the captain comes above."

Yes, please, please get dressed! Emeline gazed over the bay, the distant land, the bulwarks . . .

"Reef courses!" A shout echoed down from above. "Watch your luff!"

"If you'll excuse me." Ben slipped on his hat and left.

Why didn't Lieutenant Masters follow him? Why was he still here? *And* staring at her — with those intense eyes, his dark hair blowing in wild abandon about him. "Done entertaining your adoring sycophants?" she said curtly.

"Sycophants?" He laughed, wiped his forehead with his shirt, and glanced behind him at the men who'd gone back to their tasks. "I merely provide a diversion in their otherwise monotonous day." He leaned toward her. "I could go aloft again and show you some things that would make you squirm with delight, Miss Baratt, if it pleases you."

"It does not. Nor would it please most proper ladies. Running around half nak—unclad." She couldn't even say the word. "Behaving the pompous buffoon, risking your life for no purpose other than your own enjoyment and to gain the admiration of men more foolish than you, is no way to live your life, sir. One of these days, you will end that life prematurely, and then what have you gained?"

A sour taste filled her mouth as she realized she sounded just like her father.

His smile remained as his gaze assessed her, at first with curiosity, perhaps a little amusement, but then it narrowed as he flung his shirt over his head. "And what would a traitor know of being a proper lady?"

A knife cut deep into her heart. Without thinking, she raised her hand to slap him, but he caught her wrist. Tight at first. But then he slid his fingers to her palm and turned it over to place a kiss upon it. The horror! In the heat, she'd forgotten her gloves.

She tugged it back just as blood dripped from his hand onto the deck.

"You're hurt!" Emeline flipped over his hands. Jagged bloody trails of raw skin traveled across his palms to his fingers.

He snagged them from her grip. "It's nothing."

"Of course it is. I should tend to those immediately." Even as she said it, she wondered why she was being kind to such a brute.

"I've had worse." One brow rose. "But I appreciate your concern."

"It's my job to be —"

He took her hand again and this time successfully placed a gentle kiss on her fingers — bare fingers. A pleasant heat blossomed within her.

"I bid you adieu, miss." And off he dropped down a hatch.

Leaving Emeline in such a whirlwind of emotions, she could make no sense of any of them.

CHAPTER 10

"Here you go, Mr. Ganston. Take a spoonful twice a day for a week and you should start feeling better." Emeline handed the sailor the tonic, and he gave her a toothless grin. The poor man had spent his entire life at sea, and he resembled more an old piece of rope than a man. But at least he hadn't tried to flirt with her like the other men she'd seen that day.

An endless line of them, in fact — two cases of sunburn, one heat exhaustion, three deep cuts, one sprained ankle, nausea, one case of scurvy, and one high fever. She'd done her best to care for them with the herbs and tinctures available to her, but she felt so inadequate to the task.

Except of course, when she could tell a sailor was feigning an illness just to see her . . . to tell her how comely she was and to ask for her company on a stroll about the deck.

Fie! As if she didn't have real patients to attend. Thank goodness for the marine standing guard a few feet away or she believed some of the men would have taken liberties.

Rising, she balanced over the shifting deck and began gathering bloody rags and instruments — knives, syringes, needles and twine, forceps, and splints. The mad swoosh of the sea filled the air, drowning out snores from the gun room. Between caring for the sailors and checking on Hannah — who had somehow caught a cold — Emeline had missed supper in the captain's cabin. Just as well. She had no desire to listen to the men ramble on about boring naval tactics and how they were going to defeat America. Nor did she wish to see Lieutenant Masters. Not after their confusing encounter earlier that day. The man was a paradox. One minute he seemed to be flirting with her, the next despising her. His friend Ben Camp was much more agreeable. And godly. Not that she intended to acquaint herself further with either of them.

Releasing a heavy sigh, she moved to the table, collected the vials of herbal tinctures she had used — rosemary, mint, comfrey, sage, and angelica — and returned them to the cabinet. A moan drew her gaze to the hammock which contained the last patient from the battle that had brought her here. Had it been two weeks already? All the rest of the injured had recovered, save Mr. Thornhill, a middle-aged British seaman who continually complained of debilitating stomach pains. Yet she could find nothing wrong with him, making her suspect he preferred resting below rather than returning to the grueling work above. She would mention it to the captain on the morrow.

Emeline tilted her head to the left then right, hoping to relieve the ache that had settled there. It didn't work. Grabbing a clean cloth, she dabbed the perspiration on her forehead and the back of her neck and drew a deep breath. She instantly regretted it. By now, she should be used to the foul odors and sweltering heat belowdecks. Especially since she spent so much time attending the sick in this makeshift surgery.

The ship angled to port as a rare breeze swept in from above, fluttering the lantern flames and sending light shifting over the examination table. She dipped the cloth in a basin of water, wrung it out, then began scrubbing off the blood and other body fluids.

How had she been reduced to such gruesome work?

She wanted to be off this ship. She wanted to go home. She longed to see her father, even if he was angry with her, even if he continued to restrict and restrain her . . . or worse, marry her off to some demanding man. Odd that she would say such a thing when a few weeks ago the thought of returning home made her wish to jump overboard.

No doubt living in constant fear for her own safety and that of the crew of the *Charlotte* and then having to continually maintain her deception were beginning to take their toll on her. Perhaps that was God's plan all along — to humiliate her into submission. If only He would deem that she had suffered enough for her past rebellion, that she had learned her lesson, and send her home where she could prove to Him that she had.

But at least she'd been able to paint. "Thank You, Lord, for that small blessing."

And the blessing that she'd been able to paint in Brighton as well. Her aunt had encouraged her, in fact, but as Emeline soon discovered, only as a hobby, part of a lady's education and proof of her status.

"Ladies do not perform menial work," her aunt had said when Emeline conveyed to her how she'd been raised — cooking, cleaning, and caring for her brothers. "That is why we have servants. I must say, I'm quite surprised at your father, but then again, I warned him not to marry a common American — especially one with Indian blood."

Though Emeline bristled at the insult to her mother, she was elated to think she'd found an ally in her great-aunt, someone who would encourage her to follow her dreams and not enslave herself to a marriage of duty and submission.

But that was not the case. The life her aunt offered her was merely a different kind of prison, one of societal obligations, cloaked in wealth and privilege. Her death had left Emeline with a small inheritance but not enough to live on for very long or to allow her to follow her dreams. That and her father's insistence she return home had caused Emeline to finally make up her mind to do the right thing from here on out.

Then why was she stuck on this enemy ship?

Perhaps to aid the American cause as Hannah had said. The lady had already given the chisel to Robert. The rest was up to Emeline. Tomorrow during her painting session, perhaps God would be merciful and loosen the captain's tongue about their upcoming mission. But how to broach the subject?

She imagined how the conversation might go:

"Miss Baratt, after the war, should you ever find yourself in London, I should love it if you would visit my wife and I. We could show you all the wonderful sights of the city."

"I'd like that, Captain, and by the way, what are the British plans for the American land invasion?"

No. It simply wouldn't work.

She sighed, hung up the clean rags to dry, and tossed the hopelessly filthy ones in a corner to be taken to the laundry.

A moan sounded from behind her, and she turned to see that Mr. Thornhill was finally awake. Dipping her ladle into a barrel of water, she made her way to him.

"Good eve to you, Mr. Thornhill. How are you feeling?"

"Better today, miss." He smiled a sort of crooked smile and propped himself up on his elbows.

Emeline held the ladle to his lips as he slurped down the water. "You certainly look much better. You're regaining your strength."

She withdrew the ladle and laid the back of her hand on his forehead. Still no fever.

Good. "How is your stomach — what?!" She screeched as he clutched her wrist and swung himself up in the shifting hammock. The ladle clanged to the deck. Before she could jerk from him, he leapt to the floor and shoved her back against the surgery table.

"What are you doing?" His sudden strength shocked her as the realization of what he intended sent her heart spinning in terror.

"I've been waitin' fer this moment, missy." He pressed her hands back on the table and shoved his body against hers. "We're finally alone." His breath, hot and putrid, blasted over her.

"Help!" she managed to scream, but only the distant snores of sailors and creak and groan of the ship answered.

Thornhill grabbed a cloth and stuffed it in her mouth. "That'll be enough of that. Now how's about some lovin' for ole Thornhill."

Emeline glanced to where the marine had stood, but he was nowhere in sight.

Lifting her body as if she were naught but a sack of rice, Thornhill slammed her on top of the table then leapt on her. His weight forced the air from her lungs. She gasped and struck his chest with her fists, moaning and groaning and trying to work the cloth from her mouth, but he merely grabbed both her wrists with one hand and leaned over her.

"Yeah, I've been eyein' you, pretty one, the ways you go around playin' the wanton vixen with us men, tauntin' us with your long lashes and coy smiles. They say you're wit' us, but I don't believe 'em. You ain't nothin' but a stinkin' American whore."

Had she behaved in such a way? Horrified, she tried to rise, but his weight kept her pinned, her legs flattened beneath his.

So, this was it. Her final punishment for years of rebellion. *I'm sorry, Lord. Please, help me.*

Thornhill grunted and fumbled with her skirts, giving her a bit more leverage. She kneed him in the leg where he'd been wounded.

He arched in pain. Curses spewed from his mouth. "You'll pay for that, missy."

He continued jerking up her skirts. Emeline closed her eyes. Her thoughts spun in a cyclone of disbelief and horror. Tears sped from her eyes into her hair. He released her hands and dropped his full weight onto her chest.

She couldn't breathe.

No! No! This can't be happening. Horror

thumped so loudly in her mind, she could hear nothing else.

Thornhill began slobbering on her neck. Emeline reached to her right where she remembered there was a tall stool. Had she put away the iron pot? Squeezing her eyes shut, she groped for it. For anything . . . when . . .

There it was. Or something, anyway — something hard and heavy.

Thornhill trailed kisses down onto her chest.

She found the handle . . . strained to lift it . . .

And slammed it onto Thornhill's head.

Two things bothered Owen that night. Two things that normally he'd be able to dismiss given enough alcohol and a good game of whist. But for some reason, both things — one physical, one mental — refused to give him peace. The physical thing was the raw open sores on both of his hands, gained from his antics in the tops earlier that day. The mental thing was the frustrating Miss Baratt's absence from dinner. In the two weeks she'd been on board — and yes, he had kept track — she'd never missed dinner in the captain's cabin.

Blackwell seemed unaffected, though

disappointed, by her absence, citing the message she'd sent that she was not hungry.

Not hungry? He'd seen the woman eat. For such a tiny thing, she had the appetite of a sailor stranded on a deserted island. He smiled, but then threw down his hand of cards onto the wardroom table and slammed the remainder of his brandy to the back of his throat. "Count me out, gentlemen."

"Aw, come now, Owen," Ben said from beside him. "It's not like you to leave such a huge pot."

"I say, it is indeed like him." Dimsmore sneered. "Running away when he knows he's beat."

Owen rose, his chair scraping over the deck, and started for Dimsmore, but Ben moved between them. "On the contrary." Ben smiled. "You know as well as I that it's Owen who runs toward danger and uncertainty more than any of us."

"Humph." Dimsmore scowled, his bitter gaze shifting between them before he lowered back to his chair. "That makes him more a fool than brave."

Not in the mood for a fight, Owen ignored the insult and excused himself from his fellow officers to retire in his cabin. But his feet refused to cooperate. Instead they led him down a hall, past storage rooms, and down a ladder leading to the gun deck.

Hundreds of snores rumbled across the deck like a thunderstorm rising at sea. Hammocks, strung between guns and gear, swayed to the movement of the ship. Yet it was a light on his left that drew his attention, seeping in between cracks in the temporary bulkhead erected to separate surgery from the men. Odd. He hadn't expected anyone to be there at this hour. He'd only hoped to avoid Miss Baratt and find some bandages for his hands.

A muffled squeal sent every one of his nerves to attention. Dashing forward, he pivoted around the bulkhead, hand gripped to the pommel of his service sword, ready to fight, ready to protect, whatever was necessary.

The vision of Miss Baratt lying on the table with Thornhill on top of her had barely registered in his thoughts when he saw her strike the man on the head with a chamber pot.

The sailor moaned in agony, wobbling above her and shaking his head. Without delay, Owen dashed for him and shoved him off Miss Baratt to the deck. Thornhill's body slammed hard on the wood. He struggled to rise, groaning and gripping his head, his face twisting in rage, ready to defend himself against his attacker.

Until he saw Owen. Halting, he stared at him, hatred and defiance remaining in his eyes, but fear creeping across them as well.

"What is the meaning of this, Thornhill?" Owen shouted, drawing his sword and leveling it upon the man.

Miss Baratt struggled to rise on the table, trembling, eyes wide, and chest heaving. She yanked a cloth from her mouth and tossed it aside.

"The lady asked for it, sir." Thornhill backed against the bulkhead.

"And just how could she ask for anything with that rag in her mouth?" Owen stepped toward the man.

"She were flirting wit' me the whole time I were down here. She's a trollop, I tells ye, sir."

Sheathing his blade, Owen raised his fist and, with every ounce of his anger, slugged Thornhill across the jaw. Arms flailing, the sailor sprawled backward, struck his head on the corner of a cabinet, and toppled to the deck. He didn't move.

Owen shifted his gaze to Miss Baratt, who stared at him, wide eyes full of terror. Rushing to her side, he grabbed her waist and helped her from the table. But no sooner had he set her feet on the deck than she faltered in his grip. He caught her before she fell and held her against him.

"It's all right now, Miss Baratt."

She stiffened for a moment, seemed to have regained herself, before a rush of sobs and whimpers billowed through her entire body.

"There, there." He led her to a chair and helped her to sit, then knelt before her. Tears turned to liquid crystal in the lantern light as they sped down her cheeks. For a moment — a brief moment — he forgot this woman was a traitor to his country and longed to take her in his arms and comfort her.

"Are you injured, Miss Baratt?"

"I didn't . . . I didn't . . ." — she shifted glassy eyes toward the still figure of Thornhill — "I did not encourage that man."

Owen plucked a handkerchief from inside his coat and handed it to her. "I'm sure you did not."

"Is he dead?"

"No." Owen glanced his way. "But he'll wish he was soon enough." Especially if Owen had anything to do with it. He still could make no sense of the horror, the fury erupting within him when he first saw Thornhill attacking Miss Baratt. Much more than he'd ever felt.

She dabbed her cheeks. "Thank you, Lieutenant." Gripping the handkerchief tightly in her lap, she squeezed her eyes shut and began to shake visibly. Owen could stand it no longer. He gripped her hands in his. They were so small, his meaty palms swallowed them up whole.

"You are safe now, Miss Baratt."

"Yes, I know. Forgive me. I am out of sorts." She breathed out a sigh.

"Understandably."

She retrieved her hands, dried her eyes, and lifted her gaze to him. "Surely you came here for some other reason than to offer me your comfort." She stuck out her chin and threw back her shoulders.

He turned his hands palms up for her to see. "Indeed. But it is of little consequence now."

"Don't be silly. I will tend to them." Shoving from the chair, she moved to the cabinet on shaky legs and retrieved a bottle and some bandages.

Owen rose and sat on one of the chairs, watching her curiously. "It is all right to be distraught, Miss Baratt. You've had quite a fright. You do not have to comport yourself with poise in every situation."

She returned to sit beside him. Golden

150

strands of hair fell in disarray to her shoulders, her eyes were swollen and red, and dirt and blood stained the apron she wore over her gown. But she was lovely. Truly lovely.

Dipping some of the liquid onto a rag, she pressed it on his palm. He winced, but the pain quickly evaporated beneath her gentle ministrations.

Even amid her own pain, when most women would deflate to a sobbing mess and curl up in a corner, she thought of him. Or was it merely gratefulness after he'd saved her?

"You do not owe me this kindness for saving you, Miss Baratt."

"Saving me?" She huffed through a strangled sob. "Though I thank you for landing the final blow on Mr. Thornhill, I was doing quite well on my own before you arrived." The tremble in her voice spoke otherwise.

Owen chuckled, unsure whether she was teasing. "Clearly you did not stop the man from continuing —" He cleared his throat. "Merely stunned him momentarily."

"I would have thought of something else." She moved to tend his other hand.

He watched her, amazed. Of all the gall. The brazen chit! Yet rather than be annoyed, he found her captivating.

"It is all right for a man to rescue a woman, Miss Baratt. You are free to express your gratitude."

"Oh, am I, indeed?" She finally gazed up at him. A spark of irritation had replaced the fear in her eyes. "Would you prefer I stand and cheer for you as your crew did earlier?"

"That would be acceptable, yes." He grinned.

Groaning, she continued dabbing medicine on his hand, albeit much harder this time.

Pain throbbed, but he wouldn't give her the pleasure of knowing that. Besides, her touch was driving him mad, along with her closeness, her unique womanly scent, the wisp of her breath filling the air between them.

And when she raised those green eyes to his, so full of strength and pluck, he wanted to kiss her more than anything.

But now was certainly not the time. Nor would it ever be. She was a traitor. If she put her feet on American soil, she'd be hanged for treason.

He snagged back his hands and stood. "Thank you, Miss Baratt. If you give me the bandages, I can finish myself."

Though a tiny wrinkle of surprise formed

between her eyebrows, she nodded and stood. "Very well." She gathered the cloths and handed them to him.

"I'll escort you to your cabin." He kept his voice firm, devoid of any tenderness or playfulness it had held before.

"What of Thornhill?" She glanced at the unconscious man.

"I'll have the marines lock him up and report the incident straightaway to the captain."

Fear reappeared in her eyes. And he hated himself for behaving so callously.

They walked to her cabin in silence, though everything within him begged to offer her some words of comfort, apologize for Thornhill's behavior, assure her all would be well.

At her door, he once again advised her in the strictest terms to go nowhere on the ship unescorted.

Turning to stare at him, terror flickered on her lovely features before she raised her chin. "I am sorry to have bothered you, Lieutenant." And once again, he found himself staring at her closed door.

Regardless, Owen marched off, feeling worse than a scamp.

CHAPTER 11

Emeline handed Hannah a cup of lemon tea she'd managed to convince the cook to brew for her friend. Apparently, the captain's admiration of her had spread through the crew, and they seemed more than happy to oblige her every request. Which made her feel slightly better about her safety after the incident with Thornhill two nights ago. That and the fact that the captain was most distraught, apologizing to her for his sailor's actions over and over, and assuring her it would not happen again. Though she had not witnessed the punishment, word around the ship was that Mr. Thornhill had been flogged and assigned to a detail belowdecks, and she wondered who had tended his wounds.

She also wondered why she had not seen Lieutenant Masters since the incident. Though now that she thought about him, her anger rose.

"The man is unhinged. He's a churlish fatwit."

"Oh, I dunno, dear." Hannah sipped her tea as she sat on the cot in their tiny cabin. "I wouldn't mind some 'andsome man rescuin' me like that . . . dashin' in and punchin' out the villain." She swept her fist through the air and smiled. "Quite romantic."

Emeline frowned. "It wasn't romantic being attacked."

"No, dear, I'm sorry. I didn't mean to make light o' it. But God rescued you, after all." She smiled. "And in the form of quite the 'andsome gallant."

Emeline crossed her arms over her waist and stared out the port window. "The lieutenant didn't rescue me. I was in the process of knocking that vile sailor out when he dashed in and interfered."

"Interfered?" Hannah blew out a laugh.

Emeline returned her smile. She supposed she was being ridiculous. In truth, she'd never been so happy to see a person in her life. She'd always thought of herself as brave, but when Thornhill was slobbering all over her, she'd been overcome with more terror than she'd ever felt.

"I'll grant you," she began, lowering to one of the chairs, "Lieutenant Masters played the daring hero well, chivalrous and kind and comforting. But then in a flash, he became harsh and treated me as if he were annoyed I had been attacked. The man obviously loathes me."

She wouldn't tell Hannah that moments before his demeanor changed, Emeline actually thought he might kiss her, actually felt a stirring in her heart for his kindness and chivalry. Yes, indeed, *if* she admitted it — which she wouldn't — she'd been quite thrilled watching him dash in and slug Thornhill to the deck.

She leaned toward Hannah. "I honestly think he's mad. And it doesn't bode well for our plans to have a puddinghead in such a high position."

"Oh dear." Hannah waved her away with a sly look. " 'E's 'ardly that. 'E's probably just smitten wit' you. You know these Brits can't 'andle emotions."

"Fie! You're a silly woman sometimes, Hannah, but I'm so glad you are feeling better."

Hannah sipped her tea then cradled the cup in her hands. "Somethin' else you should know about the lieutenant. Mr. Keate tells me 'e's brung extra rations to the prisoners more'n once."

Emeline stared at her friend, unsure

whether she heard her correctly. "The American prisoners?"

"Ain't no other ones down there, dear." Hannah chuckled.

"But why would he do that?"

Hannah shrugged. "Maybe 'e's jist a kind man."

"Hmm." Emeline frowned and fingered a curl at her neck. That couldn't be it. Surely there was another explanation. And frankly, she didn't care.

"But more importantly" — Hannah set down her cup as the twinkle of mischief returned to her eyes — "Robert's been workin' on 'is irons and should have them cut through soon."

Emeline's stomach felt as though someone were slicing through it as well. "Which means I must garner some information soon." She sighed. "I will do my best. I have another painting session this afternoon."

"It's now or never, dear. Or I fear our plans are sunk."

Nerves wound tight as threads on a loom, Emeline made her way down the dimly lit companionway to the captain's cabin. The deck tilted, shoving her against the wall, but she quickly regained her balance and continued, pondering how much the action reflected the course of her life — how she attempted to stay on the straight and narrow, but something always pushed her off the path, tossing her one way or another. Events out of her control. Events that caused her to do things she wasn't sure God approved of. Like what she was planning on doing today.

The marine standing guard smiled as she approached. The door was already ajar, and her pulse raced at the thought that today was the day she must lure some information out of the captain.

It sped even faster at the sight of Dimsmore leaning over the captain's desk, examining some documents.

At the sound of her entering, he turned on his heels, and instantly the tight lines on his face softened in a smile. He took a step toward her.

Emeline gripped her hands, wondering why she always felt uneasy in the man's presence.

He halted, noting her hesitation. "Forgive me, Miss Baratt. I'm sure you are still unnerved by your . . . experience."

She was. She'd even had nightmares — most unusual for her. And she found herself jumping at every little movement and sound even though Thornhill was locked below. "I am recovering, sir."

"Such courage is rarely found in one so beautiful."

She stared at him curiously. "I was unaware that one's appearance bore any effect on bravery."

"I didn't mean . . . forgive me, yet again. I meant it as a compliment." His smile faded as annoyance gripped his features. "How fortunate that Lieutenant Masters happened upon you when he did."

Emeline narrowed her eyes. "Are you accusing him of something?"

"No, no, you misread me. I was merely noting that it was most unusual for him to be in surgery at that time of night. I had just been playing whist with the man."

"He injured his hands," she said matter-of-factly, wondering why she was defending him.

"Hmm. Well, I wouldn't put any action beyond him in order to woo a lady. He is not always what he seems."

She wouldn't tell him her theory that the poor lieutenant's sails didn't open all the way. Instead, she lifted her chin. "I am not so easily wooed."

"I am glad to hear of it. Which prompts me to apologize once again for my presumptuous behavior a week past. I had imbibed far too much brandy, but that is no excuse."

"I have forgotten it."

He smiled, and she realized that he was indeed a handsome man, cultured and educated, and she wondered why he hadn't married.

Her gaze lowered to the piece of foolscap in his hands. "I was to meet the captain here. Seems you wish to see him also."

"Indeed. I have something of import to discuss with him."

"Do not be bothered with my presence. I will prepare my paints." She moved to sit at her easel, hoping the man would leave.

"I doubt any man would be bothered by your presence, miss. Perhaps I could entice you to a stroll around the deck this afternoon?"

Before she could answer, the captain marched in, all bluster and excitement, obviously stirred up by whatever information he'd received that morning from the ship they'd anchored beside.

Emeline attempted to shrink out of sight.

"Dimsmore, good." Captain Blackwell moved to his desk.

Feet pounded above. Sails snapped, and the ship jerked forward.

"The others will be here shortly," the captain continued, studying a map spread across his desk. "We have much to discuss. This Washington campaign is most prodigious. Cockburn and Ross will lead —"

Clearing his throat, Dimsmore glanced her way, forcing the captain to look behind him.

"Ah, Miss Baratt. Forgive me. I forgot our appointment." He approached and took her hands in his.

Washington? Alarm dashed madly through her veins. "That is quite all right, Captain. Seems you have much on your mind."

"As much as I enjoy our sessions, I have more important matters to attend today." He studied her. "Are you all right? You've gone quite pale."

La! She was such a bad spy! She gulped and forced a smile. "I fear I am still out of sorts."

He flattened his lips, naught but concern on his face. "Rest assured, Thornhill has received his just dues."

She nodded. "I so hoped I could finish your portrait today. Perhaps I can paint while you and your men talk?"

The captain exchanged a glance with Dimsmore. "Nay. I fear I would be too distracted. We shall have to reschedule."

"Then I shall leave you to it." Rising, she dipped her head, smiled at both men, and left at as leisurely a pace as she could muster. *The Washington campaign?* Surely they didn't intend to march on her country's capital? How brazen! But that had to be it.

Now all she had to do was relay this information to Robert.

And pray. Pray like she never had before.

A chilled breeze rose from the foggy bay, and Emeline drew her pelisse tighter about her neck, hopelessly trying to calm her nerves. This morning, Robert would either escape to freedom with vital information for the American cause, or he'd be caught and quite possibly executed.

And she would be culpable.

In all her rebellious antics, she'd never caused anyone's death.

But she couldn't think like that. Where was her faith? Certainly God wanted the Americans to win . . . to keep their freedom. Didn't He? Or perhaps He took no interest in the governments of men.

She bowed her head to pray, as she'd been doing all night, finally ascending to the main deck just before dawn — before the prisoners were hauled up from their sleep to scrub the decks. But she had no more words to pray, no more pleas to lift to the Almighty, who seemed more silent than usual.

She had started out praying in her cabin . . . oscillating from kneeling on the deck, to leaning against the bulkhead, to pacing. She envied Hannah, who, after delivering the information to Robert and informing Emeline that he was prepared to escape the next morning, said a brief prayer and fell fast asleep. Her snores provided the only accompaniment to Emeline's prayers throughout the night. That and a sense now and then that God was indeed listening . . . and perhaps He even cared.

Perhaps that was just wishful thinking. Did people really hear from God? Hannah said she did, quite often, in fact. She claimed to even feel His divine presence. Maybe if Emeline started living her life right, doing what was expected of her, God would grant her the same blessings.

Dawn's glow lit the horizon like the blaze of a matchstick to a lantern, announcing the sun's arrival on yet another day — a day of war and despair for many. A day of nerves for her as she heard four bells, announcing the middle of the morning watch, followed by footsteps pounding the deck behind her.

Soon after came the clang and grate of chains of the prisoners and the sleepy annoyed voices of the marines. "Move on.

Move on, now!"

She glanced over her shoulder to see the crew of the *Charlotte* emerge from the hatch and slog over the deck to grab their holystones. Several glanced her way and scowled. One spit to the side. But she cared not for their misplaced hatred. Her gaze dropped to Robert's feet. In the dim light it would be impossible to tell, but the irons between his ankles were definitely cut clean through. He walked along in between Captain Lansing in front and Quartermaster Keate in back, both trying to keep him as hidden as possible.

The marine took no note. Neither did the ones standing on guard or the new watch coming on deck from below. Including Dimsmore. *What is he doing here?* Emeline faced the bay, her heart seizing in her chest. "Oh Lord, please have mercy," she whispered into the rising wind.

"I see you have not heeded my warning, Miss Baratt."

So caught up in her pleas to God, she hadn't heard the man approach. Not Dimsmore's voice, but one deeper, more genuine — Lieutenant Masters.

She faced him, ready to do battle, but suddenly found herself devoid of the energy required. Sunlight shimmered over the

164

green flecks in his brown eyes as he assessed her with impunity. Not in anger, but more in curiosity. Wind tore the tips of his hair. His uniform was a tad wrinkled, his jaw peppered with stubble, and a single ray of morning sun speared the scar along his left cheek, making him look oddly alluring.

"The captain has assured me of my safety," she said, suddenly shy beneath his intense gaze.

"Yet I do not see him here protecting you."

"That's what I have you for, isn't it, Lieutenant?" she replied curtly.

He narrowed his eyes. And she wondered whether she should keep him distracted or send him away. One glance over her shoulder showed that Robert had chosen a spot by the larboard railing to scrub. Fortunately, Dimsmore was on the foredeck talking to a group of marines.

Lieutenant Masters gave a tight smile. "I fear other more pressing duties keep me from being your ladyship's bodyguard."

Pressing duties such as making sure that every man, including each of the prisoners, was hard at work. No, she couldn't allow that. He was far too observant to miss Robert's escape. Loathing herself, she placed her hand atop his just as he was turning to leave. "I'm sorry to hear that, Lieutenant, for I always feel safe in your presence." She wanted to vomit. Instead, she smiled up at him.

His eyes lit with a twinkle of mischief and a spark of suspicion. "Is that so?"

"Yes. You can't imagine how terrifying it is on board a ship full of men." She looked down, cringing at how ridiculous she sounded.

He laughed. *Laughed!* "I find that hard to believe, Miss Baratt. Your courage puts most women, and some men, I might add, to shame."

"Then you do not know me at all." She feigned a quiver in her voice and, still looking down, glanced beneath her lashes at Robert. No one was watching him. This would be the perfect time!

Lieutenant Masters followed her gaze.

Fie! She froze, unable to swallow, unable to breathe. A shaft of morning sun thrust over the horizon and stabbed Robert's feet where the irons had been hacked through.

There was no chance the lieutenant wouldn't see it.

Hence, she did the only thing she could think to do — she fell against him. Her head hit his chest and she drew in a breath of his scent — moist linen, brandy, and the sea. It stirred something within her as she waited for his embrace and comfort. Instead, strong hands gripped her shoulders and nudged her back as if she had the plague. He laughed again, and when she looked up, his gaze was still on Robert.

He grimaced but did nothing.

Stomach sinking, she braced herself for his command that the prisoner be seized. But instead, he released her and quirked one eyebrow. "Since you are so frightened and weak, Miss Baratt, I suggest you retire to your cabin." With that, he bid her adieu and proceeded to mount the quarterdeck ladder.

Emeline glanced over the deck and saw Dimsmore's gaze shift from her to follow Lieutenant Masters until he stopped at the wheel.

She spun back around, chest heaving, and waited for her breath to settle. The sun continued its rise over the bay, illuminating the deck, betraying their plan. Yet still . . . she waited . . . and listened. . . .

Loose sails flapped. Water purled against the hull. Wood creaked interminably, and Dimsmore's voice became garbled as he continued commanding his men.

Yet through all the clamor, Emeline listened for that one sound she most desired.

Hurry, Robert, before more sailors and offi-

cers come above!

Finally, there it was. The sound of a gentle splash. *Thank God!* Emeline dared to lower her shoulders . . . dared to breathe a sigh of relief when . . .

A harrowing shout echoed over the deck, "Prisoner overboard!"

CHAPTER 12

"You have to tell 'im it were me." Hannah clutched Emeline's hands.

"Never!" Emeline snagged them back and sank into a chair. Dropping her head in her hands, she stared at the stained deck of their cabin.

"It's our only 'ope."

"For what? It's over, Hannah. Our plan has failed." Miserably. Emeline could still hear the eerie musket shots fired at poor Robert as he attempted to swim away, could still hear the demands from Dimsmore that he stop and return at once or be killed. The captain was roused from his sleep, but by the time he arrived on deck, Lieutenant Masters had ordered her to go below.

Now, hours later — after they'd heard much commotion on deck — she and Hannah had been summoned to the captain's cabin.

"They know what we did, Hannah. And

now we are to be locked up below with the others. Or worse."

"Oh posh." Hannah snorted and planted her fists at her waist. "If they knew that, we'd already be there."

"Then why does the captain wish to see both of us? And what has happened to poor Robert? I cannot bear it. This is all my fault."

"My dear, you must calm yourself. You'll do no one any good so distraught. God is in control."

A tear broke free from the corner of her eye and made a run for it down Emeline's cheek. "I knew I should have behaved. I should not have lied and deceived. Now God will punish me."

Hannah handed Emeline a handkerchief then stooped to peer up at her. "God is not like your earthly father, my dear. The sooner you believe that, the sooner you'll find peace. Now this is what we must do. . . ."

Emeline stood beside Hannah before the captain's desk, feeling as though she'd rather make a dash for it and leap out the stern windows into the bay than face the decision before her.

Lieutenant Dimsmore and two marines stood at attention to her right, ready to take them below. Lieutenants Masters and Camp stood to their left.

Captain Blackwell rose and held the infamous chisel up before him. "Which one of you can tell me how this chisel ended up in the prisoner's possession? And don't tell me he stole it on deck. We search the prisoners every time they are escorted back to the hold."

Emeline swallowed and glanced at her friend. Something sour and bitter brewed in her stomach, and she wished she'd become ill all over the deck rather than have to do what she knew she must.

But must she? What was the right thing to do? Her mind and heart spun in a wicked cauldron of confusion and angst, causing perspiration to slide down her back. The right thing to do was not lie, wasn't it? But the right thing would get them both locked below. And what good would that do the rest of the prisoners . . . or America?

She closed her eyes for a moment . . . thinking . . . praying . . . hoping they didn't see her distress. She could hear the captain's boots stomping on the deck, the breathing of the officers, the swish of water against the hull.

Hannah nudged her gently from the side.

She opened her eyes, along with her

171

mouth, and tried to get the words out. But they scrambled back down her throat.

Finally, she drew a deep breath. "I fear, Captain" — she swallowed — "that I must inform you . . . that I saw my friend in possession of this chisel not a week past." The words turned bitter on her tongue, making her want to spit and cough to be rid of them.

Blackwell's sharp eyes speared Hannah. "And you said nothing?"

"I thought nothing of it, Captain. She told me she'd found it and intended to turn it over to the first officer she saw. I had no reason to believe otherwise."

For what seemed like an eternity, Captain Blackwell stood, shoulders spread wide, brown eyes shifting to Hannah and then back to Emeline.

He approached and halted before Hannah. "And you gave this to the prisoner who escaped?"

To her credit, the woman didn't hesitate, didn't even sound nervous. "That I did, Captain. 'Twere my duty as an American."

"Then it will be your duty to watch him be flogged."

Emeline gasped.

Hannah remained steadfast, looking straight ahead.

"And it will be my duty, afterward, to see

you locked in chains with the rest of the prisoners. Escort her to the main deck. I'll be up shortly." Captain Blackwell waved a hand of dismissal toward Hannah, and Emeline's heart felt as though a thousand knives stabbed it. *No, no, no!* Everything within her wanted to take the blame, divulge her part in it, assume the punishment of her poor friend who had been naught but kind to her.

But that wouldn't do anyone any good at all. She glanced at Hannah as the marines grabbed her arms. She nodded toward Emeline, reassurance in her eyes. Not fear, not anger.

Not the weight of shame Emeline was now sinking beneath. She lowered her gaze and faced forward, waiting for whatever came next. As soon as her friend had left, the captain approached her, his harsh expression fading like a storm blown away by a soft breeze.

"I know that was not easy for you, Miss Baratt. Though an American, I realize the woman was your companion and friend."

Emeline kept her eyes on the deck by her feet. She longed to plead for mercy for Robert and Hannah, but that would only introduce suspicion. "I had to do my duty, Captain. Friend or not, she defied the

Crown."

"You have more than proven your loyalty," he replied staunchly.

Which was exactly what Hannah was counting on. But what good would it do now?

For in all probability, Emeline was never going to leave this ship.

An hour later, she stood on the quarterdeck as the August sun shot hot arrows upon the crew assembled to witness Robert's flogging. She'd wanted to beg off from watching the barbaric event, but in truth, she deserved to suffer for her part in it.

To her left stood Lieutenant Masters and the captain, while beneath her on the main deck, Hannah stood between two marines. The crew of the *Charlotte* clustered together by the larboard railing, scowls darkening their faces, while the rest of the main and foredecks were covered with British seamen, including some up in the shrouds — like ants evicted from their anthill. There had to be more than two hundred of them.

Perspiration dribbled down her back beneath her gown as she adjusted her bonnet against the raging sun. A marine appeared from belowdecks, hauling poor Robert above. A new set of irons scraped over the deck as he was led to stand before a hatch grating that had been lifted on its side. The sailors tossed curses and insults his way as the marine stripped him of his shirt and tied his hands and ankles to the grating.

Emeline felt blood rush to her head, and her breath came heavy and hard.

Captain Blackwell glanced her way. "You may go below, Miss Baratt. No need for a lady to witness this."

"I wish to stay, Captain," she managed to mumble in return.

He nodded and faced the proceedings while Lieutenant Masters eyed her curiously.

The boatswain's mate grabbed the cat-o'-nine-tails and looked up at the captain.

Captain Blackwell cleared his throat and silence swept through the ship. "For the crime of attempting to escape and as a lesson to all prisoners, this man will receive twenty lashes."

Sailors jeercd and cheered.

The boatswain's mate raised the whip and struck Robert's back. Welts rose like red volcanoes on his skin. To his credit, he did not yell out, though Emeline heard Hannah shriek.

She would do so herself. She would run

down and stop the entire heinous act if she thought she could. Instead, she closed her eyes and began whispering prayers.

Crack! The sailors continued to laugh and shout curses.

Crack! Emeline shuddered but continued her prayers, her heart growing heavy.

Crack! Oh, how she hated these Brits! Why did they have to be so cruel?

Crack! Oh Lord, help Robert endure it.

Crack! Robert finally wailed in agony.

Crack! She heard the captain of the *Charlotte* shout, "Leave him alone! Enough!"

Crack! Anger raced through her veins. Robert screamed.

Crack! She would find a way to help defeat these Brits. She would gain information and escape, God help her!

Sweat slid down her neck. Her head grew light, and she felt herself wobble. Lieutenant Masters grabbed her arm, but she tore from him and gripped the railing instead.

Crack! Robert screamed again, and Hannah began to cry.

Emeline lost count of the strikes after that and focused, instead, on her prayers, begging for God's mercy.

Finally, after an eternity of agony, the whip stopped.

"Back to your duties!" the master shouted,

and moans and groans accompanied the crew as they dispersed to their posts.

Emeline opened her eyes. She wished she hadn't, for Robert's back was naught but a lump of curdled flesh, bloody and swollen.

The biscuit she'd eaten that morning rose in her throat and filled her mouth with a putrid taste. She flung her hand over it and stumbled to leave.

Lieutenant Masters steadied her with a touch to her elbow. "You shouldn't have stayed. I'll escort you to your cabin to rest."

"No!" She jerked from him. "I will tend this poor man's wounds."

Something akin to admiration stretched across his eyes before he nodded and assigned a marine to accompany her below.

Down in surgery, she drew a deep breath and prayed for strength as she gathered bandages, water, alcohol, needles, and twine, not knowing whether she'd be able to help such a dreadfully injured man.

But she knew one thing. Even though she was a mere woman, even though proper ladies didn't do such things, she had to do something to help defeat these barbaric monsters.

Owen gripped the taffrail and stared at the inky-black waters of the Chesapeake. The half-moon he'd been admiring since he'd come above had been swallowed up by ominous clouds. The spice of rain filled his nostrils, along with the stench of blood he could not shake from earlier in the day. He'd seen floggings before, but never one done to a fellow American.

He wanted to pray to God, ask Him why He allowed such injustice in the world. Ben had told him that God was in control and everything happened for a reason. But if that was true, wouldn't God intervene more in the affairs of man, fix injustice, punish the wicked? Since Owen had seen none of that in all his five-and-twenty years, he had to conclude that God was not only distant, but perhaps even unloving. Maybe in the beginning He had intended to love His creation; however, after man fell, He abandoned them. But not before punishing them with a list of restrictive rules that kept them from enjoying the meager seventy or so years they were given.

His knuckles began to hurt, and he loosened his grip and pounded the railing instead. How much longer would he have to endure living among his enemies? Endure their arrogance, their cruelty? He wanted to fight them, not be a part of them. Not placate them or serve them.

Thunder growled in the distance, mimicking his anger. In truth, he hated the deception — especially to Ben and the captain. He longed to end the charade, but he hadn't enough information. The British planned to attack Washington, yet because HMS *Marauder* and her men were not to take part, he still knew no specifics — date, time, or armament. There was, however, talk of an attack on Baltimore as well. Owen must discover which city they meant to attack first or his information might pull much-needed troops from one city to the other, leaving one place highly vulnerable. No, it was too risky. He had to find out more. Then he could leave. Then he would be free.

Wind swirled about him, tugging at his hair and filling his lungs with the scent of the sea and the coming storm. The ship rose over a wave. He braced his feet on the deck and stared into the darkness, yearning for a glimpse of his country.

Thoughts of Miss Baratt barged unbidden into his mind. As they so often did. Baffling woman! Her insistence on viewing the flogging defied his knowledge of the weaker sex. And he knew a lot about the weaker sex. Besides, she had closed her eyes through most of it. And she had prayed. He heard snippets of her whispers in between the shouts of the men.

Yet despite her pleas and sentiments, she had betrayed a friend when she could have kept silent. When it wouldn't have really mattered since the damage was done. *What kind of person does that and then prays for her enemies — insists on tending their wounds?*

Owen withdrew his hat and ran a hand through his hair.

Lightning spiked a white fork in the distance as the sound of rain met his ears — droplets marching across the bay like ten thousand soldiers in formation. Like the British would soon do to Washington — unless Owen could get the information he needed and prevent this heinous attack on his country.

Emeline missed Hannah. Missed her comfort, her bravery, her encouragement. She needed her now more than ever. Dashing toward the chamber pot, she bent over yet again and coughed. There was nothing left in her stomach to lose.

Thankfully, Robert had lost consciousness an hour ago and was not privy to her weakness. Though she was sure the marine standing guard would spread news across the ship of her shame. No matter. The

180

shredded mass of flesh that used to be Robert's back was enough to make the bravest soldier cringe.

Besides, the marine did not have to stare at it like she did, did not have to examine every inch of it like she'd been doing the past two hours. Nor was he forced to curse himself for taking part in causing it, like she'd been doing each time she laid a bandage soaked in water and vinegar across Robert's back and had to listen to his bloodcurdling wail.

She should not have lied, not have deceived, and at the very least, not have taken part in getting the chisel to this man.

Was that what God was trying to tell her now?

Returning to the table where Robert lay facedown, she dabbed a wet cloth over his forehead and cheek. When he'd been awake, she had wanted to apologize, but with the marine there, she could not have done so. Instead, she did her best to offer him encouragements — that he would heal, that the pain would diminish.

When he'd finally lost consciousness and she no longer needed to be brave for him, the tears had spilled down her face, bursting from an endless fountain of agony and shame. She'd tossed her accounts into the chamber pot. Twice.

The marine had smiled.

The ship bucked and the water lapped and gurgled against the hull as if they had set sail, but she knew they hadn't. Perhaps the sea was as agitated as she was over the barbaric incident.

Sitting on the stool, she dipped another strip of cloth in the vinegar and lavender mixture. Only two more and Robert's back would be covered. Then it would be best to leave him here to rest or perhaps move him to a cot where he could remain facedown.

La! She batted her cheeks. Why couldn't she stop crying? She'd never been one of those weak women who sobbed over every little thing.

Thunder bellowed in the distance, thrumming through the ship's timbers. A storm was coming. Fitting somehow.

Brushing hair from her face with the back of her hand, she laid the last strip over Robert's back, pressing it down as gently as she could. Then, sitting back, she examined her work. It was all she knew to do.

Lanterns flickered as an odd breeze swept through, carrying with it the scent of rain.

"Mr. . . . Mr. . . . ," she addressed the marine. He glanced her way. "Can you move him to the surgeon's cot to rest?" She gestured toward the wooden slab attached to the bulkhead and covered with a straw-stuffed tick she assumed was for the surgeon. "He needs to lie on his front."

The man snorted. "He'll stay where he's at, miss. He deserves worse."

"He's a human being and deserves to get well."

The deck careened and Emeline clung to the table for support. Her medical knife clanked to the floor. Bending over to retrieve it, she wiped tears from her eyes as rain tapped on the deck above her.

The marine only stiffened and stared forward again.

"I will ask the captain," she announced. "I'm sure he'll agree with me." Grabbing a cloth to wipe her hands, she started out the doorway when a groan preceded the marine leaping in her way and heading out the door. "I'll see what I can do, miss."

She gave a stiff smile and returned to clean up the bloody rags and water and discard her vinegar solution. By the time she finished, the marine had returned with a sailor, and together they moved poor Robert to the cot.

After they left, she remained by his side and continued her prayers, for there was naught else she could do. Now it was up to

God to heal and Robert to get well. The lantern sputtered and seemed ready to go out. Rising, she grabbed it and headed for the ladder to go above. She had to get out of there, away from the stench of blood, pain, and death — away from the consequence of her foolish lies.

CHAPTER 13

"It's happening today, gentlemen. In fact, as we speak." Captain Blackwell's eyes sparked in excitement as he surveyed the men surrounding the desk in his cabin — Lieutenant Dimsmore and one of his marines, Mr. Ryne, Ben, and Owen himself.

Owen was still trying to process what the captain had just said when the man pointed at the map spread across his desk. "Our troops should be approaching Bladensburg at this very moment."

Bladensburg? Just five or so miles from Washington, if Owen remembered. How could this have happened? Making every attempt to school the fury exploding on his face, Owen instead fisted his hands at his sides and sucked in a breath. "Why were we not informed of the timing of this attack sooner?" *Hang it all!* His voice emerged a bit too raspy with emotion.

Dimsmore snapped his gaze to Owen, his

eyes narrowing, his lips twitching.

Captain Blackwell drew back his shoulders and turned to look out the stern windows, where noonday sun shone down upon HMS *Tonnant,* anchored yards off their port quarter. "Since we were not to partake of this battle, I was not to disclose specifics. Admiral Cockburn himself is joining Major-General Robert Ross in their march on the rebel capital." He rubbed his hands together. "The Americans don't stand a chance."

Standing beside Owen, Ben merely flattened his lips and nodded. Dimsmore's excitement could not be contained as he all but leapt in place. "That is indeed great news, Captain! When is it our turn to put these rebels in their place?"

Mr. Ryne, a young marine who followed Dimsmore around like a lost puppy, added his "Indeed!"

An unavoidable groan escaped Owen's lips, but he quickly covered it up by saying, "Are we to join a land invasion as well, Captain?"

Dimsmore faced him with a snort. "You sound less than enthusiastic, Masters."

"Do I?" Owen thumbed the scar on his cheek. "Perhaps I am not as bloodthirsty as you, Dimsmore." He turned to Captain

Blackwell and smiled. "Though I am quite pleased we will soon be victorious."

The captain spun to face them. "We are awaiting further orders, which will surely come after this Washington campaign is concluded. I should know more tomorrow. In the meantime, gentlemen, we are to remain anchored here. Hence, go about your duties as usual, and hopefully we will all be celebrating soon."

Owen was not really a praying man, but as soon as Captain Blackwell dismissed them, he made his way to his cabin, shut the door, and spoke to God, hoping beyond hope that the Almighty was listening and that He even cared.

After not hearing or sensing anything and feeling rather foolish, Owen went about his duties as best he could, which didn't amount to much since the ship was anchored — ensuring order among the crew, teaching the midshipmen, and basically maintaining an authoritative presence on deck. But his thoughts and emotions were a jumbled mess, and his gaze inadvertently drifted to the shoreline just off their port bow. How many Americans were at that moment fighting for their lives in defense of their capital? What good was he as a spy if he hadn't gotten the information soon enough to save Washington? What good was he doing here on board this ship if he couldn't fight alongside his countrymen?

The British were right. If Washington fell, it would all be over. The morale of his countrymen would plummet to the depths, and the will to fight would dissipate like the morning fog. He wanted to shout. He wanted to scream. He wanted to jump overboard and swim to shore. Instead, he smiled and nodded at Ben as they passed each other on the quarterdeck.

Emeline couldn't get the blood off her hands. No matter how hard she scrubbed, no matter how much soap she used, her fingers dripped red . . . red . . . everywhere. Oddly, she stood at the sink in her house on Hanover street in Baltimore, gazing at her mother's hibiscus flowers in the yard. Beyond them, carriages, horses, and citizens strolled by, chattering and laughing as if there wasn't a war . . . as if people weren't being killed, imprisoned on British warships. As if people weren't being flogged to near death.

Wait. How did she get home? She gazed down at her hands. Blood dripped from the tips of her fingers into the sink. She grabbed a cloth and wrapped it around both hands, but the fabric instantly saturated red. *Drip . . . drip . . . drip . . .*

She held it over the sink. The light coming through the window faded, and she glanced out to see a black cloud devour the sun. A grayish hue — the color of death — leeched all color from the world. Petals shriveled and dropped from her mother's flowers as the stems drooped and wilted into ash. People and horses passing by became skeletons, their carriages rickety coffins. Yet they continued onward, talking and laughing as if death had not made a visit.

Emeline backed away from the window, horror stealing her breath and binding every nerve until it pained her to even move.

Robert's face leapt against the panes, agony writhing on his features. *Bam!* He was struck from behind with the whip. His cheek slammed against the glass. His eyes bored into hers, questioning, pleading, incriminating . . .

Emeline screamed.

Her face jerked upward, and she bit her lip. Pain filled her mouth. She shook her head as the surgery came into view around her. Robert lay facedown on the cot beside her chair, his back covered with the bloody strips she'd just applied for the third time since his flogging.

The ship rolled over a wave, sending water sloshing against the hull. Emeline rubbed her eyes, but they still felt as heavy as if all the cares of the world sat upon them. She glanced at her hands, fully expecting them to be covered in blood, but she remembered cleaning them before she'd sat down beside Robert.

Snores rumbled across the room, and she glanced at the lantern where barely a flicker remained from the depleted oil. How long had she slept?

Sounds filtered down from above. Footsteps pounded on the deck. Shouts and huzzahs. A fiddle. Standing, she started to clean up the mess she'd made, trying to ignore whatever was happening above, but the cheering only increased. What was going on? Since Hannah was locked below, Emeline had limited her time on deck, and she especially did not go above at night, but her curiosity overcame her fears.

A warm breeze fingered through her hair as she took the last step above. Myriad stars spread across the night sky as the ship gently rocked in the bay. It had to be past midnight. Then why all the mayhem? Normally most of the sailors would be asleep below, or if they were above, they'd be attending duties in an organized fashion. Instead, they were singing and dancing to fiddle music and shouting huzzahs and pointing to something off the port side of the ship.

Off in the distance, above the jagged line of trees, a red-and-orange glow consumed the night sky . . . almost as if the sun were just about to rise. But that couldn't be. This was in the west, not the east. Above the ethereal glow, gray smoke plumed the sky. *What?* Instantly Emeline's stomach shriveled into a knot. *Washington, DC.*

Couldn't be. She spotted Lieutenant Masters standing at the railing and made her way toward him, weaving in between celebrating sailors. Not that she wanted to speak to the man, but at least he would tell her what was happening. Besides, her legs were about to give out and she needed the support of the bulwarks.

No sooner did she reach the lieutenant than Captain Blackwell's voice bellowed behind her, bringing the clamor to instant silence. She turned to see him march past the wheel and grip the quarterdeck railing.

"Men, though I have not received confirmation, it appears our forces have captured the American capital and burned it to the ground."

This brought further cheers and jeers.

"An extra ration of rum for all!" he shouted then turned to say something to Lieutenant Camp beside him.

The cheers grew even louder.

Emeline faced the bay, doing her best to keep her rage in check. Even so, tears filled her eyes as she stared at the horrid sight. She closed them, forcing back the dampness as she gripped the railing for support.

"Are you well, Miss Baratt?" Lieutenant Masters's voice bade her open her eyes and lift her chin.

"Quite," she responded as curtly as she could. But when her gaze met his, she saw agony stretching across his eyes and creating furrows in his brow. He stared back at the fire. No. She must be wrong. It was far too dark to make out his expression.

"Why are you two not celebrating?" Dimsmore's nasally voice assaulted her from behind. He leaned on the railing beside her and assessed her and Masters as if he were judge and jury.

Emeline gave a tight smile. "The revelry jarred me from a deep sleep, Lieutenant. I fear I am still not fully awake."

"And you, Masters? You seem out of sorts, even distraught I would say." His sarcastic tone grated. "Alarmed to see your nation's capital city taken so easily?"

Emeline wanted to punch the man, to unleash her fury on this sniveling Brit. But proper ladies didn't do such things.

Owen laughed and shook his head. "It is not my nation, nor my capital. In truth, I am most pleased to see it fall, for this means the war is soon at an end." He moved from beside Emeline and slapped Dimsmore on the back. Perhaps a bit too hard, for the man coughed and staggered.

"Now, about that celebrating. I could use a drink." Owen all but dragged the man away, but Emeline didn't miss the suspicious glance Dimsmore gave her over his shoulder.

Turning back to face the bay, she dropped her head. A tear slid down her cheek, and she batted it away, trying to get ahold of her emotions.

Dimsmore clearly suspected her loyalties, Washington had fallen, and her country was about to be overrun by British tyrants. "Oh Lord, help us. Help us, please."

No sooner had she whispered the words than, without warning, rain as thick as hail began pounding on them from above, dousing the revelry and sending the sailors belowdecks.

Emeline followed in their wake and

slammed the door of her cabin, happy to be alone, desperate to be off this ship, even if it meant standing arm in arm with her defeated countrymen.

After removing her gown and stockings and laying them across her chair to dry, she fell into a fitful sleep full of nightmares she didn't care to remember.

During her waking moments, lightning lit her cabin in ghoulish shadows while thunder shook the timbers and rain pelted above. Slamming her pillow atop her head, she cried like she'd never cried before and must have fallen asleep sometime before dawn.

Pain jabbed her shoulder. Someone or something shoved her into the bulkhead. She forced her eyes open just as her body rolled in the other direction and hit the edge of the cot.

Ouch! She sprang up and gripped the post. The deck teetered. The sea slammed against the hull like a battering ram. Rain hit the deck above like grapeshot.

Gray light shrouded her cabin. What time was it?

With great difficulty, Emeline donned her gown, stockings, and shoes, flung open the door, and stumbled up the companionway.

A blast of wind flung pellets of rain at her, stinging her and nearly shoving her backward. She made a dash for the capstan and clung to it as she struggled to remain upright and reach the starboard railing. Her fingers gripped the slick wood. Squinting, she stared over the churning waters of the bay. Lightning lit the scene in an eerie gray, revealing waves as high as the railing rolling toward them. A chill shivered down the length of her body.

Perhaps she'd get struck by lightning. A fitting punishment for her crimes.

"You shouldn't be above!" Lieutenant Masters suddenly appeared beside her, rain dribbling off the tip of his cocked hat.

Wiping her eyes, she glanced up at him. "I shouldn't do many things, Lieutenant!"

"I insist you go below at once!"

She could not. She would not go below with the death and blood and loneliness.

Sailors in slick coats stared at them curiously.

She backed away from him. "Leave me be. For once, just leave me be."

She'd had enough of this ship and these British ghouls. Enough! All she wanted to do was stand there and allow the rain to wash away the blood, the wind to blast away the horror of this war, and her prayers to wash the guilt and shame from her soul.

"I insist." He grabbed her arm and tugged,

but she snagged it back and retreated. The man towered over her, looking more like a sea monster in his oily jacket with rain spilling off the tips of his saturated hair. If he forced her, she didn't stand a chance. But she would not go below. Not yet.

He clutched her arm again, this time putting his other hand around her waist, and started to hoist her up on his shoulder. No! She shoved his hand away and jerked backward. The deck canted, and she gripped the railing, looking for a way of escape. To her left, the crisscross of ropes that made up the ratlines rattled in the wind.

God help me. I know I'm rebellious. Gripping them, she hoisted herself up and faced the lieutenant. "Stay away, or I swear I'll climb up and you'll have to answer to the captain for my fate." The wind whipped the ropes to and fro. She tightened her fingers on the wet twine and held fast.

"You're mad, woman. Completely and utterly mad!" The lieutenant's voice roared above the storm, but he remained in place. "Get down here at once!"

The ship lurched to port then swung to larboard. Wind flapped the lieutenant's slick coat. A wall of water crashed over him, puddling around his feet before fleeing out the scuppers. Nevertheless, his boots kept their grip on the deck. "Please, Miss Baratt. Please come down."

The man had never said please to her. Ever. Nor had he used such a conciliatory tone. And yes, she should come down. Be an obedient and proper lady and go to her cabin. But whenever she sat within its tight walls, all she could see was Robert's curdled back and the flames of her capital burning to the ground.

And she couldn't go. Not now. Tears seared her eyes and spilled down her cheeks, joining with the drops of rain lashing her skin. She couldn't go. "Let me stay a moment, please." She returned his pleading tone, but he shook his head.

"I can't do that."

Turning, she gripped the saturated ropes above her and began her ascent.

"Hang it all! What are you doing, woman?" Lieutenant Masters tore off his hat and began climbing after her.

"Go away! Leave me be!"

"You're mad!"

"Yes I am. Now go away!"

He reached her in no time and covered her with his body — in effect, shielding her from wind and rain. His hair whipped about his face, stinging her cheeks. Rain dripped from his chin onto her shoulder. "You will come down this minute or I will carry you down over my shoulder." His deep voice reverberated in her ear.

A gust of wind came out of nowhere, and the ship tilted to starboard, dipping them over the water. Lieutenant Masters lost his grip. His feet flung out from under him. He hung on with one hand.

Emeline's heart turned to ice. She reached out for him and grabbed his coat to try to bring him back.

The ship bucked over another wave, and the last thing she heard was a groan of despair as they both plunged into the sea.

CHAPTER 14

Owen could not believe the woman had done this to him. Not until he struck the cold water and was instantly assailed by salty waves buffeting him from all sides. The worst part was that he sensed another body next to his — a flailing body whose skirts wrapped around his legs, restricting his movements. Panic coursed through his veins. Had the foolish woman also fallen in?

Hang it all!

The sea rushed about him, pushing him this way and that like a band of ruffians. His lungs ached for air. He grabbed a handful of skirts and drew the woman toward him, then kicked his legs free and swam for the surface.

He broke first and gulped in air, then yanked her up beside him. Her head popped above the water, arms thrashing until they clutched him in a death grip. She heaved in air before a terrified shriek emerged from her lips.

"Hold on. Hold on. Calm yourself. I've got you!" Owen glanced around and found the ship just twenty feet away.

But the woman continued to struggle. She clawed at his chest, neck, head, trying to heave herself from the sea. A wave struck them, forcing them beneath the water again.

When Owen surfaced, they were farther from the ship. *No!* Seizing Miss Baratt, he crushed her against him and attempted to paddle back to the ship even as he heard someone shout, "Man overboard!"

Lightning flung white spears to the sea. Two ropes appeared over the railing, dangling to the water. Thunder followed with a reverberating roar.

Miss Baratt gulped for air and screamed.

Owen prided himself on being a strong swimmer, but he'd never attempted it in a storm with an oversized flopping fish strapped to his side.

"Kick your feet!" he shouted at her.

She merely wrapped her legs around his as if he were a buoy.

More lightning coated the scene in a deathly silver. Thunder bellowed out a warning. But the ship was closer, thank God. Saltwater filled his mouth, and he spit it out, gasping for air. Waves slapped his face. The woman gripped his shirt, his hair, her body trembling.

Several minutes passed. He fought the waves *and* the lady. Seawater spilled into his stomach. Still he paddled. His muscles burned. His lungs heaved. Finally, the dark hull rose before him. He reached for one of the ropes, but a wave knocked him back. Growling, he paddled forward with all his strength. There, he gripped the sodden line. After several attempts, and with great difficulty, he tied it around Miss Baratt's waist. Clutching it, he braced his shoes against the hull and signaled for the men above to pull them up.

For such a tiny thing, the woman weighed as much as a cannon in her wet clothes. With her eyes closed and her lips quivering, nothing but whimpers emerged from her mouth the entire way up.

For a moment, Owen actually felt pity for her. Storms didn't bother him. In fact, he loved them. This one in the bay was hardly a full-fledged sea storm.

But to the poor woman, it must seem like a typhoon.

Sailors reached and hauled her over the bulwarks. She landed like a dead fish on the deck. No, not dead. She rose like a drowned leviathan just as Owen swung his legs over the side. And she was just as frightening.

"You almost killed me, you bumbling oaf!"

"I almost killed *you*!?" Lieutenant Masters snorted as he nudged Emeline into her cabin. He entered behind her before she had the chance to slam the door in his face.

Which she fully intended to do.

She backed away from him. "I was trying to save you."

"Save me?" He gave a sordid chuckle and placed two blankets on the cot. "You're the one who pushed *me*!"

Emeline glanced down at her sodden attire. Water dripped from the hem of her gown onto the deck and trickled from strands of her hair that had fallen to her waist. "Why would I push you into the sea and then jump in after you? Clearly you lost your balance and grabbed me to bring me with you."

His brows rose over a sardonic grin. "I never lose my balance, miss. I had everything under control until you shoved against me."

Emeline grimaced. The man was handsome, she'd give him that, with his coat missing, his wet shirt plastered to his firm chest, water dripping from his hair hanging around his chin, and those hazel eyes of his sparking in anger . . . or was it playfulness?

"I didn't — Oh, fie." Grabbing her wet skirts, she sank onto her chair and sighed. If she kept her anger at the forefront, perhaps panic would not set in. She felt for her mother's locket around her neck and breathed a sigh when her fingers gripped the cold silver. She'd nearly drowned! The thought sent shivers through her that had naught to do with her wet attire. She would have drowned if not for this man standing before her. But she didn't want to thank him. She didn't want to owe him anything. He was the enemy.

And the enemy had just burned her capital to the ground.

"What is it you want, Lieutenant? It's been a rather long couple of days."

"Long?" He chuckled. "Is that what you call nearly drowning?" When she didn't respond, he released a sigh. "Merely to bring you these blankets."

"Well, you have done so. Now you may leave." She began playing with a saturated strand of hair hanging in her lap.

He didn't leave. Instead, he chuckled again.

"What are you laughing at?"

"You look like a drowned pelican."

"Oh, do I?" She rose and met his gaze

head-on. "And you look like a wet . . . a wet . . ." — Greek god, if she were to admit it as he raked back the hair from his face — "pirate!" she finally hissed, stomping her foot at the annoying grin on his lips. But then an odd thing occurred. She started laughing. A low rumble at first, but then it emerged rather loud and uncontrollably. The lieutenant joined in. They carried on for several minutes, staring at each other and gripping their bellies until they both swiped tears from their eyes and gasped for air.

There was something spiritual about laughter that banished all ill feelings between two people. At least for a moment. And in that moment, Emeline felt a connection to this man that extended far beyond a physical attraction.

He certainly could have left her in the sea and no one would have blamed him, especially since it was her fault he had fallen. But he had risked himself for her. Why? When she found so little honor among these British.

And now the way he was looking at her — with an intensity that both alarmed *and* thrilled her. She'd never reacted this way to any man.

He tore his gaze from her, as if he too felt

the pull between them. "I checked on your patient when I was fetching the blankets. You did a good job. He will heal nicely."

Her mood suddenly soured. "I did all I could."

"Why would you do that for an enemy?"

"Why do you give extra rations to *your* enemies?" she countered, obviously catching him off guard, as shock flashed across his face. Then a gleam of approval appeared in those daring eyes of his, and he stepped toward her. Water continued to drip from both of them onto the deck, but Emeline didn't care. Her heart sped up as he closed the distance between them. He lifted his hand, hesitated, then slid a finger down her cheek.

Why, she couldn't say, but the sensation it caused was more than pleasurable. Another sin for which God would surely punish her.

Then as if her skin burned his fingers, he yanked back his hand, turned, and darted out the door. She went to close it but not before Lieutenant Dimsmore passed by in the hall, offering her a sly smile.

Five days later with Robert mending as well as could be expected and no further encounters with Lieutenant Masters, Emeline was putting the finishing touches on the captain's portrait as he sat in his usual pose on the stern window ledge. They conversed about various topics, none of which included battle plans or tactics, and despite the fact he was her enemy, Emeline still found the man's company enjoyable. Though he was as rigid in rules as her father, he also bent those rules slightly for the sake of mercy.

For one thing, he admired her painting and did not consider it unbefitting for a lady to charge for her work. For another, he had allowed Emeline to visit Hannah in the hold and bring her extra rations and comforts. Something she was sure was not normally permitted with British prisoners.

She could learn much from this man about following rules and proper behavior, while still maintaining one's humanity, and she found herself, once again, wishing she'd had a father like him.

Sunlight streamed through the windows, highlighting the gold epaulets on his shoulders and winking at her from his row of brass buttons.

A knock on the door caused her to pause with paint-loaded brush in hand as three officers entered and surrounded the captain's desk, Lieutenant Masters among them.

"HMS *Hawk* has just signaled, Captain, with this message from Admiral Cockburn," Lieutenant Camp said.

"Very good." Blackwell slid from his perch and took the paper handed to him. "I hope it's what we've been waiting for." He took no time to break the seal and open it, perusing the contents as his officers waited.

No sound but their breathing and the creak of wood filled the cabin.

"Yes, indeed, this is it!" Blackwell tossed down the paper, plucked a map from his desk, and began rolling it out across the oak.

The men, Lieutenants Masters, Camp, and Dimsmore, listened intently as their captain laid out the plans for a land invasion of Baltimore.

Baltimore! Emeline's heart shriveled, and she nearly fell from her chair. Bracing herself, she sat frozen in place, too afraid to move, too afraid to breathe for fear they'd notice she was still there. All the while, she listened intently for any important detail, any bit of information that would help the American cause. Not that it mattered. She was stuck on this ship, and no one but Robert knew how to swim. But she listened, nonetheless.

And as she listened, her anger grew, pushing aside her fear. No doubt emboldened by their success in Washington, the British were planning a major attack on her hometown. Both by land and by sea! The thought set aflame every nerve as she pictured the beautiful buildings of her capital lying in crumbled piles of smoldering ash.

"We are being called, as is every able-bodied soldier remaining from the Washington campaign, to assist in this final endeavor."

Final? Emeline gulped.

"For the sea attack?" Lieutenant Masters shifted his stance.

"Aye, and on land." The captain rubbed the back of his neck. "We are to provide men to assist with the land invasion, both marines and sailors."

Emeline gripped the paintbrush so hard, it nearly snapped. A blob dripped onto her palette. She could not allow them to attack her home.

"By God we've got them now," Dimsmore proclaimed. "This will seal their fate."

"And end this blasted war," Camp added.

"That is our hope." Captain Blackwell rose to his full height. "Once Baltimore is taken, the rest of the country will follow, mark my words!" He stared out the stern windows. "Then it will be an easy transition once our troops and officials arrive to take over their ragtag government."

"These savage wood hicks won't know what hit them." Dimsmore chortled.

Captain Blackwell leaned back on his desk and sighed. "There's just one problem. We need information on the size of their militia in Baltimore and where their nearest army is stationed. We must discover how much armament they have and how many reinforcements they can call up from nearby cities in a moment's notice."

Emeline wanted to vomit. She set down her paintbrush, but it fell to the deck.

Blackwell glanced her way, but instead of ordering her to leave, he cocked his head. "You have relatives in Baltimore, Miss Baratt, do you not?"

She forced down a lump of terror. Unable to respond, she glanced over the surprised gazes of the men.

"I know it's a rather large town," Blackwell continued. "But surely your father knows someone in the local militia, perhaps someone of high rank?"

"What exactly are you asking me to do, Captain?" she managed to squeak out.

Turning, he gazed out the stern windows and fisted his hands at his waist. "If you are acquainted with someone in the militia, you would be able to gather the information we need and also discover how much of our plans they are privy to."

Emeline smiled to herself. Yes, she could do that. *Or* she could inform them of the upcoming invasion. "I believe I do have connections. Last I heard, a dear friend of my father's is a captain in the Maryland infantry. But I am here on the ship, Captain." She shrugged.

"A dear friend?" Dimsmore blew out a breath. "How fortuitous."

Lieutenant Masters slid a finger down his scar, unsuccessfully hiding a deepening frown.

Captain Blackwell nodded. "Fortuitous, indeed." He tapped his chin beneath a scowl. "But I could never put you in such danger."

Yet she *wanted* to be put in such danger, to do something for her country, something to prevent these men from winning the war.

"The lady has been gone a long time." Lieutenant Masters avoided her gaze. "Why would this family friend trust her? Why not just send some of our men disguised as American farmers?"

"I doubt they could get close enough to garner anything of value. Whereas Miss Baratt, a native of the city and well-known throughout I would imagine . . . well, she could walk right into the commander's tent, view maps and documents, overhear plans . . . But no matter, I would never send a lady into a war zone."

Emeline picked her paintbrush off the deck, but found it trembled so much, she immediately put it down on her tray.

It wasn't the danger or the adventure she feared. In truth, it all sounded far too enticing. It was whether a lady should be doing something like this. A double spy? Did women do such things? What would her father say? What would God say?

Still, she *had* the information, at least some of it. It was the perfect way off this ship and the perfect way to help her country. She knew the countryside and could no doubt lose whatever marine they assigned to escort her, make her way to the Baltimore militia, and warn them of the upcoming attack.

Why was she even thinking this over? Of course, she had to do it. She was the only one who could. But would her antics only cause others pain as they so often had in the past?

"I'll go," she blurted. And no sooner did the words fire from her undisciplined lips than she believed she'd lost all reason.

"What a brave girl!" Captain Blackwell

exclaimed, joy lighting his eyes. Dimsmore offered her a smile, Lieutenant Camp looked at her with concern, while Lieutenant Masters scowled. Odd.

"Begging your pardon, miss." Lieutenant Camp nodded her way but addressed the captain. "But can we trust her? She was born in America."

"So was Masters, here." Blackwell gestured toward Owen. "And they both have more than proven their loyalty in my book."

The captain circled his desk and approached her. "I will personally assure your safety, Miss Baratt. A landing party will accompany you, and I will assign my best man to protect you."

Daring to trust the sturdiness of her legs, Emeline slowly rose. "I am no spy, Captain, but I will do my best."

"The Baltimore campaign is vitally important, Miss Baratt, or I wouldn't ask. It could mean the end of the war and hence, your free passage back to England where you belong."

Forcing a smile, she nodded. Over her dead body. Britain had more rules for women than America did. Yet at the thought of finally getting off this ship, a real smile overtook the fake one.

Now, what buffoon marine would Blackwell assign to escort her? Whoever it was, she would have no trouble ditching him at her first opportunity.

CHAPTER 15

Luther Dimsmore entered the captain's cabin and shut the door behind him. Swallowing, he approached the desk, behind which Blackwell sat, and suddenly regretted his decision to speak to the man.

Blackwell looked up. "What is it, Dimsmore?"

"I've come regarding an important matter."

The man continued perusing the documents on his desk before he leaned back with a groan and stared at Dimsmore.

Dimsmore considered excusing himself and leaving. Who was he kidding? When it came to Lieutenant Masters, Blackwell had a definite log in his eye.

"Well, out with it, Lieutenant. I haven't got all day."

"It's regarding Lieutenant Masters, Captain."

The man rubbed his chin, his eyes narrowing.

"There have been a few" — Dimsmore coughed — "he has done some . . ."

Growling, Blackwell shot to his feet, impatience firing from his eyes.

Dimsmore spit out his thoughts before he changed his mind. "I believe he has given us cause to suspect his loyalties, Captain."

"Bah!" The man's face mottled. "What are you talking about?"

"I've been watching him, Captain. Closely. His behavior is definitely suspect."

Blackwell frowned, picked up a letter opener, and tapped it on the desk. "I grow weary of this feud between you two. Unless you have some proof of these accusations, I suggest you quit wasting my time and return to your duties."

"I'm offering my services to go ashore and keep an eye on him."

"For what purpose? I'm already sending Lieutenant Camp to keep him in line. Lord knows Masters oft leaps half-cocked into situations he shouldn't." He chuckled. "Though it always turns out well."

Dimsmore forced back a scowl and straightened his stance. "I have reason to suspect he remains loyal to America."

"An officer in the Royal Navy?" Blackwell

guffawed even as a twitch took residence above his right eye. "Have you taken to drinking before noon? He's been on this ship eight years and more than proven his loyalty."

"It's little things, Captain. Did you know he brings extra rations to the prisoners? And when we were all celebrating on deck as Washington burned, he seemed sad, even angry. And I'm sure he saw that prisoner escape and yet called no alarm."

Blackwell studied him for a moment . . . a long, intense moment during which Dimsmore almost regretted saying anything at all. "Pure conjecture. I don't know what you have against him, Dimsmore, but I grow weary of your disdain."

"This has naught to do with my sentiments toward the man, Captain, but more to do with my loyalty to the Crown. I'm merely asking permission to keep an eye on him. Ensure he and Miss Baratt do their duty and return safely."

"Then go." Captain Blackwell waved him away. "You may accompany them. But before you spew any further accusations, you better have solid proof, or I'll see you brought up on charges of defaming an officer. Do I make myself clear?"

"Aye, Captain." Dimsmore saluted, then

spun on his heels and marched out the door, a smile on his face.

Emeline halted and blinked, allowing her eyes to grow accustomed to the darkness. The smell was another thing altogether. She'd never get used to the putrid stench belowdecks. Covering her nose with a handkerchief, she stifled a cough. There was enough coughing coming from behind the iron bars in the distance. Holding the extra stew she'd managed to scrounge from the cook after supper, she shot the marine behind her a glance before proceeding past crates and barrels, past stacks of ropes and canvas, until finally she stood before a hatch grating and knelt. She set down the lantern and peered below where hands rose to shield blinking eyes from the brightness.

Curses also rose, like arrows to pierce her heart — "Traitor! Turncoat!" among the nicest.

"Dearest!" The voice of an angel lifted her gaze to the right, where iron bars waved at her with the teetering of the ship.

"Hannah!" Grabbing her satchel and lantern, Emeline dashed to the cage and dropped to her knees. Hands reached out and gripped Emeline's face in a loving embrace. " 'Ow are you, dear?"

"How am *I*?" Emeline wanted to cry. "How are you? What a horrid place!" She glanced over the hold. Shadows shifted over crates and barrels like hungry specters awaiting a meal. The rush of the sea was joined by the patter of tiny feet and the slosh of bilge water that smelled so foul, it brought tears to Emeline's eyes. Or perhaps the tears came because of this precious lady.

"It ain't so bad, dear." Hannah's smile remained.

Emeline handed her the food. "This is all I could get."

"Not to worry, dear. I thank ye for it. God be praised."

"How can you praise God down here?"

" 'E is worthy to be praised everywhere. It don't matter our situation."

Emeline gripped the lady's hands, cold despite the heat. "You are an inspiration." She kissed them as more tears sped down her cheeks.

"Wha's the matter? No need to cry."

"I'm to go ashore, Hannah."

"Off the ship?"

"Yes, I haven't time to explain . . . but I promise" — she glanced back at the marine who had sat on a barrel, looking rather bored — "I'll come back. I'll come back and set you all free."

"Don't you dare! If you get a chance to be free, take it an' don't look back. The good Lord'll take care of us."

Emeline squeezed her hand, knowing she couldn't stay any longer or else raise suspicion.

"I promise." Rising, she grabbed the lantern and returned to the marine standing by the ladder.

God help her, she didn't know how. But she intended to keep that promise.

September 3, 1814, off the shores of
  Maryland, just before dawn

Paddles struck the dark water again. *Swoosh, swoosh, gurgle, gurgle.* Closing her eyes, Emeline listened to the glorious sound as the marines rowed her and the landing party ashore. Freedom! At last she'd set foot on the shores of her beloved country, her home, her land. Why had she not appreciated it before? Why had she ever left? Foolish girl. And now these British ruffians intended to steal it from her . . . from her countrymen. Steal their freedom.

Not if she had a say in it.

Swoosh, swoosh, gurgle, gurgle.

She drew in a deep breath. Salty brine and earthy loam mixed in a perfume far more pleasing than anything from Paris. Another scent intruded. It was the man beside her — Lieutenant Masters — his unique scent of man, the sea, and something spicy that was far too alluring. *Fie!* Why had the captain sent him along? Surely he needed his first lieutenant on board the ship rather than on a mission to escort her to Baltimore.

Swoosh, swoosh, gurgle, gurgle.

A swath of golden light tickled her eyelids, and she opened them to find dawn's welcoming glow rippling along the horizon. The cockboat wobbled over a wavelet, and before she could grip the edge, a hand, large and firm, pressed against her back. She glanced at the lieutenant. He sat on the thwarts beside her, a mere shadow in the predawn gloom, yet she felt his eyes upon her as if he could see every detail regardless of the night. She shifted in her seat and focused ahead where dark mounds rose from the bay and leaves fluttered in the wind. *Land. Home.*

Her heart thundered in her chest. She was home, yes, but she was not free. She was still surrounded by enemies — Lieutenant Masters, Lieutenant Dimsmore, and one other marine, a Mr. Ryne. Three men. Three warriors she would have to somehow thwart, lose, disable, or God knew what. What was she thinking? How could she ever hope to

accomplish such a feat? And in a week —
all the time Blackwell had given them.

Apparently, if all went well and the information they gathered was conducive to a
British victory, the British intended to
proceed with their attack on Baltimore. But
that was all she knew. If she were to go to
the militia with only the news of an impending attack, she'd be telling them nothing
they didn't already suspect. She must know
how the British planned to attack, from
which direction, with how many troops, and
with what type of weapons. A specific date
wouldn't hurt either. She would have to get
the information out of these men before she
escaped their clutches.

Blood tore through her veins, and her
father's voice chimed in her thoughts.
"These dangerous feats are best left to men."

A breeze blew a strand of hair in her face,
and she grabbed it and twirled it around
her finger. *God, if You're there, I know what
I'm doing may not be proper, but could You
please help me?*

Swoosh, swoosh, gurgle, gurgle.

"Oars up," Lieutenant Dimsmore whispered, and the rowers lifted their paddles as
the cockboat drifted to the shore of Bird
River, a tributary off the Chesapeake. It
struck the sand with a jarring thud. Eme-

221

line lost her grip on the thwart and would have fallen if not for, once again, the firm hand of Lieutenant Masters. The marines leapt out and pulled the boat farther up on land as Mr. Ryne and Dimsmore jumped into the water.

Dimsmore spun, hand extended to assist Emeline, but Owen, without warning, swept her up in his arms and carried her onto dry land. She hadn't time to protest before he set her down and walked away. Her boot sank into the sand. She attempted a step, but her legs trembled uncontrollably, and she toppled forward. This time, Dimsmore caught her and helped her to stand. "Easy now. You still have your sea legs, Miss Baratt."

Indeed, she did, for every step she took felt like the world was shaking beneath her. He led her up the shore to lean against a tree before he returned to assist the men with supplies. Feeling slightly nauseated and as though the world were spinning, she turned to watch them just as the sun's rays speared through trees across the small inlet . . . glittering, golden rays that transformed the water into a saffron sheet, the sand into sparkling jewels, the trees into dancing emeralds.

And the three men into strangers.

Not the sailors who'd rowed them here, for they were still dressed in sailor garb, nor the midshipman in charge of them. But the men who were to accompany her no longer looked like Royal Navy officers.

But instead like American backwoodsmen.

Lieutenant Masters, his back to her, issued orders to the midshipman before the man saluted, shoved the boat from shore, leapt in, and began rowing back to the ship. Grabbing a pack of supplies, he turned to face her.

If not for that cocksure grin, she hardly recognized him. Hair freed from its queue hung to his shoulders, strands hovering over an unshaven jaw as firm and hard as the tree she leaned against. A coarse, open-collared shirt hung over his chest, covered by a brown waistcoat draped down to tight leggings stuffed within black boots. A knife perched in his belt and a brown Bess in his hand as he headed toward her, looking more ruffian and rogue than Royal Navy officer.

She warmed at the sight. No. Surely the effect came merely from the rising sun. Not this man, this enemy.

Pushing from the tree, she attempted to walk as Mr. Ryne and Dimsmore also approached, both dressed in similar garb.

To her embarrassment, she wobbled yet

again, but quickly shifted out of the way of
Lieutenant Masters's rescue. She did not
need any man's help. Especially not that
one's.

"Lead the way, Wife." He gave her a roguish grin. "You say Baltimore is over a day's
trek from here?"

Both the word *wife* and the look in his
eyes did strange things to her midsection —
things she didn't want to acknowledge.
"Roughly two days. And you'll remember,
Husband, that I am your wife in name only
and *only* for this trip." She still couldn't
believe that Blackwell had done this to her.
When she'd protested, he'd said it was the
only way to legitimize a woman traveling
with three men. She knew he was right, but
it grated on her, nonetheless. "Attempted
liberties will be dealt with swiftly," she
added, forcing her most ferocious glare at
him, which only caused his smile to widen.

"I wouldn't dream of it," he said, but she
could tell from the twinkle in his eyes that
dreaming of such things was not out of the
question with this man.

"Never fear, miss." Dimsmore joined
them. "I won't let this scoundrel touch you."

Somehow that brought her little comfort.
"The sooner we get there, the better," she
said. Clutching her skirts, she stepped over

a rock and entered the copse of trees lining the shore.

Dimsmore slid beside her. "You are a brave lady, Miss Baratt. We shall make every attempt to make the journey easy for you."

"I am no wilting flower that I have need of extra care, Lieutenant. Let us just be about our task and return unscathed."

She heard Owen chuckle behind her and felt Dimsmore's disapproval in the air.

No matter. The task before her was plain.

She just had no idea how she was going to accomplish it.

Two years. It had been two years since Owen had set foot on American soil. And it had never felt so good. If things went according to plan, he'd never have to return to HMS *Marauder* again. A pinch of regret caused him to wince at deceiving Captain Blackwell for all these years. He was a decent, honorable man . . . a good man. Owen would miss him and his wise counsel. He would also miss Benjamin Camp — another man worthy of his admiration, and his friendship, though he doubted Ben would feel the same way when he found out Owen was a spy.

That couldn't be helped.

Retrieving a handkerchief from his pocket,

he wiped the back of his neck where a constant stream of sweat did little to cool him off in the sweltering forest. They'd been walking for more than two hours in thickets of maple and elm trees, over fields of sandy soil covered with black-eyed Susans, and through foggy swampland.

Nary a complaint had issued from Miss Baratt's lips. He knew she was uncomfortable, could see the perspiration blotching her gown and gluing the fabric to her skin . . . could hear her heavy breaths as she forced herself to tread along. Wisps of honey-colored hair escaped their pins in protest and trickled down her back, seeking a breeze that never seemed to come. The homespun gown the captain had given her must have been made for an even smaller lady than she, for it clung to every curve, making her all the more alluring. If possible. Yet determination rode heavy on her brow, and though he had tried to make conversation, she had kept unusually silent.

Why did he care anyway? She was a traitor to her country, and he would have no choice but to turn her in before she gathered information and returned to the ship. He shrugged off the sudden spasm of remorse. He had no choice. Sure, he could run off to Washington and search for his uncle, providing he had survived the attack. But any information he conveyed might be too late for Baltimore. Besides, that would still leave Dimsmore and Miss Baratt to do their spying. He couldn't allow that, though he did wonder at his sudden selfless patriotism. He huffed. Or perhaps it wasn't selfless at all. He still hoped his uncle would supply him with a privateer if Owen provided good information. The only problem he faced was how to ensure the Baltimore militia commander believed he was who he said he was without his uncle's corroboration.

Yet despite the threat of being tossed in an American prison, despite even his desire for a privateer, Owen had to take the risk. For his country. He had information that could save Baltimore and thus, perhaps end the war in America's favor. He wasn't about to let a slip of a woman stop him.

In truth, he just wanted to finish the mission and get on with his life. If only they could have been dropped ashore closer to Baltimore, but they didn't want to alert the suspicions of any American farmers or woodsmen in the area. This way, it looked like they were a group of backwoods farmers seeking shelter from the British in the city.

They emerged from the trees into another

clearing. A white-tailed deer foraging in the distance lifted its head to watch them before bolting into the woods. Owen drew a deep breath. The scent of pine, oak, and earth filled his lungs — a pleasant smell that reminded him of home and lured a smile to his lips. A screech brought his gaze up to a Cooper's hawk soaring high above them. At least the bird was in a cool breeze — one that refused to grace them below.

Had he been so long at sea that he'd forgotten the heat of Maryland summers? He suddenly found himself thankful that he didn't have to wear his thick naval uniform, for he could not imagine marching in this heat beneath layers of wool. Owen was also thankful they'd not come across any troops — American or British — thus far.

Miss Baratt quickened her pace across the field, almost as if she were trying to lose them. Conversely, Dimsmore trudged behind them, cursing and grunting like an overheated sow. "Should we allow the lady to rest?" he finally said.

More like allow Dimsmore to rest. Owen smiled and glanced ahead. He could hear the slight trickle of water in the distance coming from a patch of pines.

"Miss Baratt," he shouted to the woman who was at least twenty feet in front of him.

"Let's stop up ahead by the creek."

She halted, adjusted her bonnet, and stared back at him as if he'd asked her to climb the nearest tree, before continuing onward.

Baffling woman.

The creek ambled across the edge of the field and disappeared into a cluster of pines heavily clothed with bramble bushes. As Owen approached, a trickle of unease spiraled down his back. Something wasn't right. He cocked his ear to listen, but Dimsmore began complaining behind him again.

An eagle squawked overhead. The unease increased, and Owen called out to Miss Baratt to stop, but she had already disappeared into the trees.

Her muffled shriek filled the air.

Plucking his knife from his belt, Owen dashed into the brush.

To find the muzzles of at least twenty muskets aimed their way.

CHAPTER 16

"Drop your weapons and raise your hands, you filthy rebels!" the man dressed in the royal marine uniform shouted, aiming his musket directly at Lieutenant Masters.

Emeline's heart had somehow hoisted itself into her throat, unable to beat or even move as she stared at the man. The marines had them surrounded, and behind the guns so imperiously pointed at their chests, more soldiers rustled forward. At least fifty, battle weary from what she saw of their torn, bloodstained uniforms. American blood, no doubt. Blinking back the terror and fury crowding out her thoughts, she shifted her gaze to Lieutenant Masters.

Yet the lieutenant remained as calm as a windless sea, returning the soldier's stare as if he hadn't a care in the world. Slowly he dropped his knife and placed his musket on the ground. Dimsmore and Ryne barged through the brush and froze.

Emeline felt gazes skittering over her like spiders on the loose, and her glance confirmed that several of the soldiers stared her way, ill intentions forming in their eyes. A chill wriggled up her spine. She hugged herself.

Dimsmore dared advance toward the man, whom Emeline assumed was a sergeant due to the three chevrons on his right sleeve. The white belt crisscrossing his red jacket matched his white trousers, though both were mottled with stains.

"We are British, you buffoons," Dimsmore barked. "Lower your weapons at once."

The man scowled then nodded toward the marine beside him, who promptly struck Dimsmore's head with the butt of his weapon.

Emeline gasped as the lieutenant folded to the ground like a piece of parchment.

Mr. Ryne tossed down his gun and went to assist his superior.

Lieutenant Masters shook his head and reached for something inside his waistcoat. "Completely unnecessary. The man was correct, you know."

Weapons cocked.

He halted, keeping his hands in the air. "Just retrieving proof of our loyalty."

The sergeant approached, a burly man

with eyes far too small for his face and a hook nose that rode upon a bushy mustache like a ship on a rogue wave. "You expect us to believe you are British. Where are your uniforms? Why aren't you with your regiment?"

"We have no regiment. We are spies, if you must know, sent on a secret mission by Cockburn himself." Lieutenant Masters withdrew the papers, along with what looked like a badge or perhaps a coin and handed them to the man. "A mission which you are severely compromising."

With the help of Mr. Ryne, Dimsmore rose and spewed a string of curses at the sergeant.

Ignoring him, the man unfolded the document, scanned it, and then examined the coin. Something on his face softened and then tightened again as he turned and called to a Mr. Jackson. Another man made his way through the crowd, and the sergeant handed him the parchment. "Decipher this immediately."

Stumbling, Dimsmore moaned and lifted a hand to his head. Blood saturated his hair, and Emeline headed toward him to see if she could help.

"I can tell you exactly what it says," Lieutenant Masters said as Mr. Jackson rifled through his haversack, pulled out a small leather book and a pencil, and got to work.

The sergeant frowned. "And you will, as soon as he's finished. In the meantime" — he flipped the medallion over in his hand — "where did you get this?"

"From Admiral Cockburn himself. As you can see, it bears his personal insignia as well as the crest of the Admiralty."

Removing his black shako, the sergeant ran a hand through his hair, his gaze shifting from the medallion back to Owen, then over Dimsmore, Ryne, and finally Emeline, where it remained far too long for her comfort.

Owen cleared his throat, drawing the man's gaze yet again. "First Lieutenant Owen Masters of HMS *Marauder* at your service, Sergeant. This is Mr. Ryne" — he gestured toward the marine — "and this man is, I hesitate to say, your superior, Lieutenant Luther Dimsmore."

Emeline attempted to press a handkerchief over Dimsmore's wound, but he grabbed it from her and waved her away. "And you shall pay for this affront, Sergeant," he grumbled out atop a curse.

A flicker of fear flashed in the man's eyes. "And the woman? You expect me to believe she's also a British spy?"

Some of the men behind him chuckled.

"I do." Owen glanced her way, and she thought she saw him nod as if to reassure her she was safe. "She has contacts in Baltimore we need."

"How do I know you didn't steal the admiral's medallion off the real spies?"

"If I were an American, how would I know that it bears proof of being British? It has no other value and appears to be a mere token of some sort, a cheap one at that. Why would I even steal it?"

The sergeant handed the medallion to the man beside him, a beastly fellow who looked like he could snap a neck with two fingers. He moved to a shaft of sunlight to examine it just as Mr. Jackson completed his decoding and handed the parchment to the sergeant. After perusing it, he looked up at Owen. "What does it say?"

"It says, 'By order of Admiral Cockburn, the following persons are authorized to go ashore and discover by any means possible the plans, armament, and troops of the American militia in Baltimore.' Then it lists our names . . . Lieutenant Owen Masters, Lieutenant Luther Dimsmore, Mr. Ryne, and Miss Emeline Baratt."

Owen continued with an impatient huff.

"If you detain us or if you expose us to the Americans, you'll have to answer to the admiral himself. No doubt you've heard of his brutality."

The look in the man's eyes confirmed that he had.

"He speaks the truth," Mr. Ryne, who hadn't said a word all day, added. "Lower your weapons. You're frightening the lady."

Yes, they were, though she had tried to hide it. She'd heard talk on board the *Marauder* of how vicious these marine landing parties could be — their horrific raids on civilian farmers, burning homes to the ground, slaughtering families, ravishing both goods and women.

The sergeant gestured for his men to lower their weapons. "Take the lieutenant to the creek and get him some water."

Two men snapped to attention and approached Dimsmore, but he quickly shoved them aside and speared the sergeant with hate-filled eyes. "Striking a superior is a hanging offense." He bent to retrieve his weapons, stumbled, but then finally grabbed them.

The sergeant swallowed. "I thought you were an American."

"What is your name?"

"Sergeant John Herod."

Dimsmore cursed. "Don't matter what you thought." He shook his head, blinked, and headed toward the creek.

Owen's gaze followed him, a hint of a smile on his lips. "So you believe us now?" He faced the sergeant again.

The man breathed out a weary sigh, nodded, then handed the medallion and parchment back to Owen. "Please accept my apology, Lieutenant. I'm sure you understand my mistake."

Relief settled Emeline's heart back in her chest. Still, some of the men continued to stare at her as if she sat unclad before them. Indeed, she felt as though she were in such a state beneath their intrusive gazes. Owen must have noticed for he moved to stand beside her. "I have put the matter behind me." He glanced over the troops. "No doubt you're anxious to be on your way. Let us not detain you further."

"We stopped here to rest and fill our canteens when we heard you approach. We'll do so and leave after that." With a snap of his fingers, more marines appeared from the brush and headed toward the creek, some grunting, others talking, while others kept their eyes upon Emeline and Owen. The sergeant excused himself and headed toward Dimsmore.

Owen rubbed his eyes. "We should find another place to rest. Who knows how long they'll be here?"

Emeline nodded. "In truth, I don't feel safe with these men."

"I agree." Owen retrieved his knife and musket and gave her a look of concern. "Let's fill our canteens and be on our way. Stay close to me." He gestured for Mr. Ryne to follow, and the three of them found a spot by the water a few yards from the marines.

For once, Emeline didn't mind obeying the man. And if she had to admit it, she felt safe with him by her side. She lowered to sit on a rock by the creek while Owen knelt to splash water on his face and fill her canteen. He looked nothing like he had on board the *Marauder*. Not just his attire, but his demeanor. On the ship, he'd seemed tense, out of place, almost like a caged animal pacing to be set free. Out here in the wilderness, he seemed more alive, more in his element, even calmer, though their situation was certainly not without danger. He ran his fingers back through his wet hair as he scanned their surroundings — like a predator, not prey. He turned to her, caught her staring at him, and smiled as he handed her the canteen. Against her will, her insides turned to mush.

Quickly, she shifted her gaze away. Only then did she see two wagons parked at the edge of the trees loaded with crates and sacks and over-flowing with everything imaginable — lanterns, pots, bolts of fabric, candle holders, paintings, tapestries, silverware, and even chairs. Stolen from some poor farmer, no doubt.

Her anger rose to overcome her fear, and even more so as the marines' conversation with Dimsmore echoed down the creek.

"You should have seen how easy it was to enter their capital," the sergeant said. "Daft, cow-hearted Americans! They fled like chickens before a wolf. Even that popinjay, Madison, their so-called president, took off like a spineless biddy." Other marines joined in his laughter.

Dimsmore, apparently having forgiven the sergeant's assault, nodded and smiled as he pressed a wet handkerchief to his head.

Oddly, Owen looked about ready to explode.

The water Emeline had just consumed threatened to spew from her mouth.

The sergeant took a long draft from his canteen and wiped his mouth with his sleeve. "Yes, indeed. We waltzed right into the president's dining room, all set for a feast. Ole Cockburn himself toasted the president's health with the buffoon's own claret . . . even as we were ransacking the house from cellar to garret." No doubt noticing he had an audience, the sergeant's gaze landed on Owen.

"Sorry to have missed that," Owen shouted back to him, which seemed to assuage the man.

Dimsmore swept narrowed eyes toward him.

"Then we set the mansion aflame," another marine added. "That was something to see!"

Averting her gaze to the forest, Emeline pressed a hand to her stomach.

Dimsmore rose, blinked, and wiped the wet cloth over the back of his neck. "What of the storm the next day? We felt it quite violently on the ship."

"Came out of nowhere." The sergeant shook his head. "Never saw such wind. Toppled houses and buried thirty of our men beneath the rubble."

Emeline could keep silent no longer as she faced the soldiers. "It is almost as if God Himself was defending these Americans."

Her words stole all levity from the conversation as every eye latched upon her.

"If that were so, miss," the sergeant said

with a tight smile, "He wouldn't have allowed us to burn their capital to the ground." He faced his men. "Nor raid those two farms on our way back. Taught these colonial jackals a lesson."

"They wouldn't consider themselves colonials, Sergeant." Owen knelt again to fill his own canteen. "You forget they won their independence."

"Lot of good it did them. They have no clue how to govern themselves. Why, most of them will no doubt be happy to have law and order restored."

Rising, Emeline excused herself and wandered downstream, hoping she didn't toss her accounts and give away her true sentiments.

She didn't go far enough, for she could still hear the braggarts defaming her nation. Glancing over her shoulder through the leaves, she studied Lieutenant Masters — the tightness of his lips, his ramrod stance, and the way his thumb continually rubbed over the scar on his cheek. Was he as angry as she over this injustice? But how could that be?

Unfortunately, Dimsmore seemed to notice as well, for his gaze kept finding its way toward Owen. He turned toward the sergeant. "Where are you heading now?"

"We're returning to our ship to resupply. Hear there's another attack planned on Baltimore, and we expect to be sent to help. Though they may not need that many troops. If their capital was that easy, the citizens will either run off like poltroons or throw us a party to celebrate." He laughed as if he told a grand joke, and his men joined in.

Dimsmore chuckled and nodded his approval. "That's precisely what we were sent to discover."

"Then Godspeed to you." The sergeant saluted. "And I'm sorry about the —" He pointed toward Dimsmore's head.

Dimsmore merely nodded as the sergeant ordered his men to get the wagons and fall in line.

Emeline longed to grab a musket and shoot the man. But that wouldn't be very ladylike. Instead, she closed her eyes and drew a deep breath, focusing on the rippling and splashing of the creek and the sweet warble of birdsong.

She felt Owen's presence before she heard him. The strength of him surrounded her — a barricade of comfort she didn't want to feel. Not from her enemy. Opening her eyes, she dared a glance into his hazel eyes and found naught but concern . . . and something else that made her toes tingle.

She looked away. With over a day's trek remaining, they would have to stop for the night. She'd do her best to get information about the upcoming attack from the lieutenant tonight, but regardless, she intended to escape these men and make her way to Baltimore alone, for she could no longer stand to be in the presence of her enemies.

CHAPTER 17

Clouds as dark and threatening as Owen's mood swooped in to give them a reprieve from the blaring sun. But not from the heat. The temperature only seemed to rise along with Owen's anger. Despite the beauty of sandy fields full of swamp grass and clearings dotted with Queen Anne's lace, a cauldron of emotions stirred within him. Fury, of course, at the arrogance, the cruelty of the soldiers they'd met; sorrow at what his kinsmen were suffering; fear for Baltimore and his entire country; but more than any of those, determination to fulfill his mission and save his country.

The way he saw it, there was only one thing that stood in his way. That one thing now walked in front of him, her drab brown skirts doing naught to hide her beauty nor diminish the luster of her hair trickling down her back in golden waves. And those lashes . . . a man could get lost in the forest of lashes caressing her cheek.

Hang it all. Surely he could handle such a slip of a woman, a traitor at that. But something about her . . . something he'd never encountered before . . . something caused him pause. Caused him to not want to turn her in and see her possibly executed. But he was being weak — a foreign feeling for him. And he would not let it get in his way. Not when his country's freedom was at stake.

A blue jay scolded him from above as he batted aside a leafy branch. He must stay the course, use Emeline to get close to the militia's commander, and then turn her in and tell them what he knew. He could only pray they'd believe him.

Lightning flashed across the dismal sky, crackling in the air and sending a pulse through Owen's veins . . . an evil pulse that carried more than the electric charge of a coming storm. It was the vile presence of war itself, the devastation, the loss . . . men's attempts to dominate one another. If there was a God, why did He allow such barbarity? How could a God who expected complete devotion seem so absent from the affairs of men?

A rumble of thunder brought his gaze up through the leafy canopy. Night was ap-

244

proaching. They'd have to find someplace safe to sleep.

Insects buzzed him, and he swiped them away as Emeline slowed and eased to walk beside him. Dimsmore led the way this time with Ryne guarding their flank.

"Lieutenant Masters —"

"I wish you'd call me Owen. We *are* husband and wife, are we not?" He winked.

She shifted her gaze away faster than a scared rabbit and nearly stumbled over an exposed root. *Adorable.*

After a few moments, she cleared her throat. "What are the plans for attacking Baltimore?"

Surprised by the direct question, Owen glanced behind him to make sure Mr. Ryne wasn't listening. Such a question made the lady suspect at best, at worst a spy. "Why do you need to know?"

She paused, grabbed a lock of her hair, and spun it around her finger. "After hearing those soldiers speak so boastfully, I wondered how brutal the plans are. I do still know people who live there."

Owen grimaced. People she was obviously willing to betray. "Why do you care if you're sailing back to England?"

"Surely you don't think me heartless, Owen." Her voice bore true indignance.

"This was the town of my birth."

"I would watch what you say, Miss Baratt. Especially in front of Dimsmore." Owen gripped the hilt of the knife stuffed in his belt. "Show a speck of loyalty toward this land and you may find yourself in irons with your friend Hannah."

"In front of Dimsmore but not you, sir?" She gave him a sarcastic smile.

How strange that his threat hadn't rattled her in the slightest. Oh, how he wished her loyalties lay with America! But then he remembered how quickly she'd ratted out her compatriots — her dear friend. How she'd raved to the captain about longing to live in England.

Owen stiffened his jaw and replied, "Me as well. I have no tolerance for traitors." And he didn't. He must remember that when the woman sent his senses whirling.

As she was doing now just walking beside him. Her scent — so feminine — the way she lifted her chin as if she were royalty and the world her subject. Not in an arrogant way, but in a way that said she was no ordinary woman. To that he could attest. Sweat glued his shirt and trousers to his skin, his stomach yipped at his throat like a starving dog, and his legs ached to rest. If he was that uncomfortable, what must she feel like beneath all the layers women were expected to wear? Yet she uttered not a single complaint. In addition, they hadn't eaten since the dried beef they'd consumed upon landing.

"Do you suspect my loyalties, Lieutenant?" she finally said.

"Do I have reason to?"

Distant thunder answered for her and kept her silent. A squirrel sped across the path as more clouds tumbled over the sun.

"You were born here as well, Lieutenant," she added. "What city, may I ask?"

"Portsmouth."

"So close. Do you have family there?"

"None I care to see." Owen lied, for he'd love nothing more than to see his mother and uncle again.

Moments passed. Ahead of them, Dimsmore brushed aside a final branch, and they followed him into another clearing. Wind stirred the tall grass back and forth like someone playing a harp.

Emeline drew a deep breath and then sighed as they started across. "I know what made me turn my back on my country. Pray tell, what was your reason?"

"Do I need one?"

At this she frowned, grabbed her skirts, and hastened to walk in front of him.

Grinding his teeth, he followed in her wake, wanting to apologize for his curt response, willing his anger for this turncoat to return.

Rubbing the back of his neck, he gazed up at the dark clouds and . . .

Bumped right into her.

She let out a yelp. He backed away. "My apologies. I didn't . . ."

But she wasn't listening. Both her and Dimsmore's gazes were riveted upon plumes of gray smoke curling just above the tree line to the west. A burst of wind blew the scent of charred wood past Owen's nose.

"Probably just a farm burned to the ground," Dimsmore announced before proceeding.

The man was right of course. But Owen couldn't just pass by, not if there were survivors in need of help. "There may be shelter left standing there. The sun is nearly set, and we need someplace to sleep."

Dimsmore halted again and stretched his shoulders back, then gazed up at the darkening sky. "I could sure use a rest. How far are we from Baltimore, Miss Baratt?"

"My guess is half a day."

Owen tightened his grip on his gun. "Then let's check it out. Cautiously. Guns at the ready."

■ ■ ■ ■

Raindrops fell from the night sky like tears from heaven.

Emeline hung back while the men approached the farm, guns leveled before them. She feared what they would find — feared to see her countrymen butchered, feared that she'd lose the rope of control she clung to and fall headfirst into a pool of uncontrollable rage. What she would do with that rage against three warriors, she had no idea. But then again, she wasn't much for thinking before reacting.

Night had absconded with the light, and the only thing leading their way was the smoldering embers that now sizzled and smoked beneath droplets of rain. Every inch of her body ached, including her empty stomach, but it was her heart that outdid them all when she saw the destruction left behind by a band of self-serving, arrogant soldiers who were devoid of all honor and decency.

Fences lay like firewood scattered by a child's temper tantrum. Chickens, pigs, and cows wandered aimlessly in search of food. All that remained of acres of corn were charred stalks lined up like gaunt soldiers marching to war. The barn — or what used to be the barn — was naught but a pile of smoking cinders, but off in the distance, light flickered from the window of a small house still standing.

The agony suffocating Emeline loosened its grip ever so slightly.

"Someone's still alive." Dimsmore's tone was almost one of disappointment.

"And their house remains," Mr. Ryne added.

"It'll be our house for tonight." Dimsmore chuckled.

Emeline wanted to kick him in the shin, scream a warning to these people, run as fast as she could to her house in Baltimore, and slam the door shut on this horrible world.

Instead, she watched the men start across the field. "No need for killing," Owen said. "They will think we are Americans come to help."

"They're the enemy, Masters."

"*Civilians,* Dimsmore. I will have us behave with more honor than Sergeant Herod and his men. Do I make myself clear?"

Emeline could not see Dimsmore's face in the darkness, but she could well imagine his grimace. She'd seen it enough times. Despite that, she was thankful Owen —

when had she come to think of him by his Christian name? — was in charge.

"They may have information we could use," she added her opinion to the conversation. "Plus, they might need help."

"Indeed, Miss Baratt." Owen glanced at her over his shoulder. "Kindness will go a long way in getting what we want."

"Kindness. Bah!" Dimsmore snapped. "We are at war, not attending tea and crumpets."

At the mention of crumpets, Emeline's stomach growled so loud she thought everyone would hear it. But the patter of rain and stomp of mud beneath their boots thankfully drowned out the sound.

Owen halted. "Stay here." Taking her arm, he ushered her to stand beside the thick trunk of a tall oak. "In case there's trouble."

Emeline was more than happy to remain behind. The *tap-tap* of the rain on the leaves above meant less water would reach her dress. Though it was already damp enough. A breeze sent a chill scrambling down her. Or perhaps it was her fear of what they would find in that house.

Turning, Owen crept along with Dimsmore and Ryne toward the front porch, gesturing for Mr. Ryne to go around behind.

The single lantern that shone from the

251

window barely afforded enough light to see one step ahead, let alone if there were any enemies about. Minutes passed. The three men became mere shadows floating in the darkness.

She could run. She could easily slip into the forest, find a bush to hide in during the night, and then make her way to Baltimore in the morning. But she didn't yet have the information she needed, and though she considered herself highly adventurous — much to her and God's chagrin — the thought of sleeping in a forest crowded with enemies, cold and wet, went a bit over the top. Even for her.

Besides, from the looks of things, there were most likely injured inside that house, and she intended to help them.

The raindrops grew heavier, muffling the sound of the men's footsteps. Another shadow appeared before her — and behind the men — a smaller shadow, moving ever so slowly. She held her breath, watching it, trying her best to focus in the dark. Perhaps in her exhaustion, she was seeing things. But no. The distinctive barrel of a musket rose. And she did the only thing she thought to do.

She jumped on the man.

■ ■ ■ ■

Owen heard a thump and a shout behind him. *Emeline!* Wheeling about, he charged toward the sounds, seeing only dark mounds moving on the ground. He grabbed one of them, a boy from the feel of him. The lad squirmed and kicked and attempted every which way to pound Owen in the face, but all he managed to do was punch him in the gut. Owen growled and gripped the lad's arms so tight, he squealed.

Dimsmore rushed to where Emeline lay and helped her to her feet.

"I curse you Brits! Leave my farm or die!" The young boy who had yet to reach manhood shouted with all the authority of an admiral.

Emeline groaned, and Owen started for her. "Are you all — Ouch!" The boy kicked him in the leg, squirmed from his grasp, and took off.

Mr. Ryne appeared from behind the house and brought him back within minutes.

Dimsmore laughed. "Can't even subdue a child, eh, Masters?"

"Want to try me and see?" Owen ground out as he reached for Emeline. But Dimsmore tugged her away. To the lady's credit, she jerked from his grip and stepped aside.

"Don't hurt him. He's only a boy," she pleaded, though Owen couldn't make out her expression. "I thought he was going to shoot you."

"I *was* goin' to shoot you! Stinking Brits." The boy struggled in Ryne's grip, spitting and heaving like a mad cow.

"We aren't British, boy. Calm yourself," Owen said.

Dimsmore attempted to take Emeline's arm again. "Are you all right, Miss Baratt?"

"Yes, just sore and muddy."

"Settle, lad. We aren't your enemies. We saw the smoke and came to help."

This seemed to do the trick, for the boy's shoulders deflated as if someone had forced all the air out of him. Finally, he glanced up at them. "You ain't Brits?"

"No, lad." Dimsmore adjusted his cocked hat. "We're farmers heading for Baltimore."

Emeline picked up the musket the boy had dropped and handed it to Owen.

"Then please help us, sirs." The boy's voice cracked, losing all its bluster. "My dad's hurt bad, and my mom is . . . well, she's in a family way . . . and my sister . . ." He dashed toward the house, urging them to follow.

Grabbing her skirts, Emeline charged after

him as fast as the mud would allow, but Owen caught up and grabbed her arm. "Remember we are married, Miss Baratt."

Humphing, she shrugged from his grip, but he nudged her behind him and motioned for the others to be cautious in case it was a trap. Unlikely, but one never knew in times of war.

The lad burst through the door and disappeared inside where voices could be heard.

Dimsmore mounted the steps, Mr. Ryne behind him.

A female voice shouted, "One more step and I'll shoot you clear back to England itself."

Dimsmore halted, and Owen brushed past him, hands in the air. "Ma'am, we are Americans. We saw the smoke and came to help."

"It's true, Ma. There's a lady with them too," the boy said.

Moments passed as the rain tapped on the roof and wind slapped moist air against Owen's cheek.

A groan sounded from inside. "Put down your weapons and show yourselves." The woman's voice shook.

Owen nodded toward Dimsmore and Ryne. "Do as she said —"

Before he could grab her, Miss Baratt shoved past him, her wet skirts sloshing over the porch, and rushed into the house.

"Hang it all!" Gripping his musket, Owen dashed after her to find her standing before the black barrel of a wavering musket, held by a woman quite heavy with child.

"We are friends. Let me help you," Emeline pleaded as Owen, intent on grabbing the dangerous gun from the lady, started for her.

Emeline held up a hand and gave him such a look of warning that he couldn't help but stop. She faced the woman again. "This is my husband, Owen Masters. And I'm Emeline. We are Americans heading toward Baltimore."

Dimsmore and Ryne entered behind them. The poor woman's eyes widened, fear pacing across them.

"This is my brother and cousin," Emeline added in a tone that would lure a fox out of its den. "We will do you no harm."

A moan sounded from the shadows at the far end of the one-room cabin, and a small girl no older than four crept out from beneath a table.

"Amos, get Abigail," the woman ordered. The lad who had so bravely attacked them, whom Owen could now see was no older than ten, grabbed his sister and held her tight.

"Is someone injured here? I have some medical skills." Emeline glanced past the woman into the shadows.

The woman's gaze drifted from Emeline to Owen and then over Dimsmore and Mr. Ryne. Something softened in her eyes, whether from acquiescence or sheer exhaustion, Owen couldn't tell. The musket swept downward nearly at the same time the woman started to collapse like an empty sack of potatoes. Emeline dashed toward her before she fell, and Owen grabbed her other side. Together, they led her to sit on a chair perched before an open hearth where coals from a small fire still simmered.

"My husband . . ." She gestured toward the back of the room, then squeezed her eyes shut so tight Owen thought they'd sink back into her skull. Groaning in pain, she rubbed her round belly.

"When is the babe due?" Emeline asked.

The pain passed. The woman caught her breath. "I don't know. Soon. Perhaps a week or so." She lifted pleading, pain-streaked eyes. "Please take care of my husband."

A blast of rain-laden wind spun eddies of leaves into the cabin, and Dimsmore gestured for Mr. Ryne to guard out front. After the man left, he set down his gun and shut the door.

Emeline grabbed a lantern and headed toward the far end of the room where the circle of light revealed an iron-rod bed with a man lying on top.

"What happened here?" Owen asked the woman, though he could already guess. Finding another lantern, he knelt before the fire, stirred the coals, and lit the wick.

The woman, who was around thirty years of age with curly brown hair springing from her mobcap, replied in a sullen voice, "British raiders. They took everything. Our supplies, stores of food, horses, and burned the rest." She swallowed and reached for her little girl. The toddler dashed for her and leapt into her lap, despite the size of the woman's stomach.

Dimsmore grunted as he sidled up to the fire.

Big blue eyes surrounded by a cluster of golden curls stared at Owen as if he were a monster. What the poor child must have seen. The young boy came to stand beside them in as protective a stance as any grown man.

"You've got quite the brave lad here, Mrs. . . ."

"Mrs. Oakes." The woman gazed at her

son and smiled. "Though he disobeyed me by going outside."

"Now that Papa's sick, Ma, it's up to me to be the man," the lad announced proudly.

Owen couldn't help but smile.

Tears filled the woman's eyes, and she shook her head. "I appreciate your help, mister. May God bless you for it." She glanced toward the back of the room where Emeline knelt beside the bed. "How is my husband?"

Rising, Emeline faced her. "Do you have any medical supplies?"

"A few. Bandages, needle and twine, and some laudanum . . . over there in the box on the shelf."

Emeline quickly found the box and peeked inside. Even from across the room, Owen heard her sigh of frustration. Gripping the box to her chest, she moved toward them. "Lieu . . . Luther," she addressed Dimsmore, "I need some fresh water. Rainwater will do. And any clean cloths you can find." She faced Mrs. Oakes. "Do you have any alcohol?"

Worry tightened the woman's features as she shook her head. "No. We don't drink spirits. My husband is the pastor of our local church."

Notwithstanding every attempt to keep

his reaction hidden, a bitter taste filled Owen's mouth and twisted his lips into a spiteful grimace. Just his luck, running into a man of the cloth. If not for the children, every ounce of his sympathy for this family would have instantly fled.

"Will he live? Please tell me he'll live." The woman's voice cracked as tears ran tracks in the dust on her face.

Miss Baratt set down the box and knelt before her. "I'm going to do my best, I promise. You must not stress yourself for the babe's sake." Her smile seemed to settle the poor woman.

"Got anything to eat?" Dimsmore asked.

Miss Baratt rose and leveled such a look on Dimsmore, even Owen cringed.

But Mrs. Oakes took no note. She absently shook her head. "Just some old crusty bread on the table. Help yourself."

Dimsmore didn't hesitate to do so. He broke off a piece and handed it to Emeline, but much to Owen's surprise, she didn't take it.

"If that is all they have, we should leave it to them, *Luther,* don't you think?"

"Mama, I'm hungry," the little girl said.

Mrs. Oakes rocked her back and forth. "Hush now, it's okay. These are our guests."

Emeline snagged the piece of bread from

Luther, turned, and gave it to the little girl.

Luther's eyes narrowed. He glanced around Emeline at Mrs. Oakes. "Begging your pardon, ma'am, we won't impose on you for long. We must be gone first thing in the morning."

Emeline's lips couldn't have drawn tighter. "May I have a word with you both please. Outside." Grabbing Owen, Emeline all but dragged him out the front door as Dimsmore scuffled behind.

No sooner did the door shut than she spun on them both with the fury of the storm now brewing overhead. "That man in there will die unless I help him."

"Not our problem, Miss Baratt." Dimsmore gripped the porch railing and glanced into the dark night. "We are only staying the night."

"Have you no compassion, sir? The woman is clearly about to have a child, and her husband is nearly dead."

"Then you may help him while we are here."

"That may not be enough time. And the babe is soon to be born." She crossed her arms over her chest. "How can you be so cruel?"

"Because they're rebels." Dimsmore straightened his stance. "You seem to forget what side you're on, Miss Baratt."

"You seem to forget that we are all God's creatures."

"God. Bah! We have a mission, and we will complete it."

Emeline glowered at the man. "You have no heart, sir."

"Enough." Owen finally intervened, unwilling to admit he rather enjoyed the exchange, especially the way Emeline held her own against Dimsmore. "Dimsmore, get the water she requested. We'll help them as much as we can while we are here."

With a huff and nary a glance at either of them, Emeline went back in the house. Astounding woman. Her care for these Americans, indeed for everyone she met, was eating away bit by bit at the wall of anger he'd erected against her.

Dimsmore huffed. "You'd think that lady is one of them, the way she cares for them."

"Don't be absurd, Dimsmore."

"I'm going to keep my eye on her." Dimsmore grabbed a bucket from the porch and started down the steps. "You too, Masters." He shot him a spiteful glance.

Owen stared after the man as he dove into the rain.

Regardless of Owen's superiority, he knew one thing. If Dimsmore's suspicions of either him or Miss Baratt took root, the man wouldn't hesitate to arrest them both on the spot.

Chapter 18

Emeline walked through a field of wildflowers shining in the noonday sun — marigolds, asters, and daisies, a symphony of purples, yellows, and reds. A light breeze danced through their petals as she twirled among them, enjoying the beauty and the warm sun. Birds warbled a melodious tune, frogs croaked near a distant creek that gurgled and slushed on its way. She knelt to smell a flower. How had she come to be here? She felt such peace, such freedom! She never wanted it to end.

Then the sky blotched with gray as if the Creator dabbed a paintbrush over it, blocking out the cerulean blue and casting a dismal gloom over the scene.

Stomp, stomp, stomp . . . stomp, stomp, stomp! The rhythmic sound of marching thundered across the field. Flowers shook, birds went silent. Emeline stared toward the edge of the forest where a line of redcoats

264

emerged from the green leaves like tentacles of a giant squid bursting from its cave. Before them, riding a horse, was Sergeant Herod, his malevolent gaze leveled upon her.

Lightning cracked the sky from east to west, splitting the earth in two.

Emeline spun, gathered her skirts, and sprinted across the field.

Maniacal laughter followed her, pushing her onward through pines and elms. She leapt over a creek, across a muddy clearing, terror rushing like madmen through her veins.

The *stomp, stomp* grew louder and louder, the laughter closer and closer.

She came upon the cabin, rushed through the door, closed it, and slammed the wooden bar across it, then backed away.

The stomping halted. Had they left? Silence was more frightening than noise. Slowly, she approached the window, trying not to make a sound. She peered out.

Lieutenant Dimsmore's face leapt into view on the other side of the glass, his grin evil, his eyes crazed. "You'll hang, missy. You'll hang as the traitor you are!"

She screamed and stumbled backward, tripped over a chair, and fell to the wooden floor.

Flames engulfed the house, hungry flames licking the wooden walls and creeping over the floor.

The muzzle of a cannon broke through the front window, shattering the glass.

Boom!

Emeline leapt from her chair. Her heart pounded. Her breath heaved. She shoved a hand over her mouth to keep from shrieking. Too late.

Owen was by her side within seconds. Against her will, thick arms encased her, pressing her against his chest.

"Only thunder, Emeline . . . only thunder."

She thought to push from him, but in truth, it felt far too good in his arms. Not frightening or restrictive like she'd always thought it would feel trapped next to a man, but safe, comfortable, exciting.

Raindrops pattered the roof. Wind whistled past the walls. The coals in the hearth sizzled.

The beat of Owen's heart through his waistcoat settled her nerves.

He rubbed her back, tangling his fingers in her loosened hair.

"Ouch." She half laughed and backed from him, grabbing the wayward locks.

"Forgive me." He smiled and looked

266

down. "I suppose I need practice in comforting women."

"Glad to hear it." La, had she just said that? Proper ladies didn't speak so boldly to men.

He led her to sit in the chair beside the bed and then knelt before her. Light from the fire flickered across his dark eyes as he looked at her with such admiration it set her aback. Who was this man, this enemy who seemed to despise her one minute and make her feel like a princess the next?

A day's stubble roughened his jaw, and for some strange reason she longed to run her fingers over the coarseness. Dark hair grazed his broad shoulders, still damp from the storm. They sat looking at each other far too long for propriety's sake — as if they were communicating in any way but words.

Ashamed, Emeline broke the spell between them and glanced at Mr. Oakes lying on the bed, looking so pale, his breath labored.

"You did all you could," Owen said.

"I hardly did anything." The poor man had been beaten near to death and then, from the looks of his back, dragged over rough terrain, probably by a horse. Emeline didn't want to ask his wife the details.

"All I could do was clean his wounds,

stitch him up, and give him some laudanum for the pain. But I fear he already has an infection. His fever is rising."

Owen sat on the side of the bed and stared at the man with more sympathy than Emeline would have expected.

"You disapprove of preachers?" she asked, throwing propriety to the wind yet again with this intriguing man.

He jerked his gaze up to hers. "What makes you say that?"

"I saw your reaction when Mrs. Oakes mentioned her husband's profession."

His lips flattened, and his gaze wandered back to the man.

Thunder rumbled the cabin walls, joining the snoring coming from Dimsmore as he lay before the fire, fast asleep. Poor Mrs. Oakes and both her children were snuggled up together on a quilt in a corner beyond the hearth. Thank God she was able to finally sleep. Mr. Ryne was no doubt outside on watch.

Aside from the hearth that took up an entire wall, there was a table and chairs, a wooden cabinet filled with now-broken dishes, a bench, and the bed Mr. Oakes lay upon. Shelves along the wall and in the cabinet loomed empty. Areas in the room sat vacant where furniture must have been.

The British had left a few pots, pans, and other cooking utensils, a clock, a mirror, and some clothing hung on hooks. But they had stripped this family of everything else. Emeline had difficulty quelling her anger. Though she kept repenting of it, it kept rising with more fury like a persistent storm. Like the one now blaring outside.

"My father was a preacher." Owen's deep voice drew her gaze back to him.

Emeline kept silent, waiting for him to continue, but he seemed lost in his thoughts.

"That was a bad thing?" she finally asked.

"Only if you were his son . . . *or* his wife," he added bitterly. "There were always so many rules, and I never seemed to be able to keep them." He leaned back and crossed his arms over his chest. "God's rules must be followed, Miss Baratt." His tone was cynical. "Or His wrath will be poured upon you and you will burn in hellfire."

Emeline bit her lip. "How terrifying for a child to hear such a thing."

"It was. And no matter how hard I tried to be good, I guess, well, let's just say it wasn't in my nature."

She smiled. "I don't think it's in any of our natures, for I certainly haven't been."

His brows shot up. "You? Not good? Miss Rule-follower?" He teased.

She wouldn't tell him that she often failed at following those rules. "What happened to your father? Is he still in Portsmouth?"

The fire crackled. Dimsmore's snores increased. And Owen rubbed his eyes. "He left us when I was ten. Ran off with some trollop from what we heard."

Emeline drew back, stifling her gasp.

Owen scratched his stubble. "Hypocrite down to his bones, he was. Left me and my mother without a penny in the till."

No wonder the man wanted naught to do with God and especially with His rules. "What did you do?"

"My uncle took us in, cared for us, loved us. My mother still lives with him."

"How on earth did you end up in the Royal Navy?"

He chuckled, and the sound of it settled on her like a soothing blanket. "I was nothing but trouble to my poor mother. My uncle was away often on business, and I fear I was a rather disobedient son, always getting into some kind of trouble or another. My mother had family in England with the right connections, and they got me a commission as midshipman when I was seventeen."

Emeline blew out a sigh. "What a difficult change that must have been for you."

"Indeed." He ran a thumb down his scar, started to say something, but then stopped.

Fascinating man. He'd spent so many years with the British being pruned from a rebellious youth to an obedient officer. It was no wonder his loyalties remained with them. How could she blame him for that?

Still, he was her enemy. No matter how much she was beginning to feel for him. *Fie! Insanity!* Just more proof she needed to curb her wayward emotions. For they always led her into trouble.

"Tell me some of your boyhood antics." She thought to lighten the mood.

He shook his head. "No deal, Miss . . . I mean, Emeline. It would only disparage your already low opinion of me."

I doubt it, she wanted to say, but instead she said nothing.

He stared at her hands, seeming to want to take them in his. She held her breath. He started to reach for them but pulled back and rubbed his chin.

Dawn turned the black to gray outside the window. Mr. Oakes groaned, and Emeline placed her hand atop his forehead. "Dear God, help us! He's burning with fever."

"I'm not leaving this woman to watch her husband —" Emeline slammed her mouth

271

shut and raised defiant brows toward Dimsmore.

Owen had been unable to take his eyes off her, ever since she'd stepped from the cabin onto the front porch, three-year-old Abigail in her arms. The little girl had crawled into Emeline's lap soon after they'd broken their fast with hardtack and had yet to relinquish her hold. Now, the wee one laid her head on Em's shoulder, her light curls a near match for the color of Emeline's own hair.

For some reason the sight warmed Owen to his core.

That warmth instantly dissipated when he saw Dimsmore's scowl. "We didn't come ashore to nursemaid the en— farmers," he seethed through his teeth, keeping his voice low, while his fiery gaze shot to Owen. "Surely you don't agree with her. We have a mission to perform and a captain awaiting our return."

Owen glanced over the farm. Raindrops as thick as honey continued to pound the ground that was naught but a muddy pond wherever he looked. Thick clouds rumbled overhead, dark and so low, it seemed one could reach up and touch them. Daylight revealed the total devastation the British raid had perpetrated on this poor family. Farm implements lay broken and strewn over the yard. Hay spread in the mud, fences destroyed, crops burned. So much of it done out of sheer cruelty rather than just taking plunder. It was getting increasingly difficult to keep the rage from making an appearance on his face — or in his voice.

"We can hardly travel in this storm, Dimsmore," Owen finally said. "It will not only slow our progress considerably, but we will risk becoming ill in the process. I'm in command here, and I say we wait out the storm for another day."

"Good," Emeline said. "It's settled then. While we are here, we should provide food for this poor family." She gazed over the sodden farm. "Perhaps catch a chicken or two or one of those pigs. Mr. Ryne," she addressed the marine who sat on a bench, his hat over his eyes.

He nudged it up just far enough so she could see his annoyed gaze.

"I recall Lieu— Luther here, my dear brother" — she smiled sweetly at Dimsmore — "telling me you were raised on a farm. Do you know how to catch a chicken or pig, sir? We could use your help."

The marine looked at Dimsmore, disgust shadowing his plain features.

"Order him to comply," Owen commanded. "We have to eat while we are here, don't we?"

Emeline brushed a lock of hair from the little girl's face. "And I shall find some yarrow to help bring down Mr. Oakes's fever. In addition, we should fetch dry wood for the fire and leave a stack behind when we're gone."

"Miss Baratt . . ." — Dimsmore held his temper with difficulty — "as lovely as you are, I cannot tolerate this kindness toward our enemy."

She cocked her head, green eyes flaring. "I fear you must, *Luther,* for as long as we are here, I intend to help them as much as possible."

Braver men had not stood up to Dimsmore with as much pluck as this little lady. Her green eyes sharp, her chin steel, not a tremble to be found in either her voice or stance. Poor Dimsmore seemed out of sorts, and Owen had to suppress a chuckle.

"You realize these actions make me question where your loyalties lie, *Emeline.* Suppose there's a woman with child and a sick husband at the enemy headquarters when you go to gather information. Will you suddenly tell them everything you know about our plans?"

"I know naught of your plans, Luther, nor do I wish to." She flattened her lips and hoisted the girl a little higher.

"Nap off, Dimsmore," Owen said. "The captain has already deemed her loyal. Kindness toward others, enemy or not, does not preclude loyalty to one's country."

Dimsmore's lips curled as his insolent gaze shifted between Owen and Emeline. "Have a care, Lieutenant; your rank means nothing if you are a traitor. If Captain Blackwell knew how you coddled up to the enemy, tsk-tsk-tsk" — he shook his head then pointed a finger at them — "I will keep an eye on you two rebel lovers."

"You do that, Luther." Owen growled inwardly. "For now, we need food and firewood. See to it."

Dimsmore snapped at Mr. Ryne and the marine leapt to his feet, grabbed his musket, and plunged into the rain.

Emeline stared after him and rocked the girl back and forth. "Rain or not, I must locate some yarrow root."

The young lad Amos slipped out the front door, musket nearly as tall as he was in hand. "I'll go with you."

"Too dangerous," Owen said.

The little girl whimpered in her sleep, and Emeline rubbed her back, shushing her gently.

"I'm the man of the house now, Mr.

Masters, and I don't answer to you. 'Sides, I know where some yarrow root is."

Owen glanced through the door the lad had left slightly open. Mrs. Oakes sat at her husband's bedside reading to him from a book. "Is it all right with your mother?"

Emeline brushed past them. "I'll check with her." The lad followed.

Owen watched her place the child gently on a blanket by the hearth before she approached Mrs. Oakes, where Amos was already pleading with his mother.

Owen felt Dimsmore's stare on him and faced his nemesis. "I know you don't like me, Dimsmore. But don't allow your personal sentiments to cloud your judgment. We are all on the same side here."

"Are we?" Dimsmore huffed just as Emeline appeared, the lad at her side.

"Is there no cloak inside to cover yourself with?" Owen asked the boy.

He shook his head. "They took everything."

"Then we'll have to be quick about it. Come, lad, show us where this yarrow root is."

"Yes, sir." The boy grinned.

Hence, the lady who never ceased to amaze him, amazed Owen even still by tromping ankle deep in mud in the pouring rain through sodden forest and puddle-strewn fields. The boy led the way, as brave as any soldier Owen had met. When Owen was the same age as this boy, his father had abandoned him, and thus had begun Owen's rebellion against all godliness and responsibility. Yet this lad had suffered even more, and he bore it with an honor and dignity Owen had yet to master.

"Over here!" the boy yelled above the rain as he gestured for them to follow him to the edge of a field. Emeline moved as quick as she could in her saturated skirts to the place where the boy stopped.

"There used to be some here." The boy scratched his wet hair.

Sounds that didn't belong sent alarm skittering down Owen's back.

"Oh, here it is," he heard Emeline say before she headed into the brush.

Instincts took over. Owen grabbed the lad, covered his mouth with his hand, and shoved his body against Emeline as gently as he could. Enough, however, to push her into a thicket. She stumbled in the mud, caught herself on a tree trunk, turned, no doubt, to chastise him, but then saw his face. Thank God, the woman was smart enough to keep silent. He stooped and gestured for her to do the same. The boy wiggled in his arms.

"Quiet. Be still." He removed his hand from the lad's mouth. The boy obeyed. The three of them crouched among the dripping shrubbery, their breaths mingling in the air between them.

Redcoats penetrated the forest like blood on a green blanket.

Owen could feel the lad tense in his arms. "Shh now, shh."

Twenty men traversed the field they'd just been in. Not many, but enough that Owen wouldn't be able to protect them.

Tromp, tromp, tromp. Splat, splat.

One of them coughed.

Tromp, tromp, tromp. Splat, splat.

They were nearly past . . .

Owen dared to let out his breath.

When the last man glanced their way.

CHAPTER 19

The British soldier broke rank and headed toward them. Emeline grabbed her throat to stop the shriek of terror begging for release. Owen didn't move. The boy trembled, and Owen swallowed up the lad's small hand in his large, calloused one.

Rain continued pummeling the landscape. Thunder gave a disheartened moan.

The soldier moved cautiously toward them, peering through the shrubbery.

Owen slowly withdrew a knife from his belt — a rather long knife.

Emeline's heart beat against her ribs so hard, she thought they would break.

Lord, please, make us invisible. Please protect us. She hated that she only prayed when she was desperate, but perhaps God would take pity on her and answer this time. She had been trying to be good of late.

The marine halted before the bush and poked the barrel of his musket through the leaves. It moved back and forth — a pendulum of charred death that came within an inch of hitting Owen on the cheek. He raised the knife to stab the poor man.

"Bates!" The shout ricocheted across the field from the retreating troops. "What are you doing? Get back in line."

The soldier retreated a step. So did his musket. "Thought I saw something is all."

The soldier who shouted started across the field. "Nothing's here. Come on before the colonel sees you and assigns you latrine duty."

The two slogged off in the mud, hastening to catch up with their regiment.

After they returned to the cabin — with yarrow root in hand — it took Emeline several hours before her heart settled to a steady beat. She busied herself with crushing the herb for tea while making some stew out of the chicken Mr. Ryne had caught during their absence, along with some wild turnips and a few ears of corn that had escaped the British rampage.

Since she had no change of clothes, Owen built a fire in the hearth, and the three of them frequented it often during the day to allow the heat to penetrate their damp attire. They kept the door and windows open, and through them, she could hear Dimsmore and Ryne muttering on the porch while sharpening their blades and cleaning their guns.

The rain still came down as if God were crying over the brutality of His creation. If that were the case, it may never stop. Fine by Emeline, for it kept them here helping these people.

Owen sat at the table instructing Amos how to assemble a hook and line for fishing, while poor Mrs. Oakes remained at her husband's side. Little Abigail oscillated from sitting in her mother's lap to following Emeline around, chattering like a bird set free from a cage.

"What are you doing?"

"What is that?"

"Why?"

"Can I help?"

None of her questions did Emeline mind answering, though she'd forgotten how inquisitive three-year-olds could be. This particular three-year-old was the most adorable child she'd ever seen, with a waterfall of curly blond hair framing a sweet face with big blue eyes. Children were so untainted by evil, so innocent, and Emeline longed to shield Abigail from the war raging outside her door. But it had already intruded on her peaceful childhood, threatening even now to steal her father away. Emeline glanced at Mrs. Oakes, who had opened her Bible again and was reading to her husband. He had consumed the tea hours ago, but thus far, his fever had not abated.

"Is Papa going to die?" Abigail's bottom lip quivered as she stared at Emeline.

Stooping, Emeline took her little hands in hers. "I don't know, Abigail. He's very sick. We must pray very hard for him to get well."

"Yes, Mama says God answers prayer."

Emeline smiled. "He does for good little girls like you." She tapped her on the nose and then drew her into an embrace. "Now, are you hungry?" The smile she got in response could melt the staunchest warrior.

It apparently did just that, for after they'd all eaten, Abigail crawled onto Owen's lap, book in hand. Amos drew up a chair and listened while the lieutenant read them a story. Emeline couldn't help but stare at the touching scene. What a dichotomy this man was. Adventurer, rebel, prodigal, naval officer, and warrior, taking the time to read a book to children? He even softened his voice and added emphasis and emotion when the occasion called for it in order to make the story more interesting.

Abigail and Amos adored him, obvious by

the way they looked at him and hung on his every word. Emeline went back to drying the tin plates they'd used for dinner, trying to make sense of it all. He'd come ashore to get information that would no doubt win the war for Britain, and either these children would die in the onslaught or they'd grow up under British rule. Yet they looked at him now as if he were the savior of the world.

From his position on the window ledge, Dimsmore looked at him with none of that same sentiment. As he continued sharpening his knife, he looked as though he'd love nothing more than to plant the blade in Owen's back.

Or perhaps it was just the nearness of the troops they'd spotted that day that set him on edge and put him in such a foul mood. The three men were to take turns standing watch outside. Mr. Ryne was out there now. Then after him, Owen, and lastly Dimsmore.

Rising, Dimsmore sauntered her way. "Food was delicious, *Sister.* Wherever did you learn to cook so well?"

"Taking care of my two younger brothers after my . . . our . . . mother died." She glanced at Mrs. Oakes, but she was still reading to her husband. "As you know,

283

Brother."

He glanced at the lady as well and must have decided it safe to continue. Leaning toward her, he whispered, "Yet I understood you were raised in England in a house of nobility."

Owen glanced up from his reading and motioned Dimsmore to silence.

"Indeed I was," she whispered back. "After the age of fourteen."

"Surely being a wealthy merchantman, your father could hire a staff," Dimsmore pressed. "Why leave you to cook?"

Anger and fear mixed in a brew in her stomach just as thick as her chicken stew. She faced the man with a sigh and a scowl. "We were not always wealthy. My father started out with but one ship."

Dimsmore rubbed his chin and nodded. "But your connections in England were wealthy."

Emeline tossed down her rag. "My father married against his family's wishes and was cut off."

"Then why —"

Thankfully, a moan interrupted Dimsmore's interrogation and drew Emeline over to Mrs. Oakes. Gripping her stomach, the poor woman leaned her head on the bed beside her husband.

Emeline dashed and knelt beside her. "Come now, Mrs. Oakes."

"Clara . . . please . . . call me Clara," she muttered as her face scrunched in pain.

"Clara, please come sit by the fire and eat your supper." She glanced at Mr. Oakes, who had apparently drifted back into unconsciousness. "I need to give him some more tea anyway."

Eyes brimming with sorrow met hers. "Will it help? Will he live?"

Emeline wanted to lie, wanted to tell her all would be well. "I don't know. But let me sit with him awhile, all right? You need to eat and get some rest."

She sat back and rubbed her belly, a tear breaking free down her cheek. She wiped it away. "I don't know how to thank you, Mrs. Masters."

Emeline shivered at the title, whether from pleasure or repulsion, she didn't know. Perhaps a bit of both. "Please call me Emeline."

"Emeline. You are an answer to prayer. You came when I most needed you. You've tended my dear husband, befriended and cared for my children, and provided food and protection. A godsend you are."

Emeline had never been called such, and it made her cringe at the lies they had told this woman — and a pastor's wife of all things. Something else proper ladies didn't do. Lie to godly women.

After assisting Clara to one of the comfortable chairs before the fire and serving her chicken stew, Emeline brewed a cup of yarrow tea and sat beside Mr. Oakes. It took the next hour to get but a few sips down him. And still his fever raged.

Rain pattered, fire crackled, and Clara gathered her children to ready them for bed. They both came to kiss their father good night.

"Please, Papa, get well soon." Little Abigail leaned to kiss her father's cheek. "Papa, you're so warm," the girl exclaimed as her mother drew her back and allowed Amos beside the bed. The boy stared at his father, clearly fighting back tears. He bent to kiss his forehead then hurried to join his mom and sister as they settled down for the night.

"Will you pray for him, Emeline?" Clara said. "I have no more prayers left."

Emeline nodded, longing to tell the lady that God so rarely answered her prayers. Yet hadn't He done so earlier that day when the soldiers were nigh upon them?

It certainly couldn't hurt.

Owen attempted to rub the exhaustion from

his eyes as he sat back in the chair. His belly yearned for more of Emeline's cooking, but there'd been barely enough to go around. Who knew the woman could cook like that? He smiled as his gaze shifted to Mrs. Oakes humming a sweet melody to her two children as they lay down beside her on the straw pallet. She tucked little Abigail close beside her and whispered something to Amos as he took a protective position in front of the women. They were good, decent children. Innocent children who had seen far too much misery in their short lives. A palpable pain shot through Owen's chest as he watched their sweet faces in the firelight. What would become of them in this horrid war? And where was God in all of this? How could He allow such tragedy to befall the innocent?

Whispers brought his gaze over to Emeline kneeling before Mr. Oakes's bed, head bowed and hands gripped before her. Praying? He knew she meant well, but to Owen, it seemed a waste of time. Honestly, Owen couldn't blame God for abandoning mankind. If Owen had created something so abhorrently evil, he would have forsaken it as well.

The creak of the front door opening disturbed his thoughts as Mr. Ryne entered, dragging behind him a gust of rain-spiced wind and a cyclone of leaves. Quickly shutting the door, he removed his coat and hat and headed toward the hearth to warm himself.

"You're on watch, Masters." Dimsmore's voice grated over Owen from where the man sat by the window, obviously missing nothing.

"I'm aware." Pushing to his feet, Owen grabbed his musket and coat and left, suddenly preferring the rain to sitting in the same room as Dimsmore.

Three hours later, soaked to the bone, and more tired than he'd been in a long while, he returned and got more pleasure than he should have out of waking Dimsmore from a sound sleep.

Smiling as the man grumbled and left, Owen shrugged out of his wet coat and stooped before the hot coals in the hearth. Mr. Ryne snored from his spot in the corner while deep breaths wafted from where Mrs. Oakes and her children lay fast asleep. Good. They needed their rest.

But it was the sight of Emeline still awake beside Mr. Oakes that disturbed him. Such care for her enemy! Quietly, he approached her.

"You need your sleep, Emeline. You're no

good to anyone exhausted."

She glanced up. Shadows dragged her eyes down as a sense of hopelessness hovered about her. "Neither are you." She faced Mr. Oakes once again, a brittle shadow on the bed. "His fever has risen, and he's been in and out of consciousness. I don't want to leave him alone."

"I can watch him."

When she shook her head, he squatted beside her and dared to take her hand in his. It felt good — small, soft, yet strong, just like the woman herself. "I promise to wake you should anything change."

"But what of your sleep?"

"I got a couple hours earlier, remember? Besides, I'm used to not sleeping."

She pressed her lips together.

Owen squeezed her hand, pleased she hadn't pulled it away.

"Very well." She started to rise. "Promise me you will —"

"I will. Now go lie down." He gestured with his head, wondering yet again why he was being kind to a traitor.

That traitor, though exhausted, afraid, and filthy, was quite lovely as he watched her grab a blanket and collapse on it before the hearth.

Owen took the chair she'd vacated and

the cloth she'd handed him and dipped it in the basin of cool water. He placed it back on the man's forehead and leaned forward on his knees, his wet hair hanging about his face.

Though the wind had dwindled, rain still rapped on the roof, providing a soothing melody that did naught to unwind his nerves.

"I heard you." The raspy whisper came from the bed, jerking Owen's attention up. He glanced around but everyone was asleep, including Mr. Oakes, who lay as still as death.

"I . . ." One of Mr. Oakes's eyelids cracked open. "Heard you talking about your father."

Owen frowned. "Don't try to speak. You need to rest."

An attempt at a chuckle bubbled from his mouth. "I'm tired of resting."

"Can I get you something? Water, tea?"

With great effort the man shook his head. "Listen, son. Don't blame God for your father." He stopped to catch his breath. "He had naught to do with your father's actions."

"It doesn't matter now." Owen took the cloth from the man's forehead. It felt as hot as if it had just been ironed. He dipped it in water.

Mr. Oakes coughed. "It does matter, son. It caused you to turn away from the only One who can set you free."

"Free?" Now it was Owen's turn to chuckle, though it came out rather bitter. "God's endless commandments bring anything but freedom. Thou shalt not do this, thou shalt not do that — each one is an iron bar caging in His creation."

Mr. Oakes gave a feeble smile. "Do you have children, Owen?"

Owen glanced at the little ones cuddled beside their mother, forcing down a strange yearning for some of his own. "No."

"Imagine you have a son. Would you allow him to play with a pistol without instruction?" Mr. Oakes hesitated, his breath coming fast and ragged. "Would you allow him to wander the forest alone? Take a boat out in stormy seas? Eat poison fruit?"

Owen placed the fresh cloth on Mr. Oakes's forehead. No doubt the fever had made him delirious. "Of course not."

"Yet what if your son said he wanted his freedom to do as he pleased? That he was tired of all his father's rules."

"He's just a child and doesn't know any better. He needs a father's instruction and protection."

Mr. Oakes shifted on the bed and closed his eyes. "Precisely. God is a father . . . the best father. He knows the things that would do us harm and ruin our lives, so He tells us to stay away from them. His commandments are for our own good, to keep us safe, to help us live abundantly and adventurously."

Wind howled against the logs of the cabin, sending the candle flame dancing. Adventurously? Owen rubbed his eyes. "Those rules turned my father into a miserable man who finally shirked every one of them and ran off."

"And I'll wager he's even more miserable now." Urgency shone from Mr. Oakes's eyes. "You're either a slave to sin and the devil, or you're a slave to God, Owen. There are no other choices. Yet instead of slaves, God adopts us into His family, and we become His children."

Owen groaned inwardly, hoping the man would be quiet. He'd had enough preaching as a boy to last an eternity.

"God wants you to have a full life, Owen, not restrict you. Whom the Son sets free is free indeed." Mr. Oakes winced as if in pain then drew a deep breath. "Until you repent and submit to Him, you are a slave to sin and must follow its dictates. Once free, you have a choice. And take it from me, to live for God is the most fulfilling life a man could have. Filled with purpose and joy, not momentary pleasures that leave you empty."

"Then why do all the godly people I meet seem so miserable and unable to have fun?" He glanced at Emeline, but then he remembered Ben. Good old Ben, the happiest man he knew. He never acted like he was a slave to anything. He always seemed at peace, kind, and as if he was enjoying his life.

Mr. Oakes coughed and tore the cloth from his forehead. "Unfortunately, many people are still trying to earn His favor by doing things, obeying rules, checking off some list of good deeds. They sit imprisoned in an iron cage when Jesus has already come and unlocked the door." He handed Owen the cloth and waved it away.

Owen stared at it, confused and angry. "After what has happened to you, to your family, how can you say such things?" He glanced over the cabin. "Is this loss, this devastation, adventurous? Why aren't you furious at God after you gave your life to His service? What if you should —"

"Die?" Oddly, Mr. Oakes smiled. "Though it pains me to leave my family, I know God will watch out for them. Besides, I'm going to a far better place where I will see them again someday." He stopped to take a breath. "God's timing is perfect. If I die, it will be best for me and best for my family."

Owen snorted. "You talk crazy, Preacher."

"Think on it, son. Promise me."

Owen drew a deep sigh and then nodded. "I will." But only because he could not deny a dying man's request.

"Good." A feeble hand patted Owen's. "Now leave me to sleep. Or die. Whichever God decides." He started to close his eyes, but they flew open again. "Do tell Clara how much I love her."

"I will." Owen leaned his head in his hands, his thoughts awhirl. He tried to stay awake to ponder the man's words, but exhaustion lured him to sleep. Sometime later, he woke with a start, his head jerking backward, his eyes blinking to focus. He rubbed the back of his neck and glanced over the cabin. Everyone was still asleep. Even Mr. Oakes. The man lay still . . . quiet . . . not even a breath lifted his chest. Suddenly a light rose from his body and drifted upward. Owen closed his eyes and rubbed them. He must be dreaming. But when he looked again, the light drifted to hover over Mrs. Oakes and the children snuggled up together in the corner. Then it floated upward through the roof and disappeared.

Owen knew what he would find before he reached for Mr. Oakes's hand.

It was cold as death.

CHAPTER 20

Emeline stood at the foot of the grave, arm wrapped around Mrs. Oakes, doing her best to hold up the poor woman. Amos stood on her other side, his face hidden beneath his oversized hat. Sweet Abigail lay sleeping in Owen's strong arms, her golden curls nestled against his neck.

The rain had stopped, though the skies were as gray and somber as the mood. A wooden cross, slightly askew, stood at the head of the resting place of Mr. Abe Oakes. Emeline hadn't even known his Christian name until after he'd died.

Dimsmore, of all people, held the prayer book out before him, cleared his throat, and read.

" 'Forasmuch as it hath pleased Almighty God in his wise providence to take out of this world the soul of our deceased brother, Mr. . . . Mr. . . .' " Dimsmore looked up, more in frustration than shame.

Emeline wanted to fling mud at the man. "Mr. Abe Oakes."

"Mr. Oakes," Dimsmore continued. " 'We therefore commit his body to the ground; earth to earth, ashes to ashes, dust to dust; looking for the general Resurrection in the last day, and the life of the world to come, through our Lord Jesus Christ; at whose . . .' "

Sobs racked through Mrs. Oakes's body, and she grew limp in Emeline's arms. Finally, they both slid to their knees, mud soaking through their gowns as Dimsmore continued, his tone heartless.

" '. . . And the corruptible bodies of those who sleep in him shall be changed, and made like unto his own glorious body; according to the mighty working whereby he is able to subdue all things unto himself.' "

"Amen," everyone added, and Dimsmore shut the book and ambled away, Mr. Ryne following behind.

Owen came to stand beside Amos and wrapped an arm around the boy, who was trying far too hard to be strong. They all remained, saying nothing, existing somewhere between acceptance and despondency, time and eternity. After several minutes, the sun broke through the clouds and speared a ray of golden light onto the cross at the head of the grave. Mrs. Oakes looked up, tears streaming down her red, swollen face, wisps of her brown hair fluttering beneath her bonnet.

None of them could take their eyes off the light, for there was something about it, the way it sparkled and glittered and swirled, that made it seem almost alive and not from this place. Mrs. Oakes stopped crying and wiped the tears from her face.

"Look, Mama." Amos pointed to a white dove flying down from above. It landed on the cross.

Emeline could hardly believe her eyes. She glanced up at Owen, who stared at the scene in awe.

Mrs. Oakes lifted her hands in the air. "Praise You, Father, for You have comforted me in my sorrow." She continued to worship God with exclamations of praise and snippets of songs. A huge smile lit up Amos's face even as Abigail woke up in Owen's arms. He set her down, and she ran into her mother's embrace. Mrs. Oakes drew her children close, and the three of them laughed and kissed one another.

Emeline had never seen the likes of this at any funeral she'd attended. Even Dimsmore and Mr. Ryne stared at them from the distance.

The dove took flight, and the sunlight retreated into a cloud. Though Mrs. Oakes's face was still swollen from crying, there was a new sparkle in her eyes and a glow about her that set Emeline aback.

"How can you be so happy?" she asked her.

"Of course I am sad to see my Abe leave us, but God reminded me of where he is and that I will see him again." She glanced between Emeline and Owen, no doubt sensing their skepticism. "God shone His light on the cross to remind me of the sacrifice His Son, Jesus, paid for us so that after death, we would have new life with Him. The dove? That was the Holy Spirit reminding me that God is always with me and will never forsake me."

Owen said not a word, though Emeline could tell his thoughts were spinning. Truth be told, so were hers even as a flood of tears threatened to burst free. How wonderful of God to do such a thing! But of course, why wouldn't He bless this God-fearing family?

Taking Mrs. Oakes's arm, she led her toward the house.

"We must leave posthaste," Dimsmore announced from across the yard, where he was packing his knapsack.

Ignoring him, Emeline settled Mrs. Oakes

and the children inside, then stormed out the front door toward Dimsmore. Mr. Ryne and Owen stood by his side.

"We can't very well leave this poor woman to have her baby alone."

Dimsmore fisted his hands at his hips and groaned. "First, it was the man being sick. Now it's the woman. What's next, the kids? Listen, I'm sorry for what happened to this family, but this is war. There are always casualties." He glanced into the gray skies. "The rain has stopped, and we're on our way to Baltimore today, or I'm going to report Masters here for dereliction of duty and you, Miss Baratt, for treason. We have only five more days to get the information back to Captain Blackwell and ultimately to Major-General Ross and Admiral Cockburn. And I, for one, don't intend to disappoint them."

Owen ran a hand through his hair and glanced at Emeline. "He's right. We must get going."

She wanted to slap them all in the face. But proper ladies didn't do such things.

"We'll check on them on the way back," Owen added.

"We will do no such thing." Dimsmore's face crinkled into a ball of disgust. "Miss

Baratt has turned you into a goose-livered sow."

Owen took a step toward him. "You'll watch your mouth, Dimsmore. I'm still in command here."

Dimsmore gripped the hilt of his knife, his face and eyes as hard as granite. "Until I deem otherwise, sir. I've been authorized to relieve you of your command should you exhibit any sympathy toward our enemy."

Owen didn't move, not even a flinch of his lips or jaw. Could that be true? Did Captain Blackwell suspect her or even Owen?

But they didn't have time to think about it when a mind-numbing scream blared from the cabin.

"That's good, Clara." Emeline dabbed a cloth over the woman's heated face. "You're doing well. The baby's almost here." Emeline had no idea what she was doing. She'd never birthed a baby before, never even seen it done. Proper ladies didn't witness such things. And though terror stabbed every one of her nerves when the woman had gone into labor, she knew she was the only one who could help.

It had been four hours since she'd thrown everyone, including the children, from the cabin, stoked the fire, boiled water, and made some tea. But what else could she do for the poor woman who now lay on the bed where her husband died not hours before?

The pains came again. So soon? Clara gripped the bedposts above her head and screamed in agony. Her face twisted so tight, it became unrecognizable.

Emeline felt helpless. "What can I do?" she said after the pain subsided.

"Nothing . . . please . . ." Clara breathed out. "Please, just stay. When you see the baby's head, hold it and help the rest come out, then cut the cord."

Cut the cord? Emeline gulped. Of course. She searched near the hearth for a knife then held it over the flames before wrapping it in a clean cloth and laying it beside the bed.

Clara's breath billowed rapidly. Another pain already? "It's coming now," she panted. "I'm going to push."

Emeline closed her eyes and said a silent prayer. *Lord, help me. Don't let this woman or her baby die.* Squaring her shoulders, she eased onto the bottom of the bed as Clara propped herself up on her elbows and pushed with all her might. Her face became a lump of red bloated flesh. Several minutes passed. She didn't take a breath, didn't breathe. *Fie! Please don't let her die, Lord!*

Finally, the woman exhaled. The force of it sent her shooting back onto the bed. She let out an agonizing wail, caught her breath, and then instantly she was up on her elbows again, pushing so hard, Emeline feared she'd explode.

But then miracle of miracles, the crown of a tiny head appeared.

One more giant push and the entire head was out. Emeline cradled it in her hands. Another push and a baby slid onto the clean cloth Emeline had prepared.

Clara sank onto the bed like a deflated balloon, but not too deflated to say, "Boy or girl?"

Unbidden tears streamed down Emeline's face as she quickly cut the cord and wrapped the child in the cloth. "Boy," she laughed and cried all at once. "It's a boy . . . and he's beautiful."

Clara reached out, and Emeline laid the babe against her chest. Tears of joy replaced those of pain, and Emeline knelt before the bed as they both cried and laughed and stared at the miracle God had created.

"Thank you, Emeline. Thank you."

Emeline clutched Clara's hand and squeezed. "I'm so glad I could help."

An hour later, after Emeline had cleaned everything up, she called Amos and Abigail to meet their new brother. The family snuggled together on the bed while Dimsmore scowled in the corner.

An hour after that, Emeline knelt before the fire and stirred the batch of chicken stew she'd thrown together after Mr. Ryne had caught another chicken. The man wasn't much for conversation, but at least he was useful.

"Smells good." Owen stooped beside her, his scent of earth and sea and spice temporarily intruding upon the savory smell of the stew. She dared to glance his way, though these days it seemed unsafe to do so. For every time she did, something strange happened to her insides . . . something not so unpleasant. Now as she watched him stare at the fire, his jaw tight and covered with stubble, his dark hair hanging about his face, and firelight dancing in those hazel eyes of his, she couldn't help but wonder about this man — this enemy who was so kind one minute and stern the next, a mighty warrior who was gentle with children, a man who always seemed troubled behind those intense eyes of his.

"You're an amazing woman, Emeline," he

finally said, glancing her way.

She turned back to the stew and gave it another turn, ignoring the thrill rushing through her at his words.

"Delivering that babe." He shook his head.

"I had no choice. I did what anyone would do."

"No. I don't think so." He smiled. "No English lady I've ever met would be able to do half the things you do, cooking over a fire, traipsing through forests, patching wounds, and delivering babies." He chuckled. "Oh, and lest we forget, spying for one's country during war."

Emeline sighed. "Perhaps, as a lady, I should be doing none of those things, except maybe the cooking."

"And what book of rules did you get that from?"

Emeline had no idea, neither did she wish to discuss it. At least night had fallen, and they were unable to leave yet again. But how could she abandon this lady with a new baby and two children? Perhaps she could somehow come back to help her after she delivered the British plans.

Which reminded her. She looked at Owen. She still needed to discover *those* plans.

A baby's cry brought both their gazes to Clara.

Laying down the spoon, Emeline rose and went to assist.

"He needs a change, I'm afraid." Clara handed the baby to Emeline. "If you'll hand me a nappy and a wet cloth."

"I'm happy to do it. You rest."

"I want to learn how." Amos leapt from the bed.

"Me too!" Abigail scrambled after him.

Emeline stared down at them and smiled. "Very well. We shall all do it together. Here." She spun and handed the babe to Owen.

"Wait, I don't —" His clipped words were left hanging in the air as she placed the child in his arms.

Smiling, she went to retrieve a nappy and wet cloth, but when she turned around, the sight of him froze her in place. The babe was but a speck in his muscular arms, yet he held him with such tender care, staring down at him with a look of love and protection.

And Emeline suddenly wondered what it would be like to have children with this man.

Preposterous! She didn't want to get married. She didn't want to settle down. And she most certainly didn't want to marry an enemy of her country.

Mr. Ryne burst through the door and

slammed it behind him, his frightened gaze skittering over them. "It's the British. A band of them are heading this way."

CHAPTER 21

Two British soldiers barreled through the front door before Owen could hand the baby to Mrs. Oakes and grab his gun. One of them clutched Mr. Ryne by the scruff of the neck. They leveled muskets at everyone as more men piled in behind, followed by an officer — a captain with a pointy nose and even pointier eyes placed far too close together.

Owen growled. What had Mr. Ryne been doing outside, sleeping?

"We'll be taking over your house, rebels!" The captain sneered as his gaze raked over them.

Through the open door, Owen saw at least a dozen troops filling the dark yard in front of the house. Mrs. Oakes whimpered behind him, no doubt worried for her baby, still snuggled in Owen's arms.

Dimsmore stepped forward and opened his mouth, but Owen held up his hand and gave him a stern look. This was Owen's decision, not his . . . a very tough decision as he pondered their options. He could reveal the admiral's medallion and the coded message, announce who they were, and send these greedy raiders packing. But then Mrs. Oakes would know the truth and Dimsmore would never allow her to remain behind, lest she go to Baltimore and betray them as soon as they left. *Or* he could pretend they were Americans and allow these men to do their worst. Certainly, there wasn't enough plunder left to be worth their time.

Owen glanced at the wee babe so trusting in his arms, and a sudden urge to protect him at all costs only further confused the issue.

"Captain, may I speak with you outside?" Owen finally said, turning to hand the child to Emeline, who had appeared by his side.

The man snorted. "You may not, rebel. All of you, out! Or we'll shoot you where you stand."

Owen shifted his stance. The fire crackled. "Listen, we want no trouble. Your troops already raided our farm. Took everything."

"Not that stew we smell cooking there." The man licked his lips, but his gaze wasn't on the pot steaming over the fire. It was on

Emeline handing the babe to his mother.

Owen cleared his throat. "We have nothing left for you to take."

"I beg to differ." The captain started past Owen toward the women, but Owen stepped in his way. The muzzles of five muskets locked upon him as he stared down the captain. "As I said, there's nothing left here."

Dimsmore cursed and pushed between the men. "Forget this nonsense. We are British, Captain. I'm Lieutenant Dimsmore. This is First Lieutenant Owen Masters, and Mr. Ryne. We are stationed on HMS *Marauder* under Captain Blackwell and are currently on a special mission for Admiral Cockburn."

Owen heard Mrs. Oakes gasp behind him.

Yet the muskets pointed at them remained. The captain laughed and shook his head. "Indeed? And I'm the Queen of England. Pleased to meet you." Chuckles bounded over his men.

Dimsmore stared at Owen. "Give it to him. Unless you want us all to die."

Hang it all! Dimsmore and his big mouth. Despite the many guns following him as he did so, Owen reached in his waistcoat pocket and handed the man the medallion and papers.

Opening the parchment, the captain moved to a lantern to examine both it and the medallion. After several minutes he called one of his men over, a lieutenant.

Owen took the opportunity to glance back at Emeline, who was seated on the bed with Mrs. Oakes and her children. He'd be hogtied to a ship's mast before he'd allow these men to do them harm. His musket lay against the side of the hearth, but he still had a knife tucked in his belt. It wouldn't do much good, but it was better than nothing.

"Sure looks authentic," the lieutenant said.

"It is. I assure you." Owen nodded. "What Lieutenant Dimsmore said is true. We are on a special mission."

"Spies, eh?" The captain frowned and peered around Owen at the ladies. "What's your mission?"

"I am not at liberty to say."

"And who are the ladies?"

"One is with us; the other owns this farm."

"So she and her brats are your prisoners?"

Owen bristled at the disrespect. "Yes."

"Care to spare some of that stew?"

"We haven't enough, Captain. And besides, every minute you spend here compromises our identities. Believe me, if that happens, Cockburn will hear about it."

"Hmm." The man worked his lips this way and that as he stared at Owen. The look of suspicion in his pointy eyes did not bode well for their safety. Either he didn't believe them or his appetite for food and women was stronger than his fear of Cockburn.

A soldier entered the door and pushed through the men. "Captain, our scout returned. Says there's a group of American militia just north of here."

Mr. Ryne finally jerked from the soldier's grip. "Jackson. Is that you?"

The private spun, his face instantly brightening. "Ryne. What are you doing here?" The men clasped hands.

"You know this man?" the captain asked his private.

"Yes, sir. We served aboard HMS *Charger* a few years back."

The captain scowled, his disappointment obvious. Grabbing the medallion and papers from the lieutenant, he handed them back to Owen. "Very well. Seems you are telling the truth, Lieutenant . . . Masters, was it?" His hungry gaze wandered from the women to the stew. "Sure would like a bowl of that soup."

"As I said, the longer you stay here, the more you compromise our mission." Owen cleared his throat and gestured toward the private who'd brought the news. "Besides, seems you have an engagement with the *real* enemy."

The captain nodded, his jaw stiffening. "We shall leave you to your mission, Lieutenant." He ordered his men out, and within minutes they left and shut the door behind them as if they'd never threatened to murder all within.

Owen turned to Dimsmore, attempting to restrain his fury. "Why did you have to tell them?"

"Would you rather be dead?"

"I would have thought of something." Owen went to the window and peered out, ensuring the troops were leaving. "Besides, Mr. Ryne saved the day, after all."

Ryne smiled but offered no further comment.

"What difference does it make?" Dimsmore shrugged. "Let's eat, get some sleep, and be on our way at dawn." He nodded toward Mrs. Oakes. "Course now we'll have to bring them along. First chance they get, they'll run to Baltimore and tell the authorities we're coming."

Owen growled. "Your mouth, man. Until this very moment, she didn't know where we were truly heading."

Emeline had risen from the bed and

moved toward the hearth, a horrified look on her face.

"I promise, gentlemen," Mrs. Oakes's shaky voice filled the room. "I won't go anywhere or tell anyone anything."

"There you have it," Owen said. "They stay."

"This goes beyond the pale, Masters," Dimsmore scoffed, "and borders on subversion. We take them along, and after we get the information we need, they return with us to the ship as prisoners of war."

Emeline gasped. "You will do no such thing!"

Mrs. Oakes gathered her children close, her eyes full of terror.

Emeline charged Dimsmore. "They are just babies."

But Owen knew Dimsmore was right. If he argued for anything else, more suspicion would pile onto the mountain the man already had on Owen.

And then all would be lost.

"I'm so sorry, Clara. I didn't mean to lie to you." Emeline finally got up the courage to approach the woman. "You must hate me."

Clara, remarkably calm, sat on the bed and breast-fed little Adam beneath her smock, the sight making Emeline hate herself all the more. Amos sat by the fire, scowling at everyone, while little Abigail slept by her mother's side.

"No, Emeline. You and your husband, Owen, have been kind to me."

"He's not my husband."

At this, the lady's brows rose. "Well, that much I would not have guessed was a lie, the way you look at each other."

Emeline shook the words from her mind before she allowed them to settle. "I don't know what you mean."

The lady only smiled in return.

Emeline lowered to the chair beside the bed. "I never meant for you and your children to get tangled up in this."

Clara gave a sad smile. "It's only because you cared to help that it happened."

"How can you be so kind?" Emeline fingered her mother's locket. "It was the British, *my* people, who stole everything from you, who killed your husband." Though she desperately wanted to tell her friend the truth, Emeline dared not for fear it would slip from the woman's lips in front of the others.

Clara gazed down at Abigail, asleep beside her. "Men and their wars. There are good people on both sides. And you and Owen are good people."

Emeline didn't know about that. "I hate that we are forced to take you prisoner. There must be another way."

"If you're worried about me traveling, I can walk. I helped dear Abe on the farm the day after this little angel was born." She stroked curls from Abigail's forehead.

"I'm more worried about you surviving being a prisoner. And your little ones. It isn't fair. It isn't right."

"Life isn't always fair."

Emeline agreed with that. But for this precious woman, it should be. "You are a preacher's wife. Shouldn't God be rescuing you? Helping you? Instead your husband is — and you are now British prisoners."

"God never said life would be easy, Emeline. But if we follow Him, it is an abundant life. Jesus said, 'The thief cometh not, but for to steal, and to kill, and to destroy: I am come that they might have life, and that they might have it more abundantly.' "

"Is that in the Bible?"

"Yes, indeed."

Emeline frowned and looked down. "I guess God's definition of abundance and mine are quite different."

Clara studied her. "You think my life has been boring because I do my best to obey God?" She switched little Adam to her other side. "Quite the opposite. Abe and I met down in Curacao, where I was living with my missionary parents. We had such a romance in the tropics!" Her eyes lit up, and for a moment she seemed far away. "After getting married, we traveled from island to island in the West Indies, spreading the Gospel — Barbados, Jamaica, Puerto Rico, Antigua. Most of the time we lived on the ship. One time we were even attacked by pirates. And I helped fire a cannon!"

Emeline couldn't have been more shocked. "You fired a cannon? Against pirates?" She chuckled. "And you traveled to all those exotic places with your husband?"

"Yes, but it wasn't those places that were wonderful, though the islands were gorgeous. It was doing the Lord's work, knowing I was working for the Creator and saving souls from hell. There's nothing more adventurous than that."

"I've never met a lady who led such a full life." Something Emeline had longed to do ever since she could remember.

Clara smiled. "Then Amos came along, and we settled here in Maryland, took over a church from a dying pastor, and the adventure continued."

"I don't understand. Abe is gone now, and

you're alone. How can that be adventurous?"

"Abe has gone home because the Lord called him. Since I am still here, I will carry on wherever He leads."

"Even to prison."

Adam made gurgling noises, and Clara smiled down at him. "If God desires."

Exhaustion drew Emeline's head into her hands. There must be a way out of this. She snapped her gaze up to Clara. "Was there more laudanum?"

"Some. What are you thinking?"

"I'm thinking of a way to get you out of here."

CHAPTER 22

Owen leaned back on the wooden chair, hearing it creak beneath his weight, and gazed over the dark farm. His turn for watch. Lucky for him, his mind was still spinning from the day's activities, and he needed to ponder a few things, which helped keep him awake.

Holding a newborn baby had stirred him more than he ever thought it would. Adam was so tiny, Owen could hold him in one of his hands. Being an only child, Owen had never witnessed a birth, held a wee one in his arms, or changed a nappy. All of which he'd done today. What an incredible miracle. To see such a perfectly formed human emerge from a woman's womb, where God had shaped and formed it with His own hands. At least that's what he remembered the Bible said. If anything would make Owen believe in a loving God, it was witnessing that. But then of course, his opinion had changed quickly when the British troops stormed in.

But thanks to Mr. Ryne, they'd gotten rid of them. At least for now. Yet at what cost? This poor family, who had already been through more than most people should, would become British prisoners. And he knew all too well the harsh reality of that life. Seeing Amos scowl at Owen all night after he'd found out who they were had done more damage to Owen's heart than any insult tossed his way the past eight years. Hatred, pure hatred, fired from the lad's eyes. A hatred too raging for so young a boy to feel. But Owen couldn't blame him.

How he wanted to leave right now, avoid watching this family be imprisoned, and run to Baltimore himself. But the risk was too great and the stakes too high. He still needed Emeline and her contacts. If he were honest with himself, he needed Emeline, period. But he didn't want to be honest right now. Not with his thoughts. Or his feelings.

A warm breeze sent a dried leaf fluttering over the porch and brought with it the scent of the woodland, loamy earth, and wildflowers. America. Home. For once Owen must do the right thing and turn Emeline over to the authorities. Instead of following his heart, revealing who he was, telling her that he loved her — yes, hang it all, he *did* love her! He knew that now. Then how could he even think of betraying that love? How could he choose between her and his country? Between her and what he knew to be his duty? Why was it always so hard to do the right thing?

He'd never been very good at denying his impulses . . . at putting his country — or anything, for that matter — ahead of himself. Mr. Oakes had told him he was a slave to sin, that there was true freedom in following God. Owen had never felt a slave to anything. He'd always made his own choices, choices that were best for him. How did that make him a slave?

"You are a slave to self."

The words drifted through his mind, but they didn't come from him. Gripping the sides of the chair, Owen scanned the darkness. A half-moon dripped milky light over select leaves, then spilled to shimmer in the puddles strewn over the ground. But there was nobody there.

Or was there? He remembered the strange events of the past few days — the spiral of light drifting up from Mr. Oakes's body, the shaft of sunlight on the cross at his grave, the dove. . . . Was there truly an eternal realm beyond this one? A place where spirits and angels lived . . . a heaven . . . a hell? If so, then did one's actions, what one believed — or rather, who one believed — here on earth determine one's destiny after death? Just as the Bible said? What Owen had seen recently certainly gave him pause to consider the truth of scripture.

He shook off the thoughts, allowing his mind to drift to another strange event that had occurred that night. When Emeline handed out bowls of stew for supper, neither she nor Mrs. Oakes — or her children — partook of any. Instead, they nibbled on hardtack and dried beef from the ship supplies. When Owen asked her about it, she merely said that her stomach was too upset to eat, and the Oakes's too. Seemed a reasonable explanation after all that had happened that day, so he let it go. Though somewhere deep in his gut, something told him not to eat the stew either. He gave his portion to Mr. Ryne, who was most grateful.

Now, with his stomach rumbling, Owen wondered if he'd made the right choice. He was no doubt imagining things, casting suspicions where there was no cause — a frequent occurrence ever since he'd become a spy. He'd be glad to get out of the business. And into something more lucrative but equally as dangerous and fun. Like privateering. At least he'd be his own master.

Rustling in the leaves snapped his gaze to the left where moonlight lit up the mound of Mr. Oakes's grave, bringing his thoughts back to their conversation. Was God really so intimately involved with His creation? Did He want those who followed Him to have an adventurous life? Owen could not fathom how obeying rules equated to freedom.

Thumping noises inside the house pricked his ears. They grew louder, along with harried whispers. The door creaked, and Owen slid his hat down on his face and pretended to be asleep.

The shuffle and patter of multiple feet filled the night air, along with more whispers and the closing of the door.

The footsteps halted then proceeded down the stairs and padded on the dirt.

Lifting his head slightly, Owen peered out from beneath his hat, happy that the porch kept him in the shadows, and equally happy for the moonlight that now revealed Mrs. Oakes, babe in her arms, Abigail, Amos, and, of all people, Emeline.

They halted before the house. Emeline cast a wary glance his way, then ushered them farther away. Owen turned his ear, doing his best to hear what they were saying.

"I fear you will be punished for this, Emeline," Clara said.

"Don't worry about me. My concern is for you and the children." Emeline drew Amos close and gripped young Abigail's hand.

"Mama." The little girl looked up. "Where are we going? It's dark out. I'm tired."

"I know, sweetheart. We will rest soon."

The babe in her arms let out a tiny whimper.

"The Harrison farm is only a few hours' walk," Clara said. "I couldn't go before because of Abe being so hurt. But now, what other choice do we have?"

Just when Owen didn't think Emeline could surprise him further . . . wow. He couldn't help but smile. So she was letting them escape? Amazing! Guilt prickled over him. He should have done the same, thought of a way.

"I'll protect us, Mama," Amos said.

Emeline handed the lad something. "Do you know how to use this?"

"Yes, ma'am. My papa taught me."

"Remember, if you hear anyone, hide in the shrubbery until they pass."

"We will. Don't worry, Emeline. And thank you."

"Of course. Now go! May God be with you."

Emeline embraced the woman and planted a kiss on the baby's head, then knelt and gathered the other two children close.

Who was this woman? Was it possible she was loyal to America? Or was she merely being kind to the innocent caught up in this heinous war? He found he had to know.

At least the Oakes would be safe now and not have to bear the brunt of the Royal Navy.

Emeline stood for several minutes watching the family disappear into the shadows until the forest swallowed them up. Wiping her eyes, she returned and mounted the steps.

Owen thought to have some fun. "I should arrest you right here and now," he said in his most authoritative voice.

If Emeline's heart weren't attached, it would have leapt out her throat and skittered into the woods after Clara and her children. She froze and slowly slid her gaze to Owen, waiting for her blood to stop dashing through her veins.

"Why don't you then?"

The man who was naught but a shadow sitting on the chair slid up his hat. "Because if I'd had my wits about me, I might have done the same."

She wondered if she heard him right. "I don't believe you."

Rising, he moved toward her, all muscle and man, a panther on a night prowl.

She didn't move. Refused to show this man any fear.

Stepping into the moonlight, he leaned a shoulder on the post and smiled. Yes, *smiled*. Not an I've-got-you kind of evil grin, but a smile one gives to a thing of beauty one admires. Her blood went from racing to warming.

"Why aren't you asleep like the rest of them?" she asked.

His smile remained as he removed his hat and raked his hair back. "I gave my soup to Ryne." He chuckled. "What was in it?"

Emeline released a sigh. "Laudanum."

"Brilliant." He chuckled.

Emeline raised a brow. "I don't understand. Why aren't you arresting me?"

"For allowing an innocent family to go free?" He shook his head. "That doesn't make you a traitor. Just human." He jerked his head toward the cabin. "Unlike some people we know."

Emeline swallowed and gazed at the forest where she'd last seen the Oakes. "They won't talk. They don't even know what we're after."

Owen nodded. "I must admit you are quite an enigma, Miss Baratt."

"So you keep telling me. But there is nothing special about me. I'm just trying to do the right thing. Be good as God commands." Emeline looked down and laughed. "Though I suppose proper ladies don't drug British Royal Navy officers. Hence, I have failed yet again."

He chuckled. "I'd say God will forgive you, even if He considers it an infraction."

She looked up at him. "And who made you an expert on the things of God?"

"Touché, Miss Baratt." Owen glanced across the farm, his intense gaze alert, his jaw bunching, his presence both comforting and frightening. "Our mission is almost complete. Tomorrow we'll be in Baltimore, discover their plans, and be back on the ship the next day."

She nodded, sorrow clawing at her soul — sorrow that she would have to turn this man in as a traitor. Despite his odd views of God and his unpredictability, he was decent and good. But still an enemy. Wait. Why did his tone bear none of the joy or excitement one would expect of such a victory? Odd. Could he possibly be . . .

No. Certainly her country placed no spies aboard Royal Navy ships. Such an assignment wouldn't provide enough information to warrant the risk. Only a fool or a daredevil would . . . She stared at him again, but he suddenly met her gaze and gave her a smile that made her not care where his loyalties lay.

She lowered her lashes. "I shall be glad when it is over." Snoring sounded from within the cabin, and she glanced that way. "What should we do with them?"

"Ah, let them sleep." He smiled. "They'll have a headache come morning, but they'll be none the worse for it."

"I don't know why you're being so kind. Or why you trust me still."

"Maybe I don't." He winked. "But what choice do I have? We need you."

So that was it. He needed her for access to the militia commanders. Merely a means to an end, that was all she was. She gestured toward the door. "What will you tell them?"

"That Mrs. Oakes put laudanum in the stew, and when we were all asleep, she and her children escaped."

Emeline smiled. "It was a cruel thing to do, wasn't it?"

Before she could stop him, Owen gathered a lock of her hair and eased it from her face.

Her breath caught.

He ran a thumb over her cheek. "It was a devilishly good thing to do."

"I don't think you can put the devil and —"

His lips met hers. Barely a whisper above her own — soft, testing . . . teasing. She should push him away. She should . . . but then he wrapped his arms around her and pressed her close and his kiss deepened. Madness and ecstasy! Never had she been kissed like this before. It was as if nothing in the entire world mattered but this man . . . the taste of him . . . the feel of him — all strength and honor and spice and wildness. She felt safe. Cherished.

Not like the entire world was at war around them.

La! Proper ladies didn't allow men to kiss them like this! But she couldn't stop. Didn't want to stop. He groaned, a pleasurable sound, a sound of yearning and desire. He released her lips. Stunned by the loss of him, Emeline couldn't move. She was searching for her reason, her propriety, but they had abandoned her, along with her tongue, for she tried to speak but couldn't.

His breath filled the air between them as

he cupped her chin in his thick hand and raised her gaze to his. "In another world, in a different time, I would beg you to be my lady."

Taken aback by his words, Emeline could only stare at him, searching his eyes for a spark of humor, but his tone and his look — a desperate look of longing — sent a sudden wave of terror storming through her. Covering her mouth with her hand, she opened the door and fled into the cabin.

CHAPTER 23

Angrier than a hungover pirate whose booty had been stolen, Dimsmore stomped down the path through a thicket of trees. Walking behind him, Owen hid a smile. He'd been hiding them all morning, ever since Dimsmore had woken and discovered the Oakes gone. At first, he'd blamed Owen, accused him of being a traitor, but once Emeline feigned her surprise that the laudanum was gone and then sniffed the leftover stew, Dimsmore redirected his anger toward Mrs. Oakes.

Without an apology to Owen.

"How could an ignorant farm woman concoct such a plan?" he had shouted.

He'd rumbled about the cabin, throwing things and making such a clatter that he gave himself a headache. Even Mr. Ryne, who'd been vomiting since dawn, begged him to stop.

Now the two bumbled down the trail,

complaining of nausea and muscle aches.

Of course, Owen and Emeline joined in with their own complaints, lest they draw suspicion their way.

In truth, Owen took no care for any of that. All his care was directed toward the intriguing woman walking beside him. And *all* his thoughts were on the kiss they'd shared last night. He probably shouldn't have taken liberties, but then again, there were many things he probably shouldn't do. She'd looked so lovely in the moonlight with the breeze dancing among her curls, her lustrous green eyes full of such pluck and vigor, and those lips she kept biting as if they were sweet to the taste.

He simply had to find out. And they were. Sweeter than he imagined. Her response — totally unexpected, for he'd thought she'd slap him — made it all the more sweeter, and he'd had to force himself to stop.

This was no lady to be trifled with. This was a woman to cherish and adore. Two things he would never be able to do if she remained his enemy. But what if . . . So many times she'd sided with the Americans, favored them, extended undue kindness. Dare he hope that perhaps after landing ashore her sentiments were shifting back to the country of her birth? He must find out.

At all costs.

She'd not said a word to him that morning. In fact, she avoided eye contact even now. Yet she walked beside him instead of behind or before, which gave him hope.

Morning sun trickled through branches, sparking the forest to life wherever it touched. Squirrels darted across the path, frogs chirped, lizards waddled up tree trunks. A blue jay followed them, jumping from tree to tree — an American spy, no doubt. Owen smiled.

The ground, still soft from the rain, sank beneath their boots as a breeze brought some relief from the heat already rising.

With an eye on Dimsmore and Ryne ahead of them, Owen slowed his pace.

"Would you like to talk about last night?"

"No," came the curt reply. "Nor shall anything like that happen again." She stopped and stared at him, her eyes flashing and her pert little nose curling. "You caught me at a weak moment."

"All right. What shall we talk about then?" He started forward.

"Why must we talk? We should conserve our energy for when we enter Baltimore."

"Ah, Baltimore. The city of your youth. It must be somewhat exciting to return after all these years. How long has it been, eight?"

"Ten. And I'm returning as an enemy."

"Your father will no doubt be glad to see you."

She shook her head. "What makes you think I intend to seek him out? We will discover the militia's plans and then leave. That's it."

"You don't even wish to see him? Say goodbye?"

Ah, there it was, the pain lining her face. The first hint that she still bore some affections for this place, for her family, for America. But then her expression stiffened.

"Much like your mother did when she sent you to the Royal Navy, my father sent me away to live with my great-aunt. She had been begging for me to come for years. She never approved of my father marrying my mother. She was a quarter Mohawk, and such things are unheard of in England, as you know. So my father agreed, hoping my aunt would transform me into a proper lady who would find her place in society."

Owen stared at the golden curls dangling at her neck, remembering how soft they were. But he could not reconcile the light color with the dark hair so typical among American Indians. Not that her Indian heritage disturbed him. In truth, it rather excited him and certainly explained her wild, untamed spirit. "Seems we have more in common than we thought."

She glanced at him then, and he thought he saw a smile curve her lips.

Dimsmore tripped over a fallen log up ahead, and Owen took the lady's hand to steady her as she stepped over it after him. A group of chickadees serenaded them as they passed beneath the branch of a large oak.

"I thought it would be a grand adventure," she continued. "My aunt was known to be quite eccentric, and she loved parties and traveling. I had hoped to see Europe, meet interesting people, and perhaps pursue my art."

"And meet a prospective wealthy husband?" Like most women Owen knew.

"Bite your tongue, sir. Never that. I don't ever wish to be tied down."

Owen flinched. He certainly hadn't expected that reaction. What woman didn't wish to make a good match? Extraordinary.

"Alas, my aunt became terribly ill." Emeline swept a curl from her face. "And I spent my years at her bedside, caring for her."

"How disappointing. I'm sorry."

She looked at him as if surprised by the sincerity of his tone.

But he *was* sorry. He could not see this

wild bird caged for too long. Not without breaking her spirit.

"Yet," he dared say, "it would seem that ten years living among the British *Haut-ton* was unable to strip you of your . . . hmm . . ." How to say it as a compliment and not insult this precious lady.

"Baseborn abilities?" She graced him with a smile that told him she wasn't at all insulted.

He didn't know whether to laugh or apologize. "I meant to say that the general snobbery and spoon-fed whining of the nobility found no root in your unpretentious nature."

She gave a ladylike snort. "One doesn't forget running a house and taking care of two brothers for fourteen . . . six years."

"Fourteen, six? Which is it?"

She scowled. "Six years. My mother died when I was eight, and my father sent me to my aunt's at fourteen. Ten years later, here I am."

Owen scratched his chin. Why did she seem like she was reciting a planned speech? "I'm sorry about your mother. What was she like?"

Emeline smiled and fingered the locket around her neck. "She was beautiful and full of life . . . a magnificent artist."

"So that's where you get it from."

"You flatter me, Owen. And I'm not sure why." She cocked her head at him but then faced forward again. "If I possess even half her talent, I shall be glad for it." Clutching her skirts, she stepped over a large root. "Father and she were dreadfully unhappy. He wanted a wife who acted like a wife, who tended the home and cared for the children. My mother tried her best, and she took good care of us, but she could not stop painting. It made her so happy." Emeline smiled. "She could have been famous worldwide and sold her work, she was that good."

She glanced up at him as they continued forward. "I don't know why I'm telling you this. Forgive me."

"No. Please, go on. I'm interested."

"There isn't much else to say. Perhaps it was the Indian blood in her. She wasn't suited to be a proper English wife and mother."

"And from what I gather, you don't think you are either?"

"I know I am not. But if God wills it, I will try. I'm tired of running from Him."

He dropped his gaze to the locket still gripped in her fingers. "How did she die?"

"The doctors never said. In truth, I don't think they knew. She simply grew ill, and in two days she was gone." She released the locket as if letting go of a bad memory. "My father said God punished her for not following His rules. Doing her wifely duties."

Owen ground his teeth, his fury rising.

"He said the same thing will happen to me if I don't settle down."

"Is that what you believe?" he asked, his tone a bit too angry. No wonder this woman tried so hard to be what she called a *proper lady.*

"How can I not after all the tragedies that have befallen me? I try so hard to be good, but it seems the world, or perhaps God, is against me."

"Perhaps what you consider to be good and what God considers to be good are not one and the same."

She huffed. "How would someone like you know?"

"Ouch, the lady wounds me." He pressed a hand to his chest, though he knew she was right. He had never prided himself on knowing much either about being good or about God.

"I'm sorry, Owen. You didn't deserve that. You've been kind to me."

"But I *did* deserve it."

"Well, in that case, I don't suppose you'll give me a hint of the British plan of attack?

We are nearly at Baltimore. Surely you trust me by now."

Owen wondered at both the sudden change of topic and her curiosity. But then again, perhaps, despite her declaration otherwise, she was concerned about her family's safety. What difference did it make if she knew? If she was loyal to Britain, it didn't matter. If she was loyal to America, all the better.

"All I know is that the British are planning attacks by both land and sea. They'll land four thousand troops under Ross at North Point and march to Baltimore from the east, while our ships will bombard Fort McHenry. Once the fort is taken, they'll sail into the harbor and point their guns at the city." Owen's stomach deflated even saying it. "Of course, this all depends on how many men are defending Baltimore and how much armament they have at their disposal. Which is what we are to discover."

She nodded but said nothing.

They walked on in silence, the story of her past settling in his mind. And in his heart. She was as wild and free-spirited as he. Which only made him love her more.

Love. There was that word again — a foreign word when it came to women. Desire, admiration, pleasure . . . yes. But never love. Love meant commitment, and commitment meant settling down. And he had far too many adventures planned to allow that to happen. Yet . . . as he glanced at this lady beside him — the most beautiful creature inside and out that he'd ever known — he might be persuaded to make an exception.

Proper ladies didn't think about kissing men! Proper ladies didn't feel all warm and tingly when they remembered kissing a *certain* man. Emeline glanced at that man beside her, the commanding way he walked, the way his gaze continually took in their surroundings like a protective warrior — the very presence of him, powerful, dangerous. Yet despite all that, he made her feel safe, even special.

What was happening to her?

They emerged from the trees and started across a field — like stepping from a cool kitchen into an oven as rays from a fiery sun pummeled them from above. Even the heated air seemed to buzz and crackle like sizzling coals. Plucking a handkerchief from her pocket, Emeline wiped the back of her neck. Proper ladies didn't sweat either, she supposed, but there was naught to be done about it.

Owen glanced her way and handed her the canteen. Taking it, she uncorked it and took a swig. "Thank you." Oh, what she must look like with half her hair dangling from her pins, dirt smudged on her gown and skin, and what she could only imagine were dark circles beneath her eyes.

Yet when he took back the canteen, he gave her a look as if she'd just walked into an elegant soiree in her best gown. He took a gulp of water and wiped his sleeve over his mouth. Fie! Her thoughts went to their kiss again. She sped forward and continued across the field of tall grass sprinkled with goldenrod and pink milkweed.

If he thought her unlike any British nobility he'd met, the feeling was mutual, for he certainly didn't match her notion of a Royal Navy officer. She'd always imagined them to be strict, by-the-book, heartless, and licentious. Yet during the past three days ashore, this man had disobeyed orders more than once, shown a great deal of care for Americans, and never once taken advantage of her. In fact, quite the opposite. She wished more than anything that she didn't have to turn him over to the Baltimore militia . . . that she didn't have to betray him and never see him again.

Yet now that Owen had told her the plans,

she no longer needed him. Perhaps she could lose him once they separated from Dimsmore and began their trek into Baltimore. But of course that wouldn't do. Knowing him, he'd still make every attempt to get the information he came for and then return to his ship. And she couldn't allow any knowledge to get into the hands of the British that would aid them in winning this war.

Groans brought her attention to Mr. Ryne, trudging behind them as if they had the plague.

In front of them, Dimsmore turned and dabbed his face with his cravat. "When will we see Baltimore, Miss Baratt?"

"As I told you when you inquired five minutes ago, we are nearly there. We should start seeing the outlying farms soon." She approached the man and stopped as Mr. Ryne came up from behind.

Dimsmore leaned his hands on his knees while Ryne held his head as if it would explode.

Owen and Emeline shared a smile.

"Perhaps if you didn't require so much rest," she added, "we would already be there."

The look in Dimsmore's eyes couldn't be more malevolent. "How are you two faring so well?"

Owen cradled his musket in his arms. "Made of stronger stuff than you, is my guess."

Dimsmore scowled. But the suspicion burning in his eyes gave Emeline pause.

"There's a creek up ahead, if I remember," she said. "And a wooded area in which to hide. It would be a good place for you and Mr. Ryne to remain while the lieutenant and I go ahead into Baltimore. A lone man and woman won't raise too many suspicions . . . but three armed men?"

"I remember the plan, Miss Baratt," Dimsmore quipped.

Shielding her eyes, she glanced at the sun. "Once I find the commander of the militia, it should be of no account to get the information. We could possibly even return by sundown. If not, then definitely by the next morning." Though she'd managed to keep her tone calm, her insides shook like a feather in a gale at what she was about to do.

Dimsmore's blue eyes shifted from her to Owen and back again, but he only groaned as he pushed to stand and continued onward. "I shouldn't trust you two on your own. I or Mr. Ryne should accompany you."

Emeline's heart turned to lead. *No, Lord. No.*

At the creek, he and Mr. Ryne were quite happy to collapse to the ground and splash water over their faces and necks. Too nervous to rest, Emeline peered through the woods. Indeed, she spotted a fence in the distance, which no doubt was the Henrick farm — the farthest farm from town. They were close.

She spun to find Owen looking at her oddly.

"We should get going." Grabbing a lock of hair, she spun it nervously around her finger. "Otherwise we may not make it back by nightfall." Her glance took in Dimsmore. Sweat beaded over his pale face as he leaned over the creek. "Lieutenant Dimsmore?" she said by way of invitation, hoping beyond hope he was too ill to even entertain the thought of accompanying them.

Wincing, Dimsmore struggled to rise and approached, taking a stance between her and Owen. "Very well. We will wait here. If you don't come back by tonight —"

"You'll wait until noon," Owen returned with authority. "We don't know what kind of trouble we may encounter or how long it will take to get the information we need."

Dimsmore's lips flattened, but he nodded,

then stumbled back to sit by the creek.

Owen turned to her. "Ready, Miss Baratt?"

Drawing a deep breath to mask her fear, she raised her chin. "I am." She faced Dimsmore. "Good day to you, Dimsmore. Mr. Ryne." The marine barely acknowledged her from his hands and knees beside a bush. A retching sound scraped her ears. "See you soon," she called out, hoping her cheerful tone would mock their discomfort. Actually, she hoped she'd never see these two men again.

She couldn't say the same for the man who now marched beside her. And for that, she was greatly sorry.

They entered another clearing, and the fence she'd seen appeared on their right. Beyond the wooden posts, pastures spread out, dotted with cows and horses. To their left, woods banked the Patapsco River. She heard it gurgling past even above the birdsong and flutter of leaves in the wind.

"Are you so sure, Emeline, that after ten years living in England, your friends and acquaintances or even family members will be assured of your loyalty?"

"Of course. They have no reason not to be."

"If you were such a hellcat as a child, I

don't see why."

She pursed her lips. "Hellcat, as you put it, and traitor are two different things."

Owen stared up at the sky. "Which begs the question. How does one become the other?"

Why was he questioning her loyalty now? When they were about to enter Baltimore? A niggling fear began scampering up her back. Owen Masters was no fool. She must deflect his suspicion, cast it elsewhere. The fate of Baltimore and possibly her entire country depended on it. Halting, she stared at him. "You question my loyalty, Owen, when it is yours that might very well be in doubt."

He smiled and planted the butt of his musket in the dirt. "How so?"

"You do not behave like a Royal Navy lieutenant."

"And how should a Royal Navy lieutenant behave?"

"Like Dimsmore and Ryne, I expect."

At this, his brows rose, and he began to chuckle.

"Oh, never mind." Whirling about, she grabbed her skirts and proceeded. "Let's get what we came for and return to the *Marauder.* Then your navy can proceed with its murdering and plundering."

"I believe it is your navy too, by your own account." His sarcastic voice followed her.

Something else pricked her ears — footsteps, the snap of a branch that wasn't from the wind.

Owen heard it too. They both halted, eyes locked on the shrubbery lining the field. With one hand Owen raised his musket; with the other he nudged Emeline behind him.

"Come out! Let us see you."

Seconds passed.

"I will shoot!"

Leaves rustled and a uniformed leg appeared, followed by the skinny frame of a young lad, no more than sixteen, in a private's uniform. Red hair sprang from beneath his cap and barely a whisker formed on his chin. He tossed down his musket and raised both hands, eyes stark with fear and legs trembling. "Please don't shoot, mister."

"He heard us." Owen all but growled. "He heard what we said."

"No I didn't, mister. I didn't hear nothin'."

But they could both tell from his expression that he had.

Owen kept his musket steady, his finger on the trigger. "I cannot allow you to inform your superiors."

The boy shook his head. "I won't, mister. I won't. I swear." His entire body began to shake.

No! Emeline wanted to throw herself before the boy. Surely Owen would not shoot a defenseless lad! No matter what, no matter if her actions revealed her true loyalties, she would not allow this innocent boy to die. Nothing was worth that.

"He's just a boy," she said, looking around for something to use as a weapon. Her eyes latched on the pistol stuffed in Owen's belt.

"He's in the American army," Owen answered. "He'll run and tell them."

"Please, mister, I don't want to die." The lad began to whimper.

Owen cocked the musket. "I'm sorry, boy. War is war."

So Owen would shoot an innocent lad. Perhaps he was not the man she thought he was. Plucking the pistol from Owen's belt, Emeline cocked it and leveled it at his back. "Put down the musket. Now!"

CHAPTER 24

Owen slowly turned around and smiled at the determined lady aiming a pistol at his chest. Overwhelming joy bubbled deep within him. He knew it! She was loyal to America. His ploy had worked.

Emeline narrowed her eyes. "I said, set down your weapon or I'll shoot!"

From her stance and the furious steel of her jaw, Owen figured he'd better do as she said. He lowered his musket and set it on the ground then raised his hands.

The pistol trembled in her grip, wavering over his chest. Her face was tight, her lips flat, her breath a windy storm.

"Get out of here!" she shouted to the private, but Owen could already hear the resounding echo of the boy's footsteps.

"Why are you smiling?" she asked.

"Because we are on the same side."

"Clearly, we are not, or I wouldn't be pointing this weapon at you," she spat back.

"You think I won't shoot — that a woman doesn't know how to use a pistol? Are you willing to bet your life on that?"

"I wouldn't dare." His grin remained. And as she stood so bravely risking her life for another, sticking firm to her convictions no matter the cost, Owen thought she was the loveliest woman he'd ever seen.

"I'm an American spy," he announced and watched her eyes go from fury to doubt to understanding then back to doubt again. Yet she said naught.

"After all that's happened," Owen continued in his most conciliatory tone, "I thought you might be too. So when the boy showed up, I tested you."

"You expect me to believe that? That you weren't going to shoot that poor lad?"

"I do. And I can prove it. My uncle is general counsel for the Department of the Navy. He's the one who ordered me to maintain my post on HMS *Marauder* in order to discover battle plans and bring them ashore."

He watched her mind spin behind those beautiful green eyes of hers, no doubt sorting through memories of the past month they'd spent together, searching for hints of the veracity of his story.

"So everything you told me was a lie?"

"No, not everything." Owen lowered his hands. "I'm sorry, Emeline. I wasn't sure I could trust you."

She kept the pistol raised. A breeze stirred the curls at her neck. "I don't know what to think. Fie!" She looked toward Baltimore. "I need to go and warn my city, my family, my friends." She looked back at him, tears brimming in her eyes. "I don't know who to trust."

"Trust in this . . . I've fallen in love with you, Emeline Baratt."

She stared at him, the fury seeping from her eyes along with her tears. The pistol wavered in her hand. A battle raged behind her eyes, and he wished more than anything he could allay her fears, convince her of his love and loyalty.

He reached for her. "Trust me, Emeline. You *know* me." He shook his head and laughed. "I can't believe we've been on the same side this entire time!"

She started to laugh as well . . . *and* lower her pistol. "Owen —"

"Aha! Just as I thought." An all-too-familiar voice screeched across the field, along with the cock of two pistols.

Owen quickly thrust his hands back in the air, even as his heart sank to the mud beneath his boots. He didn't have to look up to know that Dimsmore and his lackey Ryne were making their way toward them.

Why hadn't he heard them coming? Hang it all! He'd been so thrilled to finally know that Emeline was not a traitor, to realize there was nothing to stop him from expressing his love — from seeing that spark of returned affection appear in her eyes — that he'd slacked in his duties, forgotten they were at war and the enemy was close.

Emeline froze, her eyes filled with terror. Before Dimsmore got too close, Owen gestured for her to raise the pistol again.

Thank God she did.

Dimsmore and Ryne finally came into view, their weapons aimed at Owen. "Care to explain what's happening here?"

Emeline started to speak, but Owen interrupted. "She caught me. I admit it. I'm an American spy."

You'd think Owen had given Dimsmore two thousand pounds for the smile that split his face in two. "I always suspected," he slithered out in a tone of defiant victory. "You always were too soft on Americans." He snorted and shook his head. "Ryne and I saw you let that kid go and Miss Baratt here point a pistol at your head." He glanced at her. "Good work. You can lower the weapon now, Miss Baratt."

Her mouth still agape, she did as he said, but horror filled her face as she shook her head at Owen.

But Owen would not comply. Instead he faced his nemesis with a look of defeat. "Indeed, she caught me letting that private go. I didn't think she had it in her, but she grabbed my pistol."

Dimsmore faced her and smiled. "I admit, Miss Baratt, I had my doubts about you as well, but I see now that you are loyal to our country." He snapped at Ryne. "Arrest him at once!"

Mr. Ryne approached Owen, cautiously at first, but once he saw Owen acquiesce, he took his other pistol and two knives and then tied his hands behind his back. In an instant, Owen's worst fears were realized. He was not only a prisoner of war, but also a traitor whose fate was the noose.

The pistol slipped in Emeline's hands and clunked to the dirt by her boots. The sudden turn of events left her unable to move or even speak. Good thing, for she wanted to shout out her own guilt and join Owen in his chains. He had stood up for her, protected her, and it had cost him the thing he valued most — his freedom.

She still couldn't believe it. All this time

they'd been on the same side, fighting not only the same cause, but their undeniable attraction for each other. She thought back to his odd behavior on the ship when he'd found out her loyalties to Britain — how he'd kept his distance and almost seemed to hate her. Then the kindness he'd extended to the prisoners, his reaction when Washington had burned, and finally how he'd allowed her to set the Oakes family free. All the memories had started to make sense the minute he'd told her the truth, when she saw the relief, laughter, and love in his eyes. *Love.* He'd said he loved her.

How could one's heart soar to the heavens one minute and sink to the depths of the earth the next? Yet that was exactly what was happening now.

Turning, Dimsmore approached Emeline. No doubt mistaking the horrified look on her face for shock at Owen's betrayal, he knelt to pick up the pistol and stood up to take her trembling hands in his.

She wanted to tug from his grip, to spit in his face, but instead, she lowered her gaze so he wouldn't see the fury in her eyes.

"You're trembling, Miss Baratt. I'm sorry to have sent you off with the enemy. I suspected him but had no proof. But all is well now." He squeezed her hands gently.

"You are safe."

Forcing a smile, she pulled back her hands and hugged herself. Over Dimsmore's shoulder she spotted Owen, hair hanging about his face, give a barely perceptible nod. He was right of course. She had to continue on the mission, warn Baltimore of the upcoming attack. It would do no good for her to become a prisoner alongside him.

"I thank you, Lieutenant, for your quick thinking and your rescue. I'm not sure what I would have done."

Dimsmore's shoulders seemed to grow in size and stature as he holstered the pistol and glanced across the field. "If you are able, you should proceed with our plan."

Emeline drew a deep breath and followed his gaze. How could she possibly leave Owen a prisoner? If she didn't return, which she had no plans of doing, he'd be taken back to HMS *Marauder,* then eventually court-martialed and most likely hanged. She swallowed the lump forming in her throat.

"Yes, I am able." It came out scratchy and with less enthusiasm than she intended, but Dimsmore didn't seem to notice. If she didn't get this information to Baltimore, neither she nor Owen would have a country anymore.

"Brave girl." Dimsmore nodded and held

a hand to his stomach. "Mr. Ryne will accompany you."

Her heart seized. "Mr. Ryne? There is no need. Baltimore is just past that farm. I need no further escort."

Dimsmore removed a handkerchief and dabbed the sweat from his brow. "If you're worried Mr. Ryne is also a spy, I can vouch for him, Miss Baratt. And we are at war. Even a mile is dangerous for a young lady to travel alone."

"But Mr. Ryne is so . . . so" — what excuse could she use? — "British."

Dimsmore laughed. "No more than Lieutenant Masters."

"At least he was born here and can honestly say such should he be questioned." She flinched at the desperation in her tone.

Dimsmore frowned and pressed a finger to his temple. "I believe you'll find Mr. Ryne quite clever on the spur of the moment. Meanwhile, the traitor and I will be waiting at the creek where we planned."

"Ryne!"

Mr. Ryne approached, dragging Owen with him.

"Protect her with your life," Dimsmore ordered him. "Get the information and return at once."

Mr. Ryne nodded, flung his musket over

his shoulder, and took a spot beside her.

But Emeline's eyes were on Owen. He met her gaze, his expression devoid of fear. Instead she saw assurance and . . . *love.* Her heart broke. Would she ever see him again?

She averted her gaze, lest she give herself away.

"Shall we?" Mr. Ryne said.

Nodding, Emeline grabbed her skirts and proceeded.

With no idea how she was going to pull this off.

CHAPTER 25

Dimsmore shoved Owen to the muddy ground. Unable to catch his fall, he landed on his side. Pain shot into his arm and across his shoulder. He rolled to sit and spat out mud as Dimsmore kicked him against a tree, wrapped a rope around his chest, and tied him to the trunk.

"You're nothing but a crooked snake, a slimy American snake." Dimsmore looked at Owen as if he had indeed just slithered out of a hole. He called him a few more choice names that should never be said in polite company. But then again, Owen wasn't polite, nor was he company. Nor did he wish to remain in this man's company more than he had to.

Easing up against the trunk, he began scraping the ropes on his wrists against the rough bark. Slowly, methodically, stopping whenever Dimsmore looked his way. Which thankfully wasn't often.

The man pulled out a piece of dried beef and began chewing on it.

Owen's stomach grumbled. Ignoring it, he shifted his thoughts to Emeline. How was she faring with Mr. Ryne? She had a hard task before her. Not only did she have to convince the Americans that she was loyal to them, but she had to convince the staunch Mr. Ryne that she was loyal to Britain. Ryne may not say much or express much emotion, but he was no bufflehead. One slipup, one wrong word or reaction on her part, and he would . . . Well, hopefully he wouldn't harm her.

Such a brave woman! A spy of all things, though quite likely she didn't set out intending to be one. She'd no doubt made that decision on board the *Marauder,* doing her bit for her country, while most women would have never dared to put themselves in such danger. Sweet, brave Emeline. He'd told her he loved her, and he thought — dare he hope he saw affection returned in her eyes? What an incredible woman.

Yet if things went well, he'd never see her again. She'd have Ryne arrested, she'd tell the Baltimore militia the British plans, and then she'd go home where she'd be safe with her father. At least Owen hoped and prayed she would do that — for there was nothing to be done for his situation.

Minutes passed like hours. The heat of the day rose to near boiling then subsided as the sun lowered behind the trees. He was given no water, no food, and no break to relieve himself.

Dimsmore, still unwell from the laudanum, spent his time lying down on a bed of moss by the creek, his pistol in his grip.

Owen knew one thing. There was nothing stopping this man from killing him and telling Captain Blackwell that Owen had tried to escape.

Either way, dead by this man's hands or dead at the end of a rope, Owen's future looked bleak.

Which is why he continued scraping the ropes against the tree. Yet all his hard work produced was raw, bloody wrists. Despite that, the pain was nothing when compared to the ache in his heart and the emptiness in his spirit.

He tried to pray, managed a few pleas on Emeline's behalf, but in truth, he was angry at God. Owen could have taken off as soon as they'd come ashore. He could have tried to find his uncle, or he could have tried to warn Baltimore by himself. If either mission failed, who cared? He would have been free. Somehow, some way, he would have eventually made enough money to purchase a ship and fulfill his dream to sail around the world.

But he'd done the right thing. He'd followed through with the mission, put his country and the people of Baltimore above his own desires.

And look where it had gotten him. Following God's command to be unselfish had not only ripped him of his freedom; it would probably also end in his death.

Mr. Ryne was not much of a conversationalist. For that, Emeline was glad. It gave her time to plan the best way to be rid of him. The easiest way would be to find the militia commander, convince him of her loyalty, and then promptly turn in Mr. Ryne as a British spy. But plans never went that easily. At least not for her.

They passed the farm and entered another patch of trees — a brief reprieve from the searing sun. Soon they entered a clearing, and from there she could see the first buildings of Baltimore — the hospital and beyond that, the steeple of St. Patrick's church.

A mixture of excitement and terror spiraled through her. She was home. Finally. And for the first time in a long while, she was excited to see her father, her friends . . .

to feel safe and secure again, surrounded by those she loved.

She hardly remembered what that felt like. But then her thoughts drifted to Owen. *He* had made her feel that way. Squeezing back tears, she hurried her pace, longing to be done with this insane mission, longing for her heart to beat normally and not always be aflutter with fear and uncertainty.

"Over there," Mr. Ryne finally said as he pointed to a cluster of tents filling a field just south of the hospital. "That looks like their militia."

Indeed, it did. Emeline drew a deep breath and headed that way, all the while praying, *Lord, help me find someone who recognizes me, someone who will believe me and arrest Mr. Ryne.*

The tents stood in white rows like foamy waves coming on shore. Soldiers, in both army and militia uniforms, darted between them; others sat in the shade in groups, playing cards or eating. The smell of roasted meat, sweat, and gunpowder rose to join the scent of wildflowers and pine as Emeline boldly entered the camp.

Soldiers stopped to stare, their eyes latching upon her and not Mr. Ryne as they should, for clearly he was more of a threat. But men would be men, she supposed. No one stopped them to ask their purpose, which also upset her. Did these soldiers realize they were at war? Did they realize their capital had fallen and all the power and authority of the British Royal Navy was anchored just offshore?

Mr. Ryne snorted his disapproval beside her. But how could she blame him?

Anger fueled her forward, and she searched the uniforms for someone in authority.

There — a red epaulet on the right shoulder of the man's blue coat. She headed toward him. "Sergeant, if you please."

The man, who was pleasingly handsome but quite young to be a sergeant, turned to face her, his smile suddenly souring.

"May I speak to your commander, Sergeant?"

"I'm afraid General Smith is not seeing anyone, especially not" — he looked her over, his nose wrinkling — "camp trollops."

For the first time since she'd known him, Mr. Ryne cracked a smile.

"How dare you?" Heat flushed up her neck and face, fueled by anger or embarrassment, she didn't know. "I am no trollop, Sergeant. My name is Emeline Baratt. I am the daughter of Herbert Baratt."

"Humph." He cocked his head and adjusted his blue coat. "I know of Mr. Baratt, but I highly doubt he's associated with the likes of you. Now, you and your" — he spared a glance for Mr. Ryne — "man run along."

"Of all the nerve! I demand to see this General Smith, sir. I have vital information that will affect the outcome of this war."

He chuckled. "You? *You* have vital information?"

Emeline withheld a growl. Proper ladies didn't growl, after all.

"I'll handle this." Another man approached, this one in a sergeant major's uniform. "You say you're Herbert Baratt's daughter?"

"Yes, I am." Emeline studied him. "Mr. Radford, is that you?"

"How do you know my name?" the man barked back.

"I'm Emeline Baratt." She gestured to herself, but then realized with her torn and stained gown, disheveled hair, and filthy condition, she certainly didn't look like the daughter of one of the wealthiest merchants in town.

"I met Miss Baratt four years ago and you look nothing like her."

"I've been away." She glanced at Mr. Ryne. Thankfully, he didn't seem to notice the comment about four years. "In England. My ship was captured by the British. Please, I know this is most peculiar, but I must speak to your commander immediately."

"And who is this man?"

"Mr. Ryne. He was on my father's ship. We escaped together."

Radford huffed and shared a glance with the sergeant standing nearby. "You expect me to believe that you escaped from a British Royal Navy ship?"

Emeline fisted her hands and closed her eyes for a moment. This was not going well.

"Never mind, we can clear this up right now," Radford finally said, his gaze still suspicious. "Your *father* is here, I believe."

The man's words brought a wave of relief. "Thank you, sir."

Then turning, Mr. Radford started down the path. "Follow me."

Finally. Emeline's heart nearly burst in her chest. Within minutes, she would be reunited with her father. Within minutes, she could have Mr. Ryne arrested, and this entire nightmare would be over.

"That's her!" A young voice blared through the crowd, followed by a boy pushing others aside and charging toward her. It was the private Owen had released.

He pointed right at her and shouted to

everyone who could hear. "She's a British spy!"

CHAPTER 26

Emeline struggled against the ties that bound her hands so tight they were going numb. This certainly wasn't how she planned for things to turn out. She accused of being a British spy, and Owen accused of being an American one. She'd laugh at the irony if she weren't so frightened. And miserable. Was this another punishment from God for stepping outside His boundaries? Yes, she had lied. Yes, she had deceived. Yes, she had done things no proper lady should. But this was war. Certainly the Almighty would make concessions. Yet all her appeals, all the pleas she'd lifted up to heaven since being tied up, seemed to bounce off the top of the tent and drop right back into her lap.

The sun had long since set, and she could hear the crackle of fires, the chatter and laughter of men, the snort of horses, and the shouts of officers creating a frightening cacophony outside the tent. A parade of shadows, elongated and gnarled, drifted past on the canvas walls, each one threatening to enter and attack, yet each one at the last minute skipping over the flap-covered opening. She wondered if the next one wouldn't be the angel of death coming to steal her final breath.

She thanked God for one small favor. Mr. Ryne had been locked up elsewhere. Hence, she didn't have to endure his company, especially now that she would have to reveal her true mission to the first man who entered. If anyone ever did enter. Or maybe they'd just escort her to the gallows and be done with it.

A breeze stirred the tent flap, wafting in the scent of meaty stew and giving her a little reprieve from the stagnant heat. What was taking so long?

Her stomach rumbled. Uttering a rather unladylike growl, she lunged forward, trying to either tear through the ties or uproot the wooden pole behind her. But her hands struck the wood and the ropes rubbed against her raw wrists, and she cried out instead.

The tent flap opened. A lantern preceded a tall man in a sergeant's uniform, its flickering light distorting his features into an undulating mass.

She squinted from the brightness. "Please get my father. I told you I'm innocent!"

But then a voice swept past her ears, a familiar voice, a loving voice, and she looked up to see another man enter, rush forward, and drop to his knees beside her.

"Emmie!"

"Papa!" She started to cry but then laughed and then cried again. Never had she been so happy to see her father.

"Untie her at once!" he shouted behind him.

"Are you sure it's your daughter?" the man said as another soldier entered the tent.

"Of course I'm sure! Oh Emmie, I've missed you so much." He glanced over her with a worried frown, no doubt noting the stains, rips, and dirt on her gown and her tangled, loose hair and the smudges on her face. "What has happened to you?"

At a nod from the first man, the private knelt to untie Emeline. No sooner were her hands free than she fell into her father's arms, receiving his embrace with many tears. Never had she expected such a warm welcome from him. He'd always been so harsh and cold, so disappointed in her.

Nudging her back, he helped her to her feet. "What on earth are you doing here? I thought you were on the *Charlotte.*"

Emeline wiped the moisture from her face. "I was, but we were captured by the British. A Royal Navy frigate. HMS *Marauder.*"

"Captured?" The word seemed to steal the breath from him. In truth, now that she could see him in the lantern light, he looked as though he'd aged ten for the two years she'd been gone. He'd always been a handsome man, stout and well muscled, built like a sturdy ship. But now his light hair was tinged in gray, lines spread out from his eyes and over his forehead, and his thick middle stretched against the gray militia coat he wore.

Wait, militia? "You joined the militia?" She glanced at his insignia. "And a major too!"

"Indeed." One gray eyebrow rose. "But we were talking about you."

"It's a long story, Papa. I need to see General Smith. I have valuable information about an upcoming British attack."

She started for the tent flap, but her father pulled her back, sharing a glance with the sergeant.

"Please, Papa. I was on a British ship for over three weeks. The captain trusted me. There's no time to lose. Oh, and that man with me. Mr. Ryne. He's a British spy."

Her father frowned. "You were traveling alone with a British —" He interrupted himself with a growl before turning to face the sergeant. "Please inform Captain Nifton about Mr. Ryne." After the man saluted and left with the private, her father held out his arm. "Very well, I'll take you to the general. But afterward, I'm getting you some food and you're going to tell me everything. And I mean *everything.*"

Ah, there was that familiar austere tone — the one that said she was in big, big trouble.

Yet a little more than an hour later, after they entered the tent of Major General Samuel Smith and Emeline told him of the British plans to attack Baltimore, both her father's tone and the looks he gave her had changed from those of accusation and dismay to pride and admiration. Coming from her father, the sentiments were so foreign and shocking that she nearly collapsed into a nearby seat.

She did, in fact, lower to sit as the general requested.

"You've no doubt been through quite a harrowing experience, Miss Baratt." General Smith put his hands on the long table before him and leaned forward, his piercing eyes boring into hers. Around the table stood his officers, each one taking in the information she gave with a measure of gravity and appreciation.

The general glanced at the maps spread out before him, his jaw flexing and releasing. Tall, commanding, with graying hair, bushy gray eyebrows, a long face, and a large pointy nose, the man presented an imposing figure. Add to that the intelligence and confidence in his eyes, and Emeline could see why men followed him.

"To the devil with those British. They've taken Washington, but they will not take Baltimore. As God is my witness, we shall defeat these tyrannical mongrels!"

Several hear, hears and huzzahs peppered the air as the general began issuing orders. "Pull all troops from the west and reposition them here on the east side. I want earthworks built along every inch of these eastern hills and batteries with our heaviest guns positioned all along them. Call up every citizen if you have to. Tell them to bring their wheelbarrows, pickaxes, pitchforks, and shovels. Slaves, freemen, rich, poor, I care not." He pointed at the map. "I want it to stretch from Bel Air Road down to Harris Creek, a full mile."

He finally looked up at his officers. "Colonel Harrism," General Smith addressed one of the men. "Contact Major George Armistead at Fort McHenry. I want ships sunk along the North West and Ferry Branches of the Patapsco River and shoreline batteries set up along the banks. They think to take our fort. We'll see about that."

"Yes, General." The man saluted and left, and Emeline couldn't help but feel a sense of patriotism and pride in her country, along with a rabid determination to defeat those who were set on stealing their freedom.

General Smith glanced her way. "Thank you, Miss Baratt. You have done a great service for your country and by all accounts have saved Baltimore from British rule. Now, go and refresh yourself. You've well earned it."

Rising, Emeline allowed her father to lead her to the door, her mind numb and heart soaring at what the general had just said. Her? Rebellious, wild Emeline Baratt had just saved Baltimore? She could hardly believe it. But before they reached the tent flap, her elation had melted into a pool of fear and desperation.

She spun to face him. "General, if you'll permit me a small request."

"Not now, Emmie." Her father attempted to tug her along, but she stood her ground.

"There was an American spy on board HMS *Marauder,*" she blurted out before the general even agreed. "First Lieutenant Owen Masters. He was on this mission with me, but he was discovered and is now in the hands of the British marines awaiting my return. Can you please send a few men with me to rescue him? Also, the crew of Father's ship — all Americans — are still held captive on board the *Marauder*."

The general studied her for a moment, sighed, glanced at his maps, then raised his gaze once again. "I'm sorry, miss. I don't know whether this Masters fellow is on our side or not, but I've never been informed of any spies on board British ships. Besides, I can neither spare the men nor the time for someone I cannot vouch for."

"But I can vouch for him, General. I swear to you. He's not but a mile from here." Emeline dared approach the table, regardless of the intense gazes of the officers telling her to leave and bother them no longer. "It wouldn't take but an hour and two men. He's done a great service for our country, General."

"Emmie!" Her father's steely tone dug into her back, but she would not be silenced.

"And what of the Americans imprisoned on that ship?"

General Smith shook his head. "I'm sorry, miss. Many Americans have been imprisoned on British ships in this war. There is naught I can do about that. My assignment is to defend Baltimore. That is all. I have neither the resources, the time, nor the orders to do anything beyond that singular task." He gestured for her father to take her away. There was no sense in arguing further.

She barely remembered her father leading her to another tent. Neither did she remember him seating her and placing a plate of steaming food before her. Not until he took her hand in his and said grace over the food did she come out of her stupor.

"Papa, I need to help my friends."

An all-too-familiar expression hardened his face — one of disapproval, disappointment, and fear. "Eat, Emmie. You need your strength."

Grabbing the fork, she took a bite and glanced over the tent, well appointed with a desk, chairs, two cots, and several trunks. "Your home?" she asked, savoring the meaty broth and practically inhaling the chunks of meat.

"For now. Yes. I share it with another officer."

"I can't believe you joined the militia, Papa. Before I left for England, you were against war."

He smiled. "Things change. I changed.

The war changed me." He rubbed his chin and studied her. "And you are changed as well — stronger, braver, if that is possible. And more stubborn than ever."

She braced herself for the lecture, the chastisement, but instead he smiled and took a seat beside her. "Tell me of your adventures. When the *Charlotte* didn't arrive on time, I feared the worst."

Emeline took several bites before answering. Finally, after her stomach had settled and wasn't clawing her throat for more, she told him the entire story — from the attack on the *Charlotte* to her time on HMS *Marauder* and then onshore with the Oakes. Finally, she told him about Owen, how he kept her safe, saved her, even when he thought she was his enemy.

While her father pondered what she had said, she finished her meal and thought to lick her bowl. But proper ladies didn't do such things. She pushed it away and awaited her father's criticism of all she'd risked in the past month.

Instead, he took her hands in his and leaned toward her. "You have been through much, Emmie. I'm so proud of you."

"You are?"

"Of course. I would have expected nothing else from you in your situation but to take the most dangerous path." Humor twinkled in his eyes.

"You've never been pleased with that quality of mine before."

"And I'm not still. I'm just glad you're home." He looked down and squeezed her hands.

"Papa, I could still do good for my country. I could rendezvous with the marine waiting for me and Mr. Ryne. I could give him false information about the defenses of Baltimore." And rescue Owen somehow, but she wouldn't tell him that.

"Absolutely not! You've done enough. More than any lady would have done. To send you off into danger again, I won't hear of it." Releasing her hands, he stood and squared his shoulders. "You're home now, Emmie. You can rest and be safe, and when we defeat the British, you can get back to your old life."

Old life? One of following rules, obeying proper etiquette, attending parties and teas, gossiping with other ladies her age while each of them hoped to catch the eye of a wealthy man. At least she'd not have to clean and cook anymore since her father had made his fortune. But in all honesty, she didn't know which was worse.

"Lieutenant Masters saved my life. I owe

him." She lifted her most pleading gaze to him.

"Ah, that's what this is about. You're sweet on this fellow." He cocked a brow and shook his head. "Then I definitely order you not to go." When she looked down, he softened his tone. "Haven't you gotten yourself into enough trouble and danger by your disobedience? You could have been killed, Emmie. This is serious business."

A soldier cleared his throat from outside the tent.

"Yes, what is it?" her father asked.

"The general requests your presence, Major Baratt."

"Very well. Thank you." He faced her again, his expression stern, his eyes daring her to defy him. "Stay here, Emmie. Do not leave this tent. Do you hear? I'll be back soon to take you home. Won't it be good to be home again?"

"Yes. Thank you, Papa."

But she lied. It didn't sound good to her at all. It sounded like another prison. After he left, she found herself pacing up and down the tiny tent, wanting desperately to rescue Owen, but knowing in her heart it was wrong. Wasn't it? Both her father and the general had forbidden her. To be sure, blatantly disobeying one's father wasn't proper behavior. And running off in the middle of the night to rescue a man certainly wasn't proper. Proper ladies stayed home and left such wartime heroics to men. But there wasn't a man to do it. There was only her. She knew the way, and Dimsmore trusted her. How easy would it be to return, tell him Ryne had been killed, give him false information, and then when he wasn't looking, bash him over the head and free Owen?

Easy as convincing her father she could do such a feat.

She plopped down into a chair and dropped her head into her lap. "Lord, help me. Please help me. I want to do the right thing. I want to follow You. I want to behave. But why do all these situations come up in which I am forced not to?" She sighed and rubbed her eyes, weighted with exhaustion.

"Let Me lead you."

The voice came from inside her but not from her mind.

Lord? She looked up but only saw the shifting shadows on the tent cast by the lantern. "I want You to lead me. I do."

A breeze stirred the tent flap and caused the lantern to sputter.

"I have come that you might have an abundant life. Follow Me."

The words stirred a memory . . . something Mrs. Oakes had recited from the Bible. Emeline smiled. How wonderful Clara's life had been. She'd done things most women never dreamed of — living on a ship traveling the West Indies, firing a cannon at pirates. And Hannah, sweet Hannah, had led such a wonderful life, yet she was the godliest woman Emeline had ever known. Both women had told her that being adventurous did not mean she wasn't following God, that in Him was true freedom found. The verse Hannah often quoted traipsed across Emeline's mind: *"Jesus hath made me free from the law of sin and death."* God was all about freedom.

Emeline turned and paced in the other direction. But wasn't freedom from rules a bad thing? Didn't it cause people to make mistakes, sin against God?

"Not if you follow Me."

The voice halted her, made her look around again, question her sanity. Was God speaking to her? But who else could it be? "Have I been wrong all these years?" she said out loud. "Is being a proper Christian lady more about following Jesus, having a relationship with Him, rather than obeying a list of rules and requirements?"

Something inside her leapt for joy as a

breeze stirred the lantern flame into a wild dance. But there was no breeze. The air was still and stagnant, the sounds of men eating and laughing outside muted and distant. Yet the flame leapt and fluttered. Just like her heart.

She gripped her hands together. "Lord, lead me. Tell me what to do, and I'll do it."

CHAPTER 27

"Why don't you just kill me and get it over with, Dimsmore?" Owen winced as the vile man added another rope to the ones already wrapped around his raw, bloody wrists, then cinched them tight.

He forced back a wail of agony. He would not give the man the satisfaction.

Dimsmore chuckled as he retrieved another long piece of rope. "As pleasurable as that would be, Masters, I will not deny myself the joy at watching you hang." He flung it around Owen's chest and tied it behind the tree, then tightened the one already there.

Owen silently cursed himself. He'd come so close to escaping. The fire had gone out and he could hear Dimsmore's snores emanating from the shadowy lump where the man lay just a few yards away.

Owen should have been patient. He should have waited and worked through his ropes a little more. Instead, he had tugged on them with all his strength, hoping they would unravel and snap. But in the process, he made too much noise.

He should have remembered Dimsmore slept like a cat on the prowl. But Owen longed to be free. Another minute longer and he was sure he'd go mad tied up like a hog before slaughter. He needed to get to Baltimore. He longed to protect Emeline, save his country. He couldn't stand doing nothing at all. Worse — not being *able* to do anything. But his rash behavior had once again cost him dearly.

Dimsmore had leapt up like a frog tossed in the fire.

And now Owen's chances at escape drifted away with the breeze stirring the leaves around them.

Dimsmore stood beside him for a moment, and Owen was glad the darkness hid whatever heinous expression was on the man's face. He uttered a string of curses then went to stoke the fire.

Owen gazed up at the stars peeking through the canopy. It had to be well past midnight, and Emeline and Ryne had not returned. That did not bode well for her mission. A dozen horrid scenarios slunk across his mind — the worst being that

Ryne had discovered her loyalties and had been forced to kill her to keep her from revealing his identity. Was the man even capable of doing such a thing? Owen believed he was . . . that he would do anything for his country and to save his own life.

Breathing out a sigh, Owen's heart wilted. He would go mad entertaining such thoughts.

Perhaps he should pray. What could it hurt? He was out of options, and if there was a God, certainly He had the power to help. But would the God most people worshipped even listen — the God his father had worshipped, the one with more rules than the Royal Navy? Yet . . . that was not Ben's God, nor the God Mr. Oakes had spoken about. Their God was a God of love and freedom, a God who relished unconventional adventures. If such a God existed, Owen would pray to Him.

He shifted on the dirt, feeling uncomfortable, then gazed up at the heavens. *God, I don't even know how to pray, but if You're there, please help me. Please be with Emeline. Protect her and keep her safe. Don't let her come back here. Please save my country from tyranny. I'm sorry I've been rebellious. I'm sorry I haven't spoken to You much. But I promise if You protect Emeline and give her a good life, I'll follow You. I will.*

The fire crackled and the mournful sound of a whip-poor-will echoed through the trees. But something else happened. A chill skittered up Owen's back. Not just his back but over his chest and arms. A pleasurable chill, an exciting chill. And along with it, his heart seemed to swell with the oddest sensations — a love and peace he'd never known. It felt almost like acceptance would feel, if Owen had ever felt such a thing . . . acceptance from his Father in heaven. Not the disapproval and rejection Owen was accustomed to receiving from his earthly father.

God?

"What are you smiling at?" Not even Dimsmore's caustic tone diminished the joy and peace flooding Owen. He stared at the marine lieutenant, who suddenly looked somewhat pathetic.

"I believe I've had an encounter with God."

Leaning over, Dimsmore poked the fire and gave a sordid chuckle. "No, but you'll meet Him soon enough."

So this was what Ben and Mr. Oakes meant when they said knowing God was worth it — this feeling of being loved, this sensation of not being alone . . . of everything having a plan and purpose.

Owen bowed his head. *Thank You, Lord.*

"Trust Me."

The words filtered up in his spirit, and he was about to respond that he would, when leaves rustled. Dimsmore grabbed his musket just as Emeline Baratt burst into the clearing. She wore the same stained and ripped gown, her locket swayed over her bodice, twigs and leaves protruded from the tangle of golden curls falling to her waist, her face was flushed, her eyes sparkling . . . and Owen's heart both leapt and sank at the same time.

"Finally." Dimsmore lowered his musket and peered around her. "Where's Ryne?"

Emeline glanced at Owen ever so briefly, but during that second, he spotted a flash of terror cross her eyes.

To her credit, she blew out a sigh and shook her head. "He's dead."

"Dead?" Dimsmore shouted and started for her. "What do you mean, dead?"

"He was shot." Instead of backing away from the man, Emeline lifted a hand to her brow and breathed heavily. "It was horrible, Luther."

It was the first time Owen had heard her use Dimsmore's Christian name. It grated on him more than he could say. But it had the effect the lady no doubt desired, for Dimsmore took her elbow to steady her.

She fell against him, forcing him to wrap an arm around her.

Owen's grating turned to fuming as he watched the man lead her to sit on a log by the fire.

"I'm so sorry, Luther," she said breathlessly, gazing up at him as he went to get her a canteen. Were those real tears in her eyes? Amazing.

"We were heading to Baltimore, almost there, in fact, when shots rang out." Emeline took the canteen and stared at the fire. "I started running, but before long, I noticed Ryne was not beside me." She took a swig of water and handed it back to Dimsmore, who listened intently.

"Another shot rang out, so I kept running. I hid amongst the trees until whoever it was had gone." She glanced at Dimsmore. "But I could swear I saw British uniforms through the foliage. They must have thought we were Americans."

Dimsmore frowned, rubbed the back of his neck, and took up a pace before the fire.

"When I went back to find Ryne, he was . . . he was . . ." Emeline swallowed and hugged herself.

"It's all right, Miss Baratt." Dimsmore

dropped beside her. "Mr. Ryne knew the risks. Did you make it to Baltimore? Did you get the information we need?"

"Indeed, I did, Lieutenant. I have a great deal to tell Captain Blackwell. Valuable information Admiral Cockburn will want to know."

"Good." Dimsmore slapped his knee and rose. "So they believed you?"

Emeline offered Owen a quick smile while Dimsmore wasn't looking. "They did, indeed. I encountered many people who knew me years ago. Hence, it was of little consequence for them to allow me to wander about their headquarters and assess the number of troops and armament and where everything is positioned."

"Hmm." The first hint of suspicion appeared on Dimsmore's face. "America must be more barbaric than I thought to allow a lady to run about a military camp unescorted."

Emeline acted indignant. "I was not without escort. They assigned an officer to accompany me while I searched for my father. At least that was the excuse I used."

"Your father?"

"Yes, they told me he had joined the militia." Emeline clasped her hands in front of her.

"Did you find him?" Dimsmore directed a pointed gaze at her.

Still she didn't balk. In fact, her tone became sharp. "If you mean, did I reunite with him and my friends and reassess my loyalties, no I did not. Would I be here otherwise?"

Dimsmore's lips flattened. "I suppose not." He released a heavy sigh. "Very good then. We will leave at first light. With some luck, we will make it to the rendezvous point by sundown." He sneered at Owen. "Then you'll get your just dues. And you, Miss Baratt" — he smiled sweetly at her — "will be the heroine of the day."

She returned his smile. "Surely you will be a hero as well, Luther."

He rubbed his hands together. "I cannot deny this will be good for my career. Especially should your information win us this war."

"What about him?" She gestured toward Owen. "Since it is just you and me now, will he give us any trouble on the way there?"

"Don't worry about him, miss. I will ensure your safety."

She turned toward Owen, her face away from Dimsmore. "Traitor!" she shouted at him, but then winked.

He wanted to shout at the foolish lady. What sort of game did she think she was playing? If Ryne was gone and she had told the Americans the British plans, why had she returned? He could only think of one reason. And that one reason both elated him and made him steam with fury.

She'd come back for him.

"What in the name of every Royal Navy ship do you think you are doing?"

Emeline hadn't expected Owen to be completely overjoyed to see her, but she had expected some kindness, perhaps a modicum of appreciation. Certainly not the fury she was seeing now reddening his face and seething in his voice.

"I'm rescuing you of course," she retorted as she inched a bit closer to him on the dirt. One glance over her shoulder told her Dimsmore was still off relieving himself.

"We don't have much time to talk. Oh Owen . . . your wrists." Even in the dim light of the fire she could see the blood saturating the ropes around his hands.

"It's nothing. You should have stayed away." He scowled. A rather handsome scowl, if she were to say. How wonderful to see him! Even if he was filthy and bruised and tied to a tree. Blood stained his linen shirt and dribbled over his waistcoat, and his hair hung about his face like a wild savage. But just seeing him made her heart soar. He was alive and in one piece, and that was enough for her.

She leaned toward him. "This is the plan."

"There is no plan. Go home, Emeline. Live a happy life. Forget about me."

"Don't be absurd. I'll do no such thing. Dimsmore trusts me. I'll get his gun, free you, and we'll both return to Baltimore."

"*If* you can get his gun. I don't think he completely trusts you."

"It'll work, Owen. You'll see."

"Madcap woman! Please leave while you can."

"I love you, Owen." She clutched his face between her hands and dared to kiss him. She intended just a short peck for re-assurance, but the look in his eyes and the taste of him lured her to stay longer than she should. He kissed her back, but only for a moment . . . a moment too short before he nudged her away, urging her to leave with a terrified look.

As it was, Dimsmore returned just as she repositioned herself on the log, ignoring the low growl coming from Owen. Stubborn man. Would he leave *her* to hang as a trai-tor? She thought not. Besides, she'd clearly sensed the Lord leading her to rescue him. It had been more than her own desire to do so. It had been a strong urging, a sense of peace that all would be well. So she had started off on her first God-led adventure. She would do her part, and God would do His.

At least she hoped that's how it worked.

But morning came, and no matter how much she begged Dimsmore for a pistol or even a knife, citing her fear of being attacked again in the woods, he would not relent.

"I'll protect, you, Miss Baratt. You have naught to worry about." His shoulders rose and a smear of desire in his eyes caused nausea to brew in her stomach.

She offered him a sweet smile that nearly forced that nausea out of her mouth.

"Very well. Thank you for your chivalry. I am indebted, Luther."

She exchanged a glance with Owen as Dimsmore released him from the tree, and he gave her an I-told-you-so look that made her frown.

One way or another, she would get a weapon. She had a full day's journey during which to do so. If she had to, she'd resort to flirting with the beast, encouraging him, complimenting him . . . whatever it took.

Either way, she would not allow Owen to step foot on the HMS *Marauder.*

By noon, Emeline's feet ached, her throat was parched, her dress torn even more than before, and she was no closer to getting a weapon from Dimsmore than she'd been that morning. She'd given him no reason to mistrust her. She'd not once spoken to Owen, nor even looked at him. At least not when Dimsmore could see. Plenty when he could not. Even with his hands tied behind his back, Owen exuded strength and fortitude. It wouldn't take much for him to charge Dimsmore and knock him over then stomp him unconscious.

Dimsmore must have realized the danger, for he forced Owen to lead and then hung back a few yards with an ever-present pistol pointed at Owen's back. If Owen dared to try anything, he'd be dead on the spot.

Aside from the pistol in his hand, Dimsmore had a musket swung over his shoulder, a long knife tucked in his belt, and a smaller knife beside it.

Emeline must get one of those. Preferably the pistol, but the cretin never let it go. Even now, as he shoved Owen to the dirt and tied his ankles together, he set it down for only a minute.

Emeline lowered to sit in the shade of a maple tree for a much-needed rest as Dimsmore approached and handed her a piece of dried meat.

She thanked him and motioned him to sit beside her. Smiling at the invitation, he did so, much too close for her comfort, but perfect for her plan.

The poor man seemed to have suffered terribly out in the wilderness for nearly a week. A stubbly beard had grown over his smooth jaw, dirt smudged across his cheek, and his wavy dark hair hung limp about his face, but his blue eyes were as empty as always. "I'm sorry to force you to endure such a rapid pace, Miss Baratt. It is most unseemly for a lady, and I'm sure you are beyond exhausted."

"I am, but I'm anxious to get my information to the captain."

"A true patriot. I am pleased to see it." He bit off a piece of the meat. "Do you know I once suspected you of being an American spy?"

She feigned a hearty laugh. "Me? My word, Luther, you do tease me."

She glanced at Owen, who seemed ready to burst his binds. She wanted to ask Dimsmore to give him some food and water but dared not.

He handed her the canteen, and she drank freely.

"You are a remarkable woman, Miss Baratt."

"Please, call me Emeline."

"Emeline. I also thought you and Lieutenant Masters were sweet on each other."

She laughed again. "Absurd! Though he did pursue me — relentlessly and obnoxiously, I might add — I knew something was not quite right about him."

"I did warn you on board the *Marauder,* did I not?"

"You did. I should have listened. I must admit he had me quite fooled." She released a long sigh. "Who knew he was such a swaggering coxcomb?"

"Precisely! Well said, Miss Baratt. My sentiments exactly." Dimsmore swung a loathsome glance toward Owen. "Tsk-tsk. I believe you have made our traitor mad."

A ray of sunshine speared the canopy and glimmered over the knife in his belt, prompting Emeline to stand. "We should delay no further, Luther. We have a bit of a distance to traverse before dark."

"Very well, if you're rested enough. I worry about your fragile nature."

She wanted to give him a dose of that fragile nature. Instead she sidled next to him, spotted a rock in their path, and purposely tripped over it. Now if the numskull would only catch her.

He did. Not only caught her, but he took advantage of the opportunity to squeeze her against him. His breath puffed over her face, all pungent and sour.

"Get your hands off her!" Owen shouted with a growl.

Perfect timing, for it distracted Dimsmore just enough for Emeline to pluck the smaller knife from his belt.

"Shut it, Masters!" Dimsmore said. "You aren't in charge anymore."

Sliding the knife into her skirt pocket, Emeline pushed from him. "Forgive me, Luther. I must have tripped."

His smile returned. "No trouble at all."

They started out again across a field of tall grass waving in the breeze, Owen in front, Dimsmore behind, and Emeline beside him. A burst of wind brought the scent of distant rain, marshland, and the sea to her nose but did little to cool the sweat gluing her gown to her skin.

Slipping her hand in her pocket, she felt the knife. The blade was no longer than six inches. What was she supposed to do with this? She couldn't very well hold Dimsmore at knifepoint with so small a blade. He'd only laugh at her. If she stabbed him from behind, she would have to hit a vital organ, something that would debilitate him or kill him quickly, or he'd shoot both her and Owen before he bled out.

That was, even if she had the strength or the courage to stab a man.

Oh Lord, help. I need Your help.

They entered another copse of trees. For once, Dimsmore was quiet and didn't annoy her with his incessant conversation. Even so, he still glanced her way now and then with a predatory smile. Squirrels darted across the path; lizards scrambled over logs. Off in the distance the quack of ducks could be heard. Thankfully, the path narrowed, and Emeline slipped behind him.

That's when she saw it. A good-sized piece of wood, not too heavy for her to pick up, but plenty substantial for her to knock Dimsmore unconscious.

Her heart beat like a tambourine in her chest. Could she do such a thing? Leaning over, she snagged the wood as they passed and held it behind her skirt.

It was now or never. She may not have another opportunity to walk behind him. She hated the thought of hurting another human being, even Dimsmore. But Owen's life was at stake, and there was naught to be done for it.

Lord, forgive me.

Hefting the wooden club in the air, she aimed it at Dimsmore's head and gathered her strength to swing with all her might.

"Lieutenant Dimsmore?" The question came from ahead of them, clanging through the woods like a ship bell announcing a change in watch.

Dimsmore cocked his gun and pointed it over Owen's shoulder. "Who wants to know?"

Instantly, the red uniforms of three royal marines emerged from the greenery to surround them.

Emeline let the wood slip from her hand.

CHAPTER 28

Dimsmore shoved Owen — yet again — to the ground. This time into the moist sand lining the shore of Bird River.

"Don't move a muscle, Masters!" he ordered. "If you do, I'll be more than happy to shoot you."

"I wouldn't dare deprive you of watching me hang." Owen smiled up at him, though he was sure his expression was lost on the man. Darkness had fallen hours ago, draping a black curtain over the landscape and thus impeding their progress.

Now, at the rendezvous point, the marines busied themselves lighting a torch in order to signal the cockboat that would be waiting at the tip of the peninsula for their return. Dimsmore joined them while Emeline dropped to her knees before the river and splashed water over her face.

She glanced at Owen, but he couldn't make out her expression.

All through the long trek, Emeline uttered not a single complaint, as usual. Not a groan or a sigh or even a stumble. Though he could tell she was distraught over the arrival of the marines. No doubt whatever foolish plan she'd concocted had dissipated upon their arrival. Just as well. He couldn't have tolerated watching her get hurt, caught, or worse. Who knew what risks the impulsive woman would have taken? This way at least she was safe.

Owen's feet ached, and he was thirstier than a fish in a desert, but the worst part of the journey had been watching Emeline flirt with Dimsmore and seeing the way he looked at her — as he had so often looked at women on their many shore leaves in England — like a starving man looked upon a feast he was about to devour.

If he touched her . . . if he laid one finger on her . . . Owen strained against the ropes binding his hands. Not that he was in any position to do much about it. Which was the worst thing of all.

Behind him, trees stood like dark sentinels. Before him, the river spread out like shimmering ink, barely perceptible save for the rhythmic lap of waves. Dark clouds had moved in to blot out the stars. The sting of rain filled his nose. Appropriate weather for his last hours in the open air.

As far as he could see it, his fate was sealed. He'd be brought on board, have to face the captain and Ben with his guilt, get locked in irons, and then be tossed in the hold for who knew how long before his trip back to England. Once at Portsmouth, he'd be court-martialed and hanged. Not a pleasant prospect.

Yet oddly, his concern was more for Emeline. Yes, she'd be treated well on board the *Marauder,* but how would she ever escape? After the war, she'd be brought back to England where, he now knew, she had no family, no way to survive. Even worse, on the long journey across the pond, she'd be at Dimsmore's mercy with no one to protect her.

He struggled against his ropes yet again, ignoring the pain, but to no avail. Still, hope anchored in his heart. He was no longer alone. God was with him. He knew that, could feel it deep within his spirit. God had the power to either free him or to leave him in prison. But either way, Owen felt freer than he'd ever felt before.

Dimsmore snapped angrily at one of the marines, his bitter tone echoing over the sand. Finally, they lit one of the torches, and Dimsmore turned and scowled toward

Owen. The flickering light twisted his features into a maniacal grin of victory. But instead of anger, Owen felt pity for the man. As he stared at him, he saw a vision of himself in ten years, selfish, self-serving, lustful, greedy . . . and the image made him sick to his stomach. A slave to sin. A slave to self. He could see now how it only led to ugliness and misery in the end.

Emeline glanced at the men standing a few yards off, then rose and inched toward Owen. Halting a short distance away, she knelt before the water again, busying herself by pretending to wash her hands.

"Owen, I'm going to rescue you. I have a plan."

Owen would growl if it wouldn't draw attention their way. "Forget your plan and leave right now." He gestured with his head toward the forest. "While they aren't looking."

"I won't leave you."

"I order you to leave me!" he seethed out in a whisper.

She laughed. "You have no authority over me. Not yet."

It was the *not yet* that made his heart lurch. In a good way. But she couldn't have meant . . . Owen shook his head. "Please, Emeline."

She shook her hands over the water then rubbed them on her skirts. "Jump overboard."

"That's your plan? Are you mad?"

She gazed over the river. "When we are halfway to the ship, jump, and pull me over with you."

Every ounce of Owen stiffened in rebellion. "You can't swim."

"But *you* can."

"Not with ropes on my hands."

"I have a knife." She patted her skirts. "Pull me over, and I'll cut through them."

He wanted to laugh, wanted to shout, wanted to scream. Instead, he whispered in his most calm voice. "So, somehow you cut through my ropes in the dark water while we are holding our breath and floating toward the bottom of the bay, and then we gracefully swim to shore? Is that your crazy plan?"

"Perhaps not gracefully, but yes, exactly," she returned as if making plans for tea.

"Insanity."

"It's the only way."

"What if we get separated?"

"That's why you are going to hang on to me."

"They'll see us."

"It's dark and about to rain. We stay under

the water as long as possible."

"I won't. I won't risk your life. You'll be safe on board the *Marauder*."

"Perhaps, but a prisoner nonetheless. Besides, *you* will not be safe, and that is my main concern. I intend to jump. So if you want to live, jump with me."

"Miss Baratt!" Dimsmore's nasally voice made her leap as the man headed her way. "Don't get too close to him. He's more dangerous than you realize."

"Of course." She stood and made her way toward Dimsmore. "I was simply freshening up. He said not a word."

"Good." Dimsmore took her arm and drew her toward the marines, who finally had a second torch glowing brightly.

Releasing a heavy sigh, Owen bowed his head. "Please, God, tame this wild woman. Don't allow her to follow through with this foolhardy plan, or I fear we will both end up dead."

Emeline waded through the cool water beside Dimsmore and took his outstretched hand as he helped her into the wobbly boat. He'd offered to carry her, but she'd declined politely, using the excuse that her sore feet would welcome the cool moisture. Five sailors were already seated in the craft, oars at the ready, while Owen sat on the forward thwart between two of them.

Fear cinched tight around her heart.

That would never do. He must be as close to the side of the boat as possible. How would he get past an armed marine, grab her, and dive into the water? No matter. They would figure it out. She started toward him, hoping to sit as close to him as possible.

Dimsmore stepped in beside her, rocking the boat and nearly toppling her over. He caught her by the arm. "No, Miss Baratt. Sit back here with me where it's safe." He all but yanked her to the center thwart, a good four feet from Owen, where he sat and dragged her down beside him.

Desperation opened the door for fear to flood her heart. But she would not give up hope. There must be a way. God would make a way. Besides, surely things could get no worse.

As one of the remaining two marines hopped on board, Dimsmore rose, grabbed some rope, made his way to Owen, and knelt to tie his feet together at the ankles.

"Just in case you get some half-cocked idea to jump overboard. I know you're a good swimmer."

Apparently, yes, things *could* get worse.

Emeline exchanged a glance with Owen. Even in the darkness, she saw him shake his head, warning her not to go through with her plan.

"Shove off! Oars in the water," Dimsmore shouted, and the last marine pushed the boat from the sand and hopped on board.

Emeline shifted in her seat. True, the binds around his feet complicated things. They kept him from swimming at all until she could slice through them.

But she wasn't alone. God had led her to rescue Owen, and God would see it through. Wouldn't He? She had to believe that.

"We'll be safe on board HMS *Marauder* soon, Miss Baratt." Dimsmore laid a hand on her knee, but she quickly shifted from beneath his touch. *The scoundrel!*

Lanterns at fore and aft of the boat lit their way down the river as the *splash-gush* of the oars increased and sped them on their way. Each slap of the paddles in the water landed straight on Emeline's heart, causing it to pinch with fear at what she knew she must do.

Thunder growled its disapproval of her plan.

Rain splattered over the boat, the thwarts, and created dots over the black water of the bay. Yet after hiking for days in the heat with no bath, she had to admit, it felt heavenly. What didn't feel heavenly was the sight of HMS *Marauder* coming into view in the distance — rising like a monster from the deep, its jaws of death open to receive them.

She wondered how Hannah and the other Americans were doing. If only she could get back on board and help them escape. But without Owen's help and no other ally on the ship, that would be nigh impossible. Not to mention that allowing Owen back on board would seal his death. She forced back sorrow at the thought that her friends would have to stay there a little longer, but she would find another way to rescue them later. With God's help of course.

She glanced over her shoulder at the retreating mass of land. This would be the best time — close enough to land to swim but far enough away so Dimsmore's marines wouldn't dive in after them. She glanced over their faces in the shifting shadows of light and dark. How many of them could swim? The odds were not many, if any at all.

Owen once again shook his head at her. Did he not have faith in her, in God?

Her palms tingled with excitement. Her legs trembled.

It was now or never.

Emeline leapt to her feet. "American gunboat!" she shouted and pointed into the darkness. Then spreading her feet slightly apart, she began rocking the boat.

"Where?" Dimsmore tried to tug her down.

"Over there! I saw it. I saw cannons pointed our way!" She raised her voice into a hysterical pitch as she kept jarring the boat back and forth.

"Douse the lantern! Oars halt!"

Instantly everything went black. The oars no longer splashed in the water as they glided along. Only the *tap, tap* of rain accompanied the deadly silence.

Emeline screamed, "They're going to kill us!"

"Calm yourself, Miss Baratt." Dimsmore rose and reached for her, but she jumped from his grip and started toward Owen.

She tripped over something hard. Ignoring the pain shooting up her leg, she shoved marines out of the way. From behind her, Dimsmore kept calling her name. A marine gripped her arm, but someone thrust him aside, grabbed her by the fabric of her gown, and pushed her.

Thunder shook sky and sea. Her feet met air. Inhaling a big breath, she plunged into the bay. Owen's grip was tight on her gown.

Water surrounded them, muting all commotion above. Thunder rumbled again, but it sounded distant and muted. Rain tapped on the surface above them.

In an instant, she had the knife in her hand and felt her way to his hands.

But they both kept going down . . . sinking farther and farther beneath the waves. Light from a lantern shone above. Shouts seemed to come from within a dream. There — the ropes. Her lungs ached. Gripping the knife as tight as she could, she began slicing through the binds. Owen tried to stay still. Or maybe he was dead. She couldn't bear it if he died because of her!

Her lungs cried out. And still they drifted down . . . down into the murky darkness. She could no longer hear the shouts above or the patter of rain.

Would they both die here below?

She sliced some more, wanting to cry, wanting to scream. Memories passed through her frenzied mind of that morning on the *Charlotte* when she'd thought about jumping overboard and what it would feel like to sink beneath the waves. How far she'd come since then.

Lord, help. I don't want to die. I want to live! I want to live for You. And with this man You have given me.

Finally, the ropes gave. Owen grabbed her by the waist then took the knife. She felt him bending to cut the binds on his feet.

Her lungs were going to give out. *Pain! Pain!* She had no idea drowning would be so painful.

But she was with the man she loved. And God was with them both.

It would be over in a minute. Then they'd both be in heaven together . . . what a wonderful idea. She smiled even as her lungs gave out.

CHAPTER 29

No! Terror and agony ripped Owen's heart into shreds. He was taking too long with the ropes, could feel Emeline's body relax in his arms . . . heard bubbles flee her lungs out of her mouth. *No!* With a final snap of the knife, his feet were free. Clutching Emeline, he swam with every ounce of his strength through the cold water. He might as well have been wading through molasses, pushing aside globs of sticky goo, for all the progress he made. His own lungs revolted, threatened to explode . . . threatened to end it all for them both. When finally . . .

He broke the surface and heaved gulp after gulp of life-giving air. Rain pelted his face. He shoved Emeline's head above water, slapped her face. Nothing. Her forehead lobbed against his cheek, heavy as a cannonball.

From the distance, Dimsmore's angry shouts trumpeted through the rain. Oars slapped the water. Thunder bellowed. Lantern light bobbed in the darkness, heading their way.

And Owen swam. He swam with all his might, keeping Emeline's head above water and praying like he never had prayed before. Finally, his feet struck rock, then a bed of pebbles, then sand. He stood and dragged Emeline's lifeless body ashore, then collapsed to his knees beside her, his breath heaving so hard it made a wheezing sound. *No!*

"Emeline!" He shook her. Nothing. He didn't know what to do. *Lord, help!* Then he remembered. A few years back, a young sailor had fallen overboard on the *Marauder.* When they'd rescued him and brought him on deck, he wasn't breathing. The surgeon did something to him, brought him back to life. But what?

Owen flipped Emeline over onto her stomach. "Sorry, love," he said before pounding hard on her back with the heel of his hand. *Pound, pound, pound!*

Rain poured down upon them as if God Himself were crying.

No! Pound, pound, pound!

"They've got to be here somewhere. Masters can swim!" Dimsmore's voice grew nearer. Owen glanced over his shoulder.

Lantern light undulated over the dark water.

Pound, pound, pound!

Emeline coughed. Owen stood and hoisted her up, bending her at the waist.

She coughed again and water poured from her mouth.

"Thank You, Lord," Owen breathed out.

"I heard something. Over there!" Dimsmore shouted.

Emeline heaved in air and collapsed in his arms. "Owen!"

One glance back at the water revealed the lights were closer — just yards from the shore. "Shh," was all he said as he picked her up and plunged into the forest. The *tap, tap* of rain on the leaves clapped for him, urging him on.

But they weren't out of danger yet.

Diving behind a thick shrub, Owen gently lowered Emeline to the wet ground and peered through the greenery.

A circle of golden light appeared on the shore where they'd just been. The shape of the cockboat slithered behind it.

Owen readied himself to pick up Emeline and run.

"Not here, sir. They've no doubt drowned. Both of them."

Dimsmore cursed. Lightning flashed on his angry, distorted features. "Back to the

Marauder!"

Owen sank to the ground and gathered Emeline in his arms. Their breaths came hard and fast, mingling in the air between them. He kissed her forehead, unable to truly believe they were safe at last.

She started to laugh . . . a weak laugh, to be sure, but a laugh nonetheless. "I told you it would work," she finally said between raspy breaths.

Owen hugged her tight and leaned his chin on her head. "Crazy woman. I thought you were dead. You scared me to death."

"Scared the great adventurer Owen Masters?" Her tone was teasing as she pushed back and looked at him, though he could not see her expression.

"Indeed, I believe I have finally found something that frightens me more than anything." He wiped wet strands of hair from her face. "Losing you."

"Oh Owen. I love you so much." She fell against his chest. "God was with us. He told me to come rescue you."

Owen chuckled and rubbed her back. "He did, did He? But yes, I quite agree. God was with us."

"You believe now?"

"Let's just say God and I have made our peace, and I'm discovering He's quite different than I imagined Him to be."

"I have discovered the same."

Moments passed as the rain continued to serenade them and the distant sounds of the cockboat drifted upon Dimsmore's fading curses. Despite their soaked attire and the chill, Owen wished he could stay hidden in the forest with Emeline in his arms forever.

But there was a war to be won.

Emeline must have been thinking the same thing, for she pushed from him. Her hand touched his jaw, her fingers sliding down the stubble. "Are we really safe? I can hardly believe it."

"Yes." He took her hand in his and placed a kiss upon it. "I'll always protect you, Emeline."

"Seems to me I'm the one who rescued you." Her tone was playful.

"Rescued me? If not for me, you'd be at the bottom of the bay."

"If not for me —"

Owen took a guess at where her lips were and silenced her with a kiss. It seemed that was the only way to win an argument with this precious lady.

Was it possible to be soaked to the skin, sitting in a cold, wet forest, but feel as warm as if sitting before a fire? Emeline discovered that it was indeed possible as Owen kissed her with more passion and love than she ever dreamed existed. Even more than the last time he'd kissed her — the time that had sent her senses soaring into the heights. Yet this kiss held more promise, more love, and she grew heady with the sensations. She didn't want him to ever stop, would have been content to remain hidden in a bush and kiss him forever. But he pulled away, drew her to her feet, and insisted they head back to Baltimore posthaste.

Hours later after the sun had long since risen, they trudged along the sodden ground. They'd been walking all day, but it had been quite a different trek than the day before. The day before, Emeline had been terrified and desperate, loathing Dimsmore's company and conversation. Today, despite their rush, her time with Owen had been filled with laughter, teasing, engaging conversation, and more love than she'd ever felt. They'd walked most of the time hand in hand, sharing dreams and hopes and stories from their past.

She didn't care that her gown was torn and covered in mud, that her hair hung in filthy strands to her waist, or that her feet hurt and her stomach groveled for a mere ounce of food. She cared about none of those things while this man was by her side.

Twice they stopped by a creek to drink. Twice they kissed, and twice they prayed together for God to save America.

Yet now, their time together was coming to an end. They'd be in Baltimore within minutes. For some reason, the thought saddened Emeline as she cast one last glance toward Owen. He'd long since lost his cocked hat, freeing his dark hair to blow in the breeze behind him. Still wet, his stained linen shirt clung to his body, as did his breeches. But he might as well have been wearing kingly garb for the way he held his head high, stretched his shoulders wide, and stomped through the mud as if he owned the world.

He looked at her, his hazel eyes brimming with love. Slipping his hand in hers, they proceeded forward, when suddenly, he halted.

"What is it?"

"Shh." He placed a finger on her lips. But it was too late; the barrels of three muskets emerged from the trees.

"Halt or we'll shoot!" one of the soldiers said.

American soldiers. Emeline breathed a sigh of relief.

"We're Americans," Owen returned. Even so, he slid his hands in the air.

Emeline was far too weary to do the same. "Take us to General Smith at once." She surprised herself at her commanding tone. But it did the trick.

An hour later, she and Owen stood in General Smith's tent.

"This is the man I told you about, General. I can vouch for him."

General Smith rose from his chair and approached Owen. "I am sending word today to this uncle of yours in DC. Hopefully, he's still alive."

"That is my hope as well." Owen nodded as General Smith directed his attention to Emeline.

"Your information aided us greatly, Miss Baratt. The Committee of Vigilance and Safety divided all nonmilitary males into four labor districts to work day and night on the earthworks along the city's eastern hills. Now we have strong batteries with heavy guns guarding our Eastern Heights. We've proclaimed martial law as well and have recruited women to help with the wounded and roll bandages."

"What of Fort McHenry?" Owen asked.

The general studied him for a moment before proceeding. "We've sunk twenty-four schooners, brigs, and ships across the North West and Ferry Branches. Also, I'm positioning a fleet of twelve small, one-gun boats in the North West Branch with 360 men."

He pointed at the map spread across the table. "We have seamen and marines on the sloop of war *Erie* and also on our frigates *Java* and *Guerriere*. I'm assigning two hundred gunners up on the range of hills rising from the north edge of Inner Harbor and parallel to Fort McHenry."

Emeline didn't know much about military strategy, but the plans seemed good to her. Owen must have agreed because he crossed his arms over his chest, studied the map, and then nodded. "I believe you've done all you can, General."

The general rubbed his eyes. "You have told me what you know of their armament and troops. Now, tell me, young man, do we stand a chance against them?"

Owen nodded. "With God's help, aye, sir, I believe we do." Though Emeline could tell from his voice, he wasn't so sure. "In the meantime, I want to fight," Owen added. "I've been too long on the enemy's side."

The flap opened and in rushed Emeline's father.

"Emmie!" He flew into her arms, gave her a tight squeeze, but then pushed her back.

"You will be the death of me, child! Are you ever going to listen to my orders?"

"I'm sorry to disobey you, Papa. I had to go get my friend. This is Owen Masters."

Her father barely afforded Owen a glance. "You had me worried sick. I should have known you would go and assigned a guard to watch over you." He glanced up at General Smith, as if just realizing he was there. "Forgive me, sir."

The general smiled. "No need, Major. I have children . . . daughters, in fact."

Emeline's father chuckled, then finally focused on Owen, sizing him up from head to toe. "So, you're the man my Emmie risked her life to save. I hope you won't be a disappointment."

To his credit, Owen returned his firm stare without so much as a flinch. In fact, a slow smile curved his lips as he said, "You've got quite an incredible daughter, sir." He glanced at Emeline. "With your permission, I'd like to marry her."

Emeline's legs turned to mush. She stumbled, and Owen reached out to steady her. "That is, if she'll have me."

The look in his eyes told her he was quite serious. She wanted to scream, shout, cry! Had she heard him correctly? "I'll more than have you," she breathed out in a chuckle.

Her father fingered the bristle on his chin. General Smith laughed.

"I'll tell you what, Mr. Masters," Emeline's father said. "You help us kick the British back to England, and I just might let you have her." He huffed and grinned her way. "Though I'm not sure you realize the trouble you'll be getting."

"Oh, I realize it, sir." Owen winked at her, but the love and desire in his eyes nearly melted her on the spot. He faced the general. "What do you say, General? Can I join the fight?"

"We'd be honored to have you," the general said. "Major Baratt, get this man a weapon and assign him a post. In fact, put him under General Stricker."

Emeline's breath caught. "Isn't he leading the troops at the front?"

"Yes, he'll lead the first advance." General Smith cocked a brow at Owen. "If your man wants to do the most damage, that's where he should be."

Owen smiled. "Indeed. I wouldn't have it any other way."

Emeline's father faced her with one of his stern looks. "Now, you go home. Clean yourself up, and get some rest. Please. And pray while you're at it." He gave her a look that said he doubted she'd do any of that.

The praying she did. The resting? She was sure God had more important things for her to do. But she did go home as ordered, where she bathed, donned a new gown, and slept for a few hours. First thing in the morning, she was back on the front lines, where she joined the other women helping to feed and supply the soldiers and prepare the hospital to receive the injured.

She did not see Owen or her father the entire day, nor during the long night, but she did maintain a constant prayer for them and for Baltimore and her country.

The British landed at North Point the next day with more than four thousand men, the scouts reported. The fighting started soon after, and though she longed to grab a musket and join the battle, Emeline retreated a slight distance to pray and to help with the wounded as they began to pour in. The first day lagged on, her prayers serenaded by the peppering sound of gunfire, the thunder of cannons, the squawk of bugles, and the shouts and screams of men. By the time the sun set, twenty-four Americans were dead and over a hundred were wounded.

Then the rain began. Relentless, pounding, pummeling rain that transformed the militia camp into a lake and the tents into sieves. She and the other women did their best to tend the wounded in the nearby hospital, all while General Smith sent men out to fell trees to block the British advance.

Sometime just before dawn, distant cannons woke Emeline from a fitful sleep where she'd sat down just an hour earlier in a chair by a patient. A soldier ran inside the hospital and announced that the British were attacking Fort McHenry.

Leaning forward, Emeline dropped her head in her hands and continued her prayers. Thankfully, dawn's light revealed a sopping wet landscape, drenched soldiers, but no British troops. Emeline stood by the door of the hospital, cup of hot tea in hand, and stared into the distant trees, longing for a glimpse of Owen, praying he was well and in one piece.

All during the day, the shelling continued over Fort McHenry, reminding them every few minutes that the British had not given up. The constant whine and boom of rockets set everyone on edge.

And still it rained, as if God were trying to stop the madness with a deluge from heaven.

The enemy arrived late that afternoon and halted in the distance, a line of red and gray like an advancing thundercloud of fire. Emeline braced herself for the onslaught, but as darkness shoved the day away, the British still had not fired a single shot. Could it be they were deterred by the twenty thousand men and hundred cannons General Smith had positioned in their way? Emeline could only hope, for that was the last defense before they marched into Baltimore.

Whatever the reason for the delay in their advance, they camped for the night. Emeline watched their campfires spark the landscape like fireflies on a summer night.

And still the rockets bombarded the fort.

Between prayers and attending to the wounded, Emeline managed to catch a few hours of sleep.

She awoke a little after dawn on September 14th, not due to an attack or the blaring sound of cannon fire, but due to silence — pure, peaceful silence. Even the rain had stopped.

Rubbing her eyes, she dashed from the hospital, shielded her gaze from the rising sun, and glanced toward the earthworks. The British troops were gone.

Huzzahs and cheers blared from the American camp.

She darted toward them and grabbed the

first soldier she passed. "What's happening?"

"The British are retreating, miss. They could not take Fort McHenry. Our flag still flies!"

A band of soldiers joined him, raising their muskets in the air. "Long live America. Long live our republic!" they cheered as they continued onward.

Emeline dropped to her knees in the mud and lifted her hands to heaven. "Praise You, Father. Thank You!"

That's when she saw him. Owen, black blotches on his face, muddy streaks on his shirt, and a bloodied bandage around his arm, walking with musket in hand alongside a band of troops.

His gaze scanned the camp in search of something . . . or someone. He spotted her and halted. The men he walked with moved on, leaving him standing there staring at her. Moments passed, yet somehow they didn't — as if time stood still.

She smiled. He ran. She dashed toward him. They fell together, embracing, kissing, laughing.

"We won, Owen. We won!"

Holding her face in his hands, he said, "God won. And now we are free."

"Free, indeed!"

CHAPTER 30

Two days later . . .

"Permission to come aboard, Captain."
Emeline stood on the wharf just off Thames
Street and admired the graceful lines of her
father's two-masted schooner. She admired
other graceful lines as well when her eyes
landed on Owen, standing amidships in his
breeches, boots, open-collared shirt, and
cocked hat. She had thought him handsome
in his lieutenant's uniform, then even more
so as an American pioneer, but this? A
privateer captain? Oh my. Well, if she was
the swooning type . . .

With a grin to melt a glacier, Owen approached the gangplank and held out a
hand. "Permission granted, my lady. But it
is as much your schooner as mine."

Clutching her skirts, she allowed him to
lead her aboard, though she needed no help.
After six weeks on the *Charlotte* and a
month on board the *Marauder,* she'd grown

quite proficient at balancing on a shifting deck.

Two sailors emerged from below, sailcloth and rope in hand. After tipping their hats her way, they went about their work.

Emeline admired the schooner once again. Plain bow without a gammon knee, a square tuck stern and outside rudder steered with a tiller. On deck, a large hatchway opened between the masts, a capstan aft, and a windlass abaft the foremast. She had easy lines with rounded bilges, and her masts held a square-sail yard, a topsail yard, and a royal yard. Even as Emeline noticed all that, she realized how much she'd learned of ships the past few months. "I can't believe my father gave this to us. She's a beauty."

"Yes, she is *quite* a beauty."

By the tone of his voice, she could tell he wasn't talking about the schooner. When she raised her gaze to his, the look in his eyes set every inch of her on fire.

Were they really getting married that night?

As if reading her mind, he ran a finger down her cheek. "I can't wait."

Lowering her lashes, she stepped aside. "Well, Captain, you shall have to — at least for a few more hours."

"And here I thought you never wished to

be imprisoned in marriage." He arched a brow.

She frowned and tapped a finger on her lips. "You're right. What am I thinking?" She let out a heavy sigh. "Well, I suppose it depends on whether you intend to keep me chained to the stove with a swarm of wee ones nipping at my heels."

"Chained to the stove? No, I have better plans for you." His eyes twinkled with desire before he shrugged and smiled. "But as for the wee ones, well, I was hoping we could have a ship full."

Emeline was sure her face had turned the color of a Maryland apple. "Why, Captain. Such talk before the wedding."

"You do want children, do you not?"

She eased beside him and threaded her fingers in his. "If it's a ship full you want, it is a ship full I'm happy to give, as long as you're the father."

He smiled, wrapped an arm around her waist, and gazed up at the men repairing the sheets. "It was rather kind of your father to give us this as a wedding present."

She ran a finger over the smooth wood railing and gazed at Fort McHenry, where the American flag waved in the breeze. "After he met your uncle and confirmed your story, I believe he is quite proud to have you in the family."

Owen huffed. "If he only knew my past, he might reconsider."

"We all have a past, Owen."

Removing his hat, he raked back his hair. "Regardless, I am glad he trusts me with such a prize." His gaze met hers again, and he caressed her cheek with his thumb. "And I don't mean the schooner. Not only does he give me your hand in marriage, but he's allowing you to sail off with me."

Emeline smiled. "I think he realizes by now that I would find a way onto the ship anyway."

His brows rose. "But you *will* obey me as your husband, will you not?"

She pouted. "Of course. But only when we are in agreement."

"Hmm." He feigned a frown of concern.

The schooner creaked over a wavelet, and she glanced past the fort into the bay. "Like rescuing Hannah and my father's crew. How could we not at least try?"

"Agreed. Good of my uncle to send along the USS *Constitution* to help us."

"How long before we catch up to the *Marauder*?"

"Word is, they left the Chesapeake just yesterday. So a day or two at most. We will set sail first thing in the morning. I'm only waiting on the guns my uncle sent to arrive."

Emeline spun a curl around her finger and smiled coyly up at Owen. "And after we perform a daring rescue of our compatriots, where to after that?"

"Anywhere you want to go, love. Or should I say, anywhere God leads." A warm breeze swirled around them as he gestured toward the open bay where sunlight transformed wavelets into lines of glittering silver. "He's made the world for us to explore."

Emeline gripped Owen's hands in hers, hardly able to contain her excitement. "I wish to paint a masterpiece of every port city."

"Then you shall! And while you're doing that, we will tell the people who live there of God's love and forgiveness."

"It sounds too marvelous to be true." Emeline fingered the locket around her neck. "If only my mother had known such freedom. There is true freedom in following God, isn't there? I always thought the Christian life was so confining."

"Me as well. What a pair we were." He laughed. "I ran from the confining rules and you tried to abide by them. Neither of us were right."

She nodded and squeezed his hand.

"Ah, the adventures we shall have, my lady." He leaned to kiss her. Someone cleared their throat. Yet as Owen's lips touched hers, Emeline thought to ignore it, but a murmured question gave her pause. "Do proper ladies kiss gentlemen in public?"

That voice! Emeline spun to find her dear friend standing on the wharf, gripping her hands together in glee.

"Hannah!" Arms out, Emeline darted across the wobbling gangplank and swallowed up her friend in her arms. "I can't believe . . . how . . . where . . . ?"

"Slow down, dear." Hannah kissed her cheek and nudged her back. "We were put ashore day afore yesterday. Cap'n Blackwell hisself bid us farewell, an' his men rowed us to land."

Emeline's mouth hung open. Owen approached the railing, his grin wide.

Hannah glanced his way then continued. "I went ri' to your home an' your father told me you was here."

Emeline gripped Hannah's hands and looked up at Owen. "But we were coming to rescue you."

"That's wha' he said! Wha' are you thinkin' embarkin' on such a foolish mission,

431

dear? God took care o' us." She squinted at the setting sun, her eyes sparkling with mischief. "I hear you had quite the adventure."

Emeline smiled and lowered her gaze. "Indeed, we did."

Hannah pointed a finger at Owen. "I knew you was a good man. I knew it!"

"We're getting married right here on the ship. Today at sunset," Emeline all but squealed out.

"Today?" Hannah's face lit. "How wonderful!"

"You must come. I insist. You and Abner. Oh my, is everyone else from the *Charlotte* well?"

"Yes. They are all in good health, happy to be home." Hannah suddenly frowned. "All 'cept the ones what went off with the *Charlotte,* that is."

Emeline sighed. "They should be freed once the war is over."

Gripping one of the lines, Owen planted a boot on the bulwarks. "Your husband is a quartermaster?"

Shielding her eyes, Hannah gazed up at him. "Aye, he is."

"Thing is, I'm looking for a good quartermaster." He shared a smile with Emeline.

"What are you saying?" Hannah asked.

"I'm asking you and your husband to join us. We'll be merchants part of the time, missionaries part time, artists" — he smiled at Emeline — "and privateers when the occasion calls for it."

Hannah's face split in a wide grin. "Sounds like an adventure I can't pass up. Oh, I can't wait to tell Abner." She started down the wharf, waving a hand over her shoulder. "We'll be back for the wedding."

Emeline crossed back over the plank and fell against Owen, inhaling a deep breath of his unique scent. She could hardly believe she'd be his wife in just a few hours. A ray of sunshine angled over the scar on his cheek.

"You never told me how you got that scar."

Owen grinned, a mischievous sparkle in his eyes. "Let's just say the story is not one to be told to a proper lady."

"Well, I do believe I've given up trying to be proper. Instead, I will simply follow my Lord and let Him show me what to do."

"Hmm. I suppose I should change the name of the ship then."

"Why? What have you called her?"

"The *Proper Lady* of course."

Emeline laughed. "No. No. That will never do. Let me think." She tapped her chin and gazed over the schooner, then over her

433

beloved hometown of Baltimore, then at the other ships anchored in the bay, and finally back to Owen. "I know. We must call her *Liberty*. For not only has our country found liberty, but we have as well."

Owen nodded his agreement. "*Liberty* it is, my lady." Then, drawing her close, he leaned down and kissed her.

AUTHOR'S HISTORICAL NOTE

After the British marched on Washington, DC, in August 1814 and effectively conquered and burned much of it to the ground, they set their sights on Baltimore. The port city had been nothing but an annoyance during the war, sending out more privateers who wreaked havoc among British merchants than any other city. Overconfident and filled with pride after the ease with which they had conquered Washington, the British were positive that a victory in Baltimore would put an end to the War of 1812 and to the rebellious Americans.

Their plan of attack was twofold. By sea, British ships would pummel the tiny Fort McHenry protecting the city and then sail into the harbor, where they would point their cannons at Baltimore until they surrendered. By land, they would send four thousand troops to storm the city and force its citizens into submission.

On September 12, 1814, under the cover of night, some 4,200 British soldiers landed at North Point just outside Baltimore. General Ross and Rear Admiral Cockburn, who led the forces, enjoyed breakfast at the Gorsuch house five miles from the landing place. So confident were they of victory that when asked if they would be back for dinner, General Ross replied, "I'll sup in Baltimore tonight — or in hell."

The generals were unaware of the American militia forces awaiting them just four miles away under the very competent command of General John Stricker and General Samuel Smith. Even so, the British troops were able to advance toward Baltimore, though they suffered several casualties, including General Ross himself. Rain also impeded their progress, transforming the landscape into mud and their uniforms into heavy, cold armor. Once they arrived at the outskirts of the city, they were met unexpectedly by twenty thousand American troops, more than one hundred cannons on heights covered by breastworks, and a line of fortified redoubts.

Unwilling to advance and lose more men, the British camped within two miles of the American defenses, waiting for their ships to defeat Fort McHenry and sail into the harbor, where they would hold the city hostage at cannon point.

With the American flag flying above Fort McHenry visible to both sides, British ships began their bombardment of the fort at dawn on September 13th. For the next twenty-five hours they would hurl more than 1,800 exploding shells at the fort, shaking the entire town for miles. Still, they were unable to take the fort, and on the morning of September 14th, the Royal Navy ships withdrew. (Check out my novel *Surrender the Dawn* for more information on the battle for Fort McHenry!)

Seeing that they would not have the support of their ships, the commanders of the British troops decided to retreat rather than risk more casualties and a humiliating defeat. With the flag waving over Fort McHenry and Francis Scott Key writing our national anthem aboard a ship in the bay, the citizens of Baltimore celebrated their miraculous victory over the greatest military force at that time. Just three months later, the Treaty of Ghent was signed in Belgium, ending the War of 1812. Long live the Republic!

BIBLIOGRAPHY

George, Christopher T. *Terror on the Chesa-peake: The War of 1812 on the Bay.* Shippensburg, PA: White Mane Books, 2000.

Healey, David. *1812: Rediscovering Chesapeake Bay's Forgotten War.* Rock Hill, SC: Bella Rosa Books, 2005.

Hickey, Donald R. *The War of 1812: A Short History.* Bicentennial ed. Champaign: University of Illinois Press, 2012.

Muller, Charles G. *The Darkest Day.* Philadelphia: University of Pennsylvania, 2003.

Sheads, Scott. *Fort McHenry: A History.* Baltimore: Nautical & Aviation Publishing Company of America, 1995.

ABOUT THE AUTHOR

MaryLu Tyndall, a Christy Award finalist and bestselling author of the Legacy of the King's Pirates series, is known for her adventurous historical romances filled with deep spiritual themes. She holds a degree in math and worked as a software engineer for fifteen years before testing the waters as a writer. MaryLu currently writes full-time and makes her home on the California coast with her husband, six kids, and four cats. Her passion is to write page-turning, romantic adventures that not only entertain but open people's eyes to their God-given potential. MaryLu is a member of American Christian Fiction Writers and Romance Writers of America.

The employees of Thorndike Press hope you have enjoyed this Large Print book. All our Thorndike, Wheeler, and Kennebec Large Print titles are designed for easy reading, and all our books are made to last. Other Thorndike Press Large Print books are available at your library, through selected bookstores, or directly from us.

For information about titles, please call:
(800) 223-1244

or visit our website at:
gale.com/thorndike

To share your comments, please write:
Publisher
Thorndike Press
10 Water St., Suite 310
Waterville, ME 04901